TOME
OF THE
PALADINS

MARSHAL

MYERS

MW00983254

This book is dedicated to Macie, Miriam, Eliana, and especially Jo, whose God-given knowledge foretold the compiling of this work. Dream on, old chum.

And to my God, who made me a knight.

For my niece, Eliana Connor

1. Berserker Moon

A blank stillness hungover the silver city of Auraheim. For over 8 months, Irminsul, the Kingdom of Men, had known peace after the Battle of the Plains. The battle was the final defeat of the forces of the dark army under the treacherous Gollmorn, vying for kingship. This had ended the War of the One Generation, led by the great Sword Dreamer and now-legendary seer, Leofric. The red-whiskered, 19-summered man was also son and heir of the recently crowned Battle-King Rothgaric. The Kingdom it would seem, was entering a golden, or, rather, a Neo-Elven Age, as Prince Leofric had of recent taken the ebon-skinned and captivatingly beautiful Elven warrioress, Sundea Surgessarsdottir, as his wife. As in love as they were, caressing publicly, both nobleman and commoner alike were hoping for a new half-elven grandson for Queen Ragna and King Rothgaric, who would eventually succeed the new red-bearded royal line, and continue the newly named House of Wulf.

However...

Tonight, was the night of the Berserkr moon. On that ensorcelled night, the wolves of Firbolg Forest bayed for fresh blood at the steel-blued, heavenly-bound body. Strange things happened in that forest of the southlands, things that I could concern myself with imparting to you, dear reader. Erm, but for the sake of the love of my God, known here in as the king that is, I will not. I must simply suffice to say that, especially upon the night of the Berserker moon, fell deeds awaited anyone who passed through those forest doors. The aura of that former dwelling place of the dark enemy was so pregnant with evil that those in the Silver City, near as it was to the Elvenlands to the north of the mountains, felt as if someone was going to give birth to a devil.

Mayhaps, I think. As the unholy moon of the Firbolg grinned down in malevolence, strange things were happening in the palace of the king.

For you see, gentle readers, Queen Ragna, aided by the sisterhood of healers had founded an hostelry for the poor and destitute of the northern cities. It so happened that one night not so many moons ago, a strange young lady had come into that House of the poor. She could not remember her origins nor her recent past only that she was named Herkata.

Sometimes as a morality lesson, gentle readers, it seems that pity on strangers can be a bad thing, which precipitates fell deeds in the night. But if there is one indeed for the silvercity of men; That remains to be seen, for even I Lamathrath called the wise, cannot foresee all ends. That belongs only to the mind of the God of the Angel armies, and I am not even a soldier, but I am His scribe only. Though I have some foresight, I am no seraph paladin. even they only smite those whom the king of heaven tells them. Would they have struck her down that orphan, great giants. I'm getting ahead of myself, I beg pardon, my Lord, back to the matters at hand with as little more extraneous commentary as I can muster. My mind wanders at times, you know. Come now, Angel Scribe, back to your story.

There are an infinite number of universes beyond the mind of mortal man. I, Lamathrath, scribe of all universes, have compiled the tales of three of these universes so that you might know the light of the Master in all worlds. First follows the tale, in part, of Geoffrey de Dunnmouth, scribe of the world of Unterheofa and his tales of the Paladins Nine.

Paladins Nine

Prelude: The Forging

Brunhild looked out across the shining fields of Middenheofa, the realm separating heaven from the middle-earth of Unterheofa and the other worlds created by the Master. She was armor bearer to the Great King and this day He had charged her with a supreme task. She was to forge a Golden Blade, a blade so magnificent that its equal had never been seen in the lands of Unterheofa. A mortal warrior in Unterheofa needed it to best Skrael, one of the lesser demons of Helheim who served the Dark Enemy. The Dark Enemy was indeed powerful but not powerful enough to escape defeat by the Son of the King as the Son had defeated him in the sphere of Naofatir as well as in the sphere of Veritia in the city of Silvardrassil. The Son would someday come to the world of Unterheofa, as he also would to Éalindé of the four races, and even to worlds which the Master had not yet given birth in the mind of man.

But, her task, which filled Brunhild's mind, was this deed for the cause of the Light in Unterheofa, not the numerous other worlds created by the Master. And so she stood at her forge at the door of the Nexus and beat forth, by the power of the Spirit of the Master, a Golden Blade that would rival even the blades of the sons of heaven. *Dring-Ring-Dring!* The once half-dwarven angel smith beat out a singsong timpani in praise to her God, as her azure eyes flashed brighter than the sea blue mail she wore. Her radiant golden curls blew on the winds of praise gathered up from all the realms, both new and old, the praises of the children of God. The fire of the Spirit of God danced on the holy ore as it took shape and burned with sanctified splendor greater than any other magic of the realms, for it was the "magic" of God, or rather the power of the spirit of God, which has often been mistaken for magic of the Enemy. And so she bound the hilt with the gossamer spun long ago in the garden of life. Though it was for a mortal, she felt it wise to test its balance. And so the blade sang through the air with a joyous song of righteous fury. Though it may be broken someday it would still accomplish the purpose for which the dwarven seraph had forged it. She unfurled her silver gold wings and flew through the Nexus to deliver the blade to her King. He would be pleased. Yes. He would be pleased. And so her great duty for the cause of God in Unterheofa was complete.

Prologue

Roderick Goldenbeard, Tenth Marshall of the kingdom of Kyngesrelm, strode methodically along Baerynthine's Wall, which marked the northernmost border of the kingdom, hand twitching at the hilt of his sword. Though it was almost spring, he wondered why the snow just due south of the wall showed no sign of melting. His men were becoming increasingly uneasy and dour. Not even their usual supply of malt beer could brighten their mood. Pagh! The enemy take it, the very master of Skrael take all of it! There was foul work afoot, though he could not face a mail-backed finger. Two of the man on watch, wiry menby the names of Hakkar and Thorst, were gambling away the rest of their ale by playing Vaering chess. Their painted black gambeson's bore a golden broadsword insignia, the Golden angelic sword of the old Paladin King Baerynthine, founder of the kingdom of Kyngerelm and builder of his eponymous wall, which kept the forces of the dark one at bay ever in a long sleep.

The old Marshall was watching the snow-battered brazier flicker, when suddenly the flame turned a ruddy color. There in the midst of the flame stood a woman who appeared to be a dwarf by her size but her ears were long and tapering like those of an elf. She was actually rather short even for a dwarf. A long cloak seemingly made of fire was clasped with an orange ruby at her neck. Her hair was long and golden red, and it hung in wavy curls. The Marshall's eyes darted over to the chess-playing watchmen and started to speak but he saw with a curious note that they had neither seen the flare nor sensed the presence of the strange visitor. Could this be an omen? A voice that Roderick knew instantly to be the spirit's, echoed in his head. Her pale blue eyes burned into him yet her mouth did not move. "I am Geld-Ruada, a daughter of heaven. I am one of the Eight, the Fae of the North. My God and your God has sent me here with a message of great importance. Fear the worst. For the way of darkness is open. The enemy has returned, has awakened from his long sleep. Once I was a mortal like you. So I value the lives of God's mortal children. Heed my warning and go to your King. Make haste. I must go." Then as quickly as she had come, the fae vanished. It was a moment before the old MarshallMarshall shook himself from his trance.

The Fae of the eight points of the compass, the eight sisters, were known mostly in legend, as guardians placed over mortals and guardians of the welfare of all of Unterheofa, the great orb of earth, stone, air, wind, water and fire, upon which Kyngesrelm and the whole of Pallanon rested. They were half Angel, so the lore said, that they, who had once been mortals now became powerful subservient immortals to their great immortal and invisible God. Surely, this Geld-Ruada, who, if what she said was true was the guardian of the North and that the enemy had awakened, it was imperative that Roderick bear word south to Castle Pallanon. He alone had seen the Fae, and so he alone could speak of this. The task had been appointed to him. "Joffrey!" He barked to his chief lieutenant. "I am leaving the wall in your care, as I will be journeying south to Castle Pallanon." He held up his hand as he saw the younger man's bewildered stare. "You will just have to trust me, but I speak true when I say the fate of the entire kingdom may depend on it."

The Marshall made preparations to leave in less than half an hour. His midnight black horse galloped forth from the barbican of the wall and burned down across the snow like a black flame. The Fae, standing invisibly on one of the southern merlons, watched for a time as he disappeared into the distance. She wondered what she would have done, had she still been mortal, and the vision had come to her. She smiled as she remembered fondly the painful yet wondrous days she had spent as Heather Luinn, the dwarf cleric. But that is another tale.

A Rhyme of Old King Baerynthine's Minstrel, Quinnery Quicksilver, composed at the paladin king's coronation, in honor of King Baerynthine and his knights, and their victory over the shadow-raiser Skrael in the Everfrost War.

A paladin is a warrior of Light

From the arm of the Lord does he draw his might

His heart more powerful than his sword

A holy weapon in the hand of the Lord

An empty vessel though his shoulders be broad,

A humble, poor fellow servant of God.

There once was a Sword

Forged by the Angel of the Lord

Of blessed golden steel.

Worthy of those of the seraph host,

Caused the forces of darkness and ice to reel.

Shall the noble power of this sword one day be thine?
If thou art

Baptised of heart

Like noble Baerynthine.

The hour now comes to be

Winter upon the land.

Lest evil rise, our souls to freeze,

Let us sharpen the holy brand.

Pallanon

Varluckhild

Faerynthine's wall

Alf-anon Plains

Gateway to Varluck — Castle Roldfring

Dwarvenhomn

Village of Ofermod

Kyngesrefse

Villageof Vayloghlin

Afferton Trollveins Forest

Delvins Fen

Darkmort Village

Castle Palisera

Reftkirk

Priory of Bott Lamb

1.   Whisper of Everfrost

The crystal white veil of winter blanketed Kyngesrelm, the kingdom of Southern Pallanon. It was not unlike any other winter of the last five centuries, save that perhaps the wind carried with it a colder chill, almost a sense of foreboding. A snow flurry had sprung up around Castle Pallanon, making it nigh impossible for the guards standing on the four turrets to see very far into the confused, floury mass.

The captain of the guard, a broad-shouldered unkempt man clad in a fur-lined gambeson and mail coif, squinted out at the driving snow. He thought he saw a speck through the flurry. *Could it be a horse and rider?* The burly captain rubbed his eyes and scratched his graying whiskers. "I was sure I saw something out there, Alisdair," he remarked to the Alfanonian elf youth standing at battlement beside him. "Me old eyes must be seeing things."

"Well, I dunna ken the state of your eyes, but I wouldn't doubt it on account of the snow, old Ector," the strawberry-haired elf said. He squinted in the same direction as the older man. "You can hardly see a yard beyond the stone of the battlement. And the cold!" He blew into his cupped hands and patted them together. "Aye! truly 'tis worse than the land north of Baerynthine's Wall, where lies the magical curse of eternal winter, though I really cannot say that for certain, for nobody has been in the north of Pallanon for almost five centuries. Still, if we did not have these furs, we would freeze to our deaths, and no mistake. I tell you, captain, I could surely do with a spot of spiced wine about now."

"But no, Young Alisdair. We must stay here at the battlement, needlessly, while King Jaerython and his knights sit at Winter's Last Feast in the great hall below us. Ah, yes. Such is our lot, my friend. Such is our lot."

Even though it was said with an attitude of complaint, Captain Ector's statement was true. Below, the great hall was bedecked with decorations that spoke of the spring to come. The minstrels played lutes and harps lively in the corners underneath tapestries sewn with the bright blues, yellows and pinks of the life-bringing season. A glowing, golden fire crackled and blazed on the hearth in the center of the hall. Venison, boar and fowl roasted on irons spits above it. King Jaerython sat at the great semicircular feasting table against the northern wall.

Unlike what Ector's statement had implied, Jaerython deserved to celebrate. Under his rule, all three sectors of Pallanon's population, elves, dwarves and humans alike, thrived to the greatest extent since the days of King Baerynthine, Jaerython's ancestor. Although the King claimed supreme rule over the Elvish, dwarvish and human population, he left the governing of the specific towns and cities to their councils and rulers. The peace was only occasionally disrupted by raids upon small towns by tribes of forest trolls, goblins and the like, who had been created by the Enemy and did not submit to Jaerython's authority. The maintaining of the peace was principally overseen by the King's nine bravest and most trustworthy paladins.

Lengar Faldron, the king's dwarf minstrel, was singing the song of Bartholas Bristlemane, The first paladin to die in the Everfrost War five hundred years past.

'Old Bartholas Bristlemane rode through the dark of night

Through the biting cut of Everfrost.

His pupiless golden eyes, despite the dark had sight

This first Paladin of Baerynthine

Did not know how fate would entwine

Before returned the light

He needed blood of a great-wolf heart

To save his lover, Britomart De Vaelen Vavriel.

The only priestess of the light

Who had ever sought to fight the shadow-raiser Skrael

Only fell blood of the Wolf

Would her precious life engulf

To redeem her body frail

And on the bite of the wind

Came not a voice not of human ken,

'Twould make a heart leap from mail

I am hunger, I am thirst

I am everything accursed.

I'll grind your heart like shale

Forward came the dog of Helheim

And the pure knight of Baerynthine

Met him with a great mace

The round spiked head would surely to ribbons, turn the great-wolf's face

Alas, however, wolfish tooth rent through Elven mail

Cried St. Bar, "I'll have your blood,

And send you to lord of Skrael!"

With the last breath of life

He called to his wife

And struck the Wolf dead

So great was the blow

That through the snow

Spun the Wolf's head

Though he laid clawed and reven

Two angels from heaven

Came down to where he lay.

One bore the blood to Bris'mane's wife

The other bore him away.

Hearken ye all ye knights

Speak well of your forebear

For God Himself gave him last rites

Beneath the Everfrost air.'

His brogue-filled recitation caused a kerchief-dabbed tear in the eye of many a fair lady, and a libation of courageous fervor in the breast of many a young man-at-arms.

The knights sat with Old King Jaer at his feasting table that night. There was Sir Leofred, Sir Hersker, Sir Fréalást, Sir Waldon, Sir Cedric, Sir Godfrey, Sir Elliend, Sir Liddegond, and Sir Vaelen. They had won many battles together against the trolls and goblins. But after each battle, each knight felt in his heart that the greatest proof of his valor, his greatest service to God, was yet to come.

Each knight was clad in gleaming ceremonial mail, his standard hanging from the wall behind his tall chair. Leofred's was a white broadsword on a blood-red field. Sir Hersker's was a rearing gray stallion on a field of gold. Sir Fréalást's was a golden-hilted sword in a matching sheath and baldric, all on a field of rich purple. Sir Waldon's was a great seraph in white on a field of blue, his sounding horn at his side. On Sir Cedric's white standard and surcoat were the images of a silver hand holding a silver chalice. Sir Godfrey's heraldry consisted of two arms, one white, and one black, each gripping the forearm of the other over a field of light green. Sir Elliend's silver tabard was bedecked with golden stars, which seemed to be shining ever on in the firelight. Sir Liddegond's orange surcoat showed a silver sword with the blade broken near the hilt. Sir Vaelen's bright yellow standard bore two green arms. The right held an upraised sword. The other held the first by the wrist, staying it. In this regalia, the nine noble warriors sat at the feast with their King.

King Jaerython stood as the great fire crackled, and raising his goblet, declared, "My good lords and ladies, knights and servants all, we are glad to take part in tonight's festivities, but we must sober you somewhat, for tonight we remember those who died those long centuries ago in the fight against the enemy, the shadow-raiser Skrael. Hail to the valiant dead!"

"Hail!" echoed the assembly.

"Let us pray. Oh, Lord God…."

Meanwhile, on the turret above the gate, Ector squinted into the flurry. The speck he had seen in the distance had reappeared and was growing larger. *Could it be? Yes! It was! A horse and rider were approaching Castle Pallanon. Who could be on the high road on a night such as this?*

The figure stopped short of the drawbridge, cupped its hands around its mouth and bellowed up a wind-muffled cry of "Halloa!"

"Halloa!" roared Ector in reply. "Who goes there?"

"It is Marshall Roderick! I come from Baerynthine's Wall with a message of great import for the King."

Though the aging Ector did not want to be rebuked for interrupting the night's festivities, he knew that a message that merited Roderick coming himself to Castle Pallanon must be of the highest importance, just as the Marshall had said. He turned back to the staircase leading down from the turret and called, "Raise the portcullis!"

The guards obeyed and the sounds of the grating and wheezing of chains groaned forth from the barbican as the iron gate rose.

"…And we pray that You would continue to shield this land from the evil that once threatened to engulf it. Amen!"

Jaerython had barely finished leading the prayer when Marshalll Roderick X, Commander of the Force at Baerynthine's Wall, burst unannounced into the great hall. The man was of powerful build, clad in snow-caked mail over which he wore a fur-padded gambeson for warmth rather than protection. He held his cylindrical great helm in leather-gloved hands. A coif of mail was on his head. A thick golden beard, a characteristic trait of the house of the Marshall of Pallanon, accented his visage. Light blue eyes holding a stern gaze fixed themselves on the King.

King Jaerython appeared surprised though not overly vexed at Roderick's coming. Many noblemen and ladies, however, stared in shock at the battle-hardened soldier. A mistake such as this would never do.

"Marshall Roderick," the King began, "how is it that you abandon your post at Baerynthine's Wall to come to Castle Pallanon?"

"I come with a message of import, sire, one that may concern the whole kingdom."

Taking cautious note of the noble guests, he moved closer and whispered in the King's ear. "Just to the south of the Wall, the wind grows colder, the snow piles higher, though the spring thaw should already be upon us. Every night, my men hear fell voices on the wind, and the wind itself carries an evil, almost arcane sting. Though I know my history, and all that your ancestor King Baerynthine did to ensure the safety of the South, I fear…"

He swallowed hard before continuing, "Several weeks ago, a holy messenger confirmed my suspicions. The Everfrost is returning. The chief minion of the Dark One, the shadow-raiser Skrael, has awoken."

2.   Much-Needed Council

The graying king's face blanched for a mere second. He closed his eyes and heaved a long but inaudible sigh. As quickly as the look of shock appeared, it was replaced by a façade of regal authority. He turned back to his noble guests and said with a forced weak smile. "Noble lords and ladies, we beg your forgiveness, but we must take our leave, together with our knights, to confer upon affairs of state. Therefore we bid you good night." He bowed and, motioning for the paladins to follow, strode toward the door leading into the inner reaches of the castle. Before he left, he whispered to Geldbjorn Gold Bear, tawny-haired War-Leader of the Vaering barbarian warband that had sworn to protect the king, "Keep my noble guests entertained. A sword dance or mock *holmgangr* should keep their minds from my absence."

"Jah, my King," the golden-locked giant whispered, inclining his head. The towering northman motioned to his men, and the bearded warriors fell to swinging axe and sword in staged combat. The king thought in passing that they looked much like angel warriors, clad in gilded mail and silvered conical helms with nasals.

King Jaerython hurried toward the hall of records, as the knights and Marshall Roderick followed close behind. Catching sight of a young porter, the King snapped his fingers and ordered. "Awaken Master Scribe Geoffrey de Dunnmouth, and tell him that his king requires his presence in the Hall of Records this very moment."

The young servant bowed and scampered off to the master scribe's quarters. Meanwhile, the small party reached its destination and Roderick used his battle-hardened muscles to open the massive lacquered doors, which were etched with the

Golden Blade of King Baerynthine, the battle standard of the Kings of Kyngesrelm.

The Hall of Records was a large octagonal room with forty-foot high walls. The marble walls themselves were carved in the shapes of book cases and held many time-worn tomes, most of them yellowed records of the deeds of Jaerython's ancestors. There were no ladders in sight. Rather, a walkway of burnished bronze weaved up the walls to the different levels of the bookshelves. There were many torch rings set in enclaves in between the shelves to provide light. There was a long table at the center of the room surrounded by upholstered chairs.

The knights and their King had already taken their seats when Geoffrey de Dunnmouth burst into the room. He was a short man with a head of flat, close-cropped graying hair, a round mouth bedecked with a grayish black goatee topped by a round nose, and large brown eyes.

He was dressed in a heavy robe of blood crimson, the sleeves hung down in a loose fashion, for he had thrown it on hurriedly. "You sent for me, m'lord?" he asked, stifling a yawn.

"Yes, Master Scribe. Shake the sleep from your mind, for I have something very important to say. But first you, Geoffrey de Dunnmouth, must swear that you will forget everything you hear at this gathering tonight. For if the people of Kyngesrelm should gain wind of this council, it could spell panic, or even, the Lord forbid, insurrection. Will you swear to this?"

The gravity of the statement shook the last remnants of sleep from Geoffrey's mind. "I swear."

"It is done. Marshall Roderick, would you now disclose to these men what you told me in secret in the great hall?"

The golden-haired Marshall surveyed his audience with a stony gaze before clearing his throat and venturing to speak.

"Gentlemen, as you all well know, I have my lodging at Baerynthine's Wall, as all previous Marshalls of Kyngesrelm have before me since King Baerynthine's victory in the Everfrost War five hundred years ago. Those under my command along the northern side of the wall have always detected a difference between the seasonal winter chill of Southern Pallanon and the winds that blow down without ceasing from the land of Varluckhuld to the north. This current winter, the difference has become blurred."

All those assembled, with the exception of the King, stared at Roderick, not comprehending. "Permit me to explain further. Each night after sunset, my men and I hear fell voices on the air coupled with the howling of nocturnal beasts. Were it not for the hot fires and stew, the cold of the night would have killed us long ago. It was not always thus. My men behold strange visions as they sleep, vision of ravenous wolves, and other creatures given life and movement out of an unholy power, as those creatures dwelling in the evil Forest of Trillven, except these are inconcrete beings, not trolls or goblins; I fear they be far more powerful, minions of a Great Evil, a Nameless Fear. It seems to me that the balance of the elements and of sanity have been twisted against us. I believe the laws of nature are being upset, by an unseen foe, a foe only known to us in our history books."

"Ah, it is late, and our minds are not used to riddles," chided Sir Liddegond in a coaxing tone. "Please speak plainly, good Marshall. What are you trying to tell us?"

"I fear that an evil shadow shall once again descend over this land. May God grant that I interpreted the vision wrong but the night I set forth for Castle Pallanon I was visited by one of the Eight Sisters, Geld-Ruada, the Fae of the north. They only deliver messages at pivotal points in history. I fear that that at which the immortal Fae hinted is true. The ancient enemy of God, the shadow-raiser Skrael, most terrible of all the minions of the Dark One, has awoken."

A stunned silence followed the Marshall's last statement and for what seemed a long time the men of the Council struggled to comprehend this serious news.

At last, the King broke the silence. "I know not if what the Marshall says is true. In order to gain any sense of certainty, we must turn back to hallowed antiquity. And that, Master Geoffrey, is why you have been invited to this meeting. Fetch the *Annals of the Everfrost War*."

"As you wish, my liege."

Geoffrey de Dunnmouth ascended the winding ramp to the top level of the library. He returned with a timeworn volume and, moving very slowly, set it on the long table. "My apologies, my lord. But this book dates from the reign of Baerynthine and therefore I must handle it with the utmost care." He sat down and asked. "Where shall I begin?"

"At the beginning; for any word may hold a clue."

The record keeper blew a cloud of dust from the cover and opened the book. Placing a gentle finger on the yellowed, cracked page, he began to read:

"In the Second Spring of Pallanon, there arose in the hills of the North a Black Tower with a turret in the semblance of a skull. The creator of the tower, who laid its foundation by dark magic, was known in the common tongue of the free races as Skrael, the beautiful deceiver who was an

enemy of the God of elves, dwarves and men. From his dark chamber he wove a curse that laid the land bare and frozen. This spell, driven by the ice of water and of Skrael's heart, soon covered all of Pallanon. Aided by the supernatural frost, the wraith army of the shadow-raiser swept down across the land, putting many to the sword. Soon Pallanon fell into the mire of defeat and despair. But there was one who did not waver in his trust in the Lord. Baerynthine, a simple soldier, said to his friend, Roderick Goldenbeard, 'Let us rally the three oppressed races to us and strike a blow for the Lord.'

God was pleased with Baerynthine and entrusted him with a sword, forged in the halls of heaven, of sacred golden steel, with which to defeat the shadow-raiser. The Lord sent the sacred blade down in a bolt of lightning and spoke to Baerynthine's heart, saying , "By this blessed steel, the Enemy shall fall". The faithful Baerynthine led an army of elves, dwarves and men in an assault on the Black Tower, and used the sacred power of the holy sword to seal Skrael away in his tower.

After the victory, the paladin Baerynthine was proclaimed King over all the land of Pallanon. The newly proclaimed King did not possess a power great enough to destroy the Black Tower. So he commissioned Roderick Goldenbeard, now Marshall of the kingdom, to oversee the building of a high wall. Baerynthine's Wall, as it came to be known thereafter, separated the south of Pallanon from Skrael's former seat of power in the north. Spring later returned to the Southern kingdom, which was called Kyngesrelm. But before the wall was finished, tragedy befell the King. One night during a storm, while standing on a high section of the wall, he dropped the sacred sword which God had given him. From the Black Tower, the remaining magics that the shadow-raiser had loosed before his defeat drove a Black Wind, which cut quicker than the keenest broadsword, down upon the golden blade. The blessed brand shattered at the hilt and the shards scattered to the four winds. Roderick the Marshall rode the length and breadth of the kingdom over many months and recovered all of the shards. But alas, even the forging skill of the dwarves could not reforge it. The golden shards are kept in the vault of Castle Pallanon to this very day."

King Jaerython held up his hand as a signal for the old record keeper to stop.

Sir Leofred, who was the eldest of the paladins, asked, "If I may make so bold, my liege, how does this tale of hallowed antiquity help us now? In truth, we have known our history since we were lads. How does this affect our current situation?"

There was a short pause. All heads turned at the sound of old Geoffrey clearing his throat. "Er, I know it is not my place to offer advice on affairs of state, but it appears to me that the shattering of Baerynthine's heavenly weapon may have something to do with the supposed awakening of the shadow-raiser. With no blade to contain it, the holy power of Baerynthine's blade has surely waned over the centuries. This may be what has allowed Skrael to arise again."

"But," said Sir Waldon, "it has been five hundred years since the breaking of the sword. Would not Skrael have arisen before now?"

"The power of the sword of the king drained the Enemy of his potency. It is probable that he has been amassing his former strength in secrecy."

"This arising of Everfrost may forebode the coming of his master, the Dark One who canted him into being from an unholy, dark fire. Let us pray that we will not have to face that all-encompassing Darkness, for only the One-Born, the avatar begotten by God Himself, the only one to be truly begotten and not created, and one with the Creator, could save us. Only he could defeat the Dark One, as the sacred tomes say he did long ago when this midden-realm was shapeless and empty."

"The answer is simple, then," said Sir Liddegond, rising from his seat. "We must reforge the holy sword of Baerynthine and use it to seal the shadow-raiser Skrael in his tower once again."

The King raised his hand. "Baerynthine's blade was forged in the halls of heaven. Not even the skill of the master dwarven smith Dunnir of Veylandin, who forged the alchemical sword Ettin-Bane, wielded by the troll-slayer Sir Peter von Wulfbain, the Lord of Veylandin. No, not even Master Smith Dunnir could reforge King Baerynthine's blade."

Sir Leofred had been listening carefully to the discourse, stroking his auburn beard. Suddenly he stood, and said, "Therefore, we know it to be impossible for one knight to wield the holy sword of Baerynthine, but it could be done by nine standing in unison." Everyone, including the King, looked quite puzzled.

Endeavoring to explain, Sir Leofred continued, "Listen, my friends. There are nine shards, kept here in Castle Pallanon, which once made up the blade of Baerynthine's holy sword. Is this true?" All nodded.

"And there are we, the nine chief knights of Kyngesrelm under your personal command, O King. I therefore set forth this motion that on the morrow at first light, all of us will ride out, each in a different direction, much as the first Marshall of the kingdom did centuries ago. We will ride throughout the kingdom to rendezvous within two months at the Gateway to Varluckhuld in the north. We shall each take with us a shard of Baerynthine's holy brand, while gathering the other tools of war with which to assault the Black Tower. With the blessing of God it may be that our ancient Enemy shall be vanquished once and for all and his hold over the north of Pallanon will be broken at last. However, we must understand that this mission must be accomplished in secret to prevent panic and insurrection. With your permission, my lord, I shall commit my life, strength and honor to this just and holy cause. Who shall stand with me?"

After a lengthy pause, young Sir Hersker stood and declared with a glad heart, "I shall bear my banner to the north!"

"As will I!" shouted Fréalást, in a calm, yet determined voice.

"And I!" said Sir Waldon, eager to give his all to the sacred quest.

The five remaining knights cried aloud in acclamation and pounded the pommels of their swords on the table.

King Jaerython held up his hand for silence. "This shall be your quest, likely the greatest of your generation. You shall go with my blessing and we shall pray for the blessing of God on this sacred endeavor."

The knights took their leave and went to their chambers to rest and pray. Leofred dreamt that night of the cold, howling winter wind and of the righteous swords that would vanquish it at last. He awoke in the early hours before dawn and prayed that it was in truth God who had planted the seed of this stratagem in his mind.

The next day, clad in full battle armor, the nine paladins of Kyngesrelm gathered before the barbican of Castle Pallanon. King Jaerython led them in the singing of a hymn and then lifted his eyes to heaven and prayed aloud.

"O Lord God, send your angel host to ride with these paladins, your faithful servants. Keep them from evil and let righteous fruit, the fruit of victory, come through their endeavors. May your own Spirit give them guidance and victory over the Enemy. Amen."

Then the nine paladins rode forth from Castle Pallanon, each following his own path.

Sir Leofred rode directly north from Castle Pallanon. He was clad in a padded leather jerkin to ward off the chill of winter. He also wore a gleaming hauberk, and his bright red surcoat emblazoned on the chest with a white broadsword, his heraldric insignia. His hands were covered with gauntlets of wine red leather. On his head he wore a leather arming cap, mail coif and open-faced bascinet. He also wore a mighty broadsword at his belt and carried a red kite shield, also emblazoned with his heraldry, on his back. A great nagging had told the knight to place his shard of the sword of Baerynthine directly over his heart. He kept it in place with a thick strip of white linen tied around his chest. Having the shard so close warmed his soul. Still, his nose was stabbed by the chill of the winter wind. Even worse, his bluish gray eyes were somewhat blinded by the driving snow, which also served to turn his auburn beard white.

He was at this time recently come into his thirty-third year, making him the youngest lord ever to have lordship of Lufien Hall, just to the west of Castle Pallanon, the warmest and friendliest hold in all the south of the kingdom of Kyngesrelm. He was the only married paladin among the Nine Peers. He and his wife, who was three years his junior, allowed a betrothed vassal every year from one of Leofred's shires to bring their betrothed to listen to the beautiful ballads of minstrel, Danton "Merry Danny" Quicksilver, sing his ballads of chivalry and romance, of the great deeds of knights of old and of their ladies fair. He sang with as much gusto for Sir Leofred and his guests as his ancestor, Quinnery Quicksilver, did for King Baerynthine and his court. The most popular of his self-composed ballads was the lay concerning Sir Peter von Wulfbain, Lord of Veylandin, and how he slew a great troll from Trillven Forest with his mighty alchemical sword, Ettin-Bane. More often though, Merry Danton would strum a ballad of love on his elf-made harp, and both the betrothed couple and the lord and lady of Lufien Hall would embrace and share a kiss.

Sir Leofred's infant son, Madoc, had been born the previous fall. He painfully relived the last time he parted with sweet young Lily, his wife. He had walked with her down to the gates of the manor, Lily carrying his infant son, Madoc, close to her. Her eyes were like burnished emerald stones set in the ivory of her pale complexion. Her features were somewhat angular. Some had told Leofred when he was first courting the Lady Lily Eldonine that her family had one of the fair folk, an unnamed Elven courtier, in their bloodline. But no one knew for certain.

On the day of Leofred's departure, the Lady Lily's long, chestnut hair was partially hidden by the hood of her bronze-colored, fur-lined winter cloak. She had worn a light summer riding dress as emerald green as her gem-like eyes on their first courting, her chestnut hair shining like burrone alchemist gold tempered with the philosopher's stone.

Leofred could not help remembering the way she had looked on the first day of their courtship. She had ridden her highland pony, Star-kindler, a rare Alfanonian white, shaggy clumps of hair draping over his hooves like melting ice sickles. The young knight's heart was pierced by the arrow of love at that very moment. He decided then that he would soon seek her hand in marriage.

After she had taken her leave that night, he stayed a while at the manor house to speak with her father. Lord Gairard

Eldonine was a stern old nobleman, a widower, whose wife had died giving birth to their only child. Doubtlessly, he loved his daughter more than his own life, and though he was becoming somewhat feeble in his advancing years, he would give his last ounce of strength fighting to avenge her if he thought her wronged.

When the young knight asked his blessing in seeking her hand, he mused a long time in silence and said at last, "Answer me this one riddle, young knight, and you shall have my blessing and much more, 'I am a tower men seek to rebuild, but no stonemason hath enough stone. I am a moat men seek to fill, but the whole ocean sea hath not enough water. I am fallow ground men seek to plant but the strongest plow cannot break my loam. What am I?"

Sir Leofred was greatly troubled by Lord Gairard's riddle, and lay awake the whole night trying to comprehend its meaning. At last, as dawn was breaking in the east, the Lord God gave clarity to his mind.

He arose, saddled his horse and galloped to the manor of Lord Gairard Eldonine. He was nearly out of breath in his excitement as the serving man ushered him into Lord Gairard's presence. "The answer to your riddle, my lord, is your daughter's broken heart were I to abandon her, for nothing could rebuild it, fill it or make it soft once more were I to foolishly and cold-heartedly forsake her. I love your daughter Lily with all my heart, and may I be accursed if I ever bring shame to her name or her honor.

"Now," the young man said, looking intently at Lord Gairard, "may I humbly ask your blessing in seeking your daughter Lily's hand in marriage, my lord?"

"Please," the old nobleman smiled, laying a friendly hand on the young man's shoulder. "Call me 'father', my son!" When Leofred offered a betrothal ring, young Lily was overjoyed. By special arrangement of Lord Gairard, their engagement was very brief. They married less than two months after the betrothal, and began a life of great joy together, their love deepening with each passing day.

As he rode out that cold winter day, he remembered some of his wife's parting words, and they stung him to the heart. "My lord, husband, and lover," she had said, her eyes misting, slipping her hand into his mighty grip. "I wish you were not going to the feast of winter's ending this year, for, though Castle Pallanon is near to our manor and you will be gone but a short time, I dreamed a vile dream last night. I saw you riding your horse to the north, and a great shadow rose up to meet you and though I ran after you and called your name many times, I could not find you." A tear trailed down her pale cheek. Wiping it away and kissing her, the knight said softly, "Do not fret my love. The Greatest Love watches over us and He will keep me safe. And, what is more, often enough dreams are only just dreams. The mind is a capricious thing."

He embraced his wife and kissed her once more. In that moment, he seemed to be even more taken with this woman with whom he had entwined souls than on the very first day of their enrapturing courtship. Holding his son in his strong arms, he blessed the child. Then he mounted his steed and rode for Castle Pallanon, raising his hand in a final farewell as he disappeared over the horizon.

Now, he reflected, the prophecies of fair Lily's dream were coming to pass.

Often Sir Leofred would think of little Madoc, and of his wife, Lily, as he rode out to survey his shires as required by King Jaerython. He thought of them with a tinge of sadness as he rode forth from Castle Pallanon that day, for he knew that he may not return from this uncertain quest. Shaking the morbid thoughts from his mind, he began to pray:

"Father God, shield me from harm and give me safe passage that I might live to embrace my wife and son once again. Yet if it be your will that I should come home to you in your Blessed Kingdom, I pray that you might provide for Lily and for little Madoc. I love them more than life itself. But even more do I love you and pray that you would aid me in surrendering to your will. Guide me by your Holy Light. Amen."

As soon as the auburn-haired knight had sent his entreaty heavenward, his ears caught the faint sound of a roar, somewhat like that of a lion, on the wind. He looked to the left. Nothing. To the right. There was nothing but the snow-laden wind. He suddenly felt a singeing blast of heat barreling down from above, very shocking, especially in the full tide of winter. So great was the force of the blast, that it almost toppled the mail-clad knight from his mount. Struggling to regain his center of balance, he looked up through the searing wind and discerned a blood red figure, winged and serpentine in shape, riding against the turbulent gale. All dragons in Pallanon were malevolent, so Sir Leofred knew he was in danger. He reached back instinctively for a crossbow and finding none, whispered, "Agh, troll's teeth! If I but had an Elven longbow, I could bring the fell serpent down in one shot, and even do so without fully nocking the shaft." He quietly clicked his tongue to his horse and rode back several paces to a formation of two boulders that formed a giant, natural lean-to. He held his breath for what seemed like hours, praying that the dragon could not see him, for keen were the eyes of fire wyrms. He held his breath all the more when he heard a great *thud*. The dragon had perched on the formation, and was now directly above him. Leofred's brow began to bead with sweat despite the cold. He could hear the cracking and biting sounds as bits of shale broke off beneath the wyrm's talons. He could both hear and feel the hot huff of its breath. *Oh Lord God, shield me with a mighty battalion of seraph knights*, the knight silently pleaded. The wyrm sniffed. Then Sir Leofred heard a deafening *VAROOSH* as the dragon's wings beat the air and it ascended back into the sky.

Leofred sighed in relief, patted his stallion's neck and prayed a silent prayer of thanks. He knew then that he would be forced to reach Baerynthine's Wall by another road. Just as he was about to spur his mount back the way he had come, the paladin heard a still small voice inside his head. *"Follow the dragon. Soon you will know what to do."* Leofred held no liking for confronting a wyrm. But his all-consuming love of the Lord, his God, cast out all his fear and trepidation. Spurring on his stallion, the foal of a supernaturally swift mare bred by the famous Elven riders of the Alf-anon Plains, the knight followed close behind the red wyrm, riding against the bitter wind. To keep his mount from panicking or overexerting itself, he began to croon softly in its ear:

"As you love me

And as I love thee,

And more so my wife

Beneath the tall oak tree,

Carry me, ever swiftly

To where my God-given quest be."

This song, though somewhat simple and foppish, seemed to

hearten the grey beast, and it pressed on, faster and faster, though the chilling snow caked its maw.

Leofred and his faithful mount pressed on for days on end, stopping only for a few precious moments each day for the horse to drink, and for the knight to bolt down a few pieces of hard tack, and to rest, keeping one eye open, looking toward the sky. Strangely, when the crimson fire wyrm began to descend at last, it was very near the village of Drakinon near central Kyngesrelm. A more characteristic place for a fire wyrm to dwell would be in the dark recesses of a cave or atop a high mountain. The land surrounding the village contained neither. As he neared the small village, the knight saw that the crimson wyrm was descending faster and faster. He knew not what work was afoot, but whatever it was, it was foul. That much he could sense.

The dragon landed suddenly in the town square. Leofred reined the stallion to a halt outside the town limits, raising a confused eyebrow. A dragon had just landed in the middle of the village, yet there were no cries of terror coming from the populace. Wondering at this phenomenon, Leofred rode at a soft canter, and came around into the town square from the side. A group of about a score of young girls and boys were gathered before a tall bald man of late middle age. From the black robe he wore and the wooden crosier he carried, the knight knew the other man to be a priest. And behind the priest, perched on a pedestal before an altar, sat the dragon. Why would a man of God enter into a pact with a creature of darkness?

As Sir Leofred drew closer, he noticed that all the children were holding small wooden blocks, such as one would find in a carpenter's shop. The priest held a burlap sack, and from it he produced a wooden block identical to the ones the children held. He looked down at it and sighed. He then called out in a shaking voice, "Mairead."

Then the dragon rose into the sky and disappeared. A small girl of about six years of age with a head of dusky curls looked around in bewilderment at the calling of her name. A woman standing in the doorway, who closely resembled the girl, ran to the young child, weeping frantically, and scooped the girl up, pressing her tear-stained cheek to her daughter's. All the while, she was wailing, "No! No! Not my Mairead! Someone please help us! Have you forgotten how to love?"

Leofred could bear it no longer. He galloped into the square, swung out of the saddle, and embraced the child and her mother, saying to the woman, "Calm yourself, dear lady. There, there. No one is going to hurt your little girl." He fixed the priest with an icy glare. "You. How can you call yourself a man of God and ally yourself with a minion of darkness? What have you done?"

A tear rolled down the priest's cheek as he listened to Sir Leofred's rebuke.

"Alas, what you say is true, good sir knight. I, Father Brennan of Drakinon, am the most wretched man to tarnish the holy cloth in all the history of Kyngesrelm. But before you judge me further, I beg you to hear me out. And before we discuss my sins, I believe I have the right to know the name of my accuser. Who are you? I have never seen you before. Are you new in this area of the kingdom?"

"Yes. I am Sir Leofred, one of the Nine Peers. My shires are near Castle Pallanon."

"Then you have never heard of the recent sad plight of the village of Drakinon. That red wyrm that just now ascended into the sky is bound to the wizard Kaermoth. Six months ago, Kaermoth appeared, demanding tribute and slaves to feed his dragon. This compulsory tax, which if we do not pay, the wizard will use his dragon to turn the village into nothing more than a heap of ashes, has drained us of our already meager resources. With every innocent life the dragon takes, the wizard grows stronger, and the power of his magic increases."

"But," queried the knight, "why not speak to a fletcher about this?"

"I suppose you mean to say, Sir Leofred, that we should slay the dragon with a bow and arrow?" Not waiting for the knight to reply, the despondent priest continued. "We do not have a fletcher. What is more, we are tradesmen, not marksmen or hunters."

Sir Leofred again despised himself for not having brought his crossbow or an Elven longbow on his journey.

"So I," the melancholy priest continued, "acting as an inadvertent tool of the darkness, chose the lesser evil, and invented the seasonal lottery of death. Every three months, we write the names of the remaining children on small blocks of wood. The dragon comes and I produce one of the children's names and read it aloud to the dragon. A week after the drawing, that enemy of God, Kaermoth, comes, plunges his evil knife into the poor child's breast, and feeds the child's flesh to his accursed magical pet. I am making our enemies stronger, and, much worse, I am killing the next generation. I deserve a fate worse than death..." the priest sat down on the ground and began to sob into his hands.

Leofred knelt by the grieving father and lifted the man's head, looking deep into his eyes and placing a strong hand on his shoulder. "Do not weep so, Father Brennan. Gods loves you and will not abandon you. I will help in every way I can. I would be ashamed to call myself a paladin of Kyngesrelm and be unwilling to defend the weak."

3. Kaermoth

As soon as Sir Leofred had finished consoling the priest, a man of powerful build approached the knight and grasped his forearm tightly. He was dressed in a leather apron and his belt held awls, hammers and sturdy cutting knives. His long hair and mustache were dusky like the child's. He bared his teeth in a thankful yet sad smile. "Thank you, good sir knight, for comforting my family. We are thankful for your offer of aid. But I know not what one mere knight can do against the wizard Kaermoth and his fire wyrm."

"Have faith in the love of the Lord our God. I do not know what I am to do. But I swear to you that I will not let your daughter die."

The man smiled a tired smile . "I am Connor Wallace, the village leather worker. You look spent, Sir Leofred. Rhona, Mairead and I would be honored to have a guest at our table this night."

"And gratefully, I accept. I feel that God has called me to this place, for the time being at least."

The big craftsman took the knight by the hand and led him across the village square to his house.

That night as he ate supper, Sir Leofred watched little Mairead as she ate, talked and laughed, seemingly oblivious of her terrible fate; a fate that threatened to blot out the light of her life before it had the chance to shine. He wiped a solitary tear from his eye as he thought of the terrible images that must be coursing through the minds of the leather worker and his wife. What if a dragon should come to his castle and demand the life of his infant son as tribute? Should he be willing to give him up to purchase the lives and safety of his vassals? Although his bed in the loft above the leather worker's shop was warm and soft, Sir Leofred tossed and turned restlessly before finally sinking into an exhausted and dream-haunted sleep.

He dreamed that he was back in his manor near Castle Pallanon. Yet something was different. Instead of the banqueting table in the great hall, there was a bloodstained altar. On top of the bloodstained altar sat the crimson dragon of Kaermoth. The paladin gasped as he saw the sacrifice upon it. It was little Madoc, whimpering in terror. Lily stood before the altar, hands clasped, many tears staining her alabaster cheeks as she pleaded, "No! No! I beg of you, please!"

"The boy must die!" boomed an unseen, mighty voice.

Sir Leofred cried out, "No! Spare him! Take me in his stead!"

Father Brennan appeared before him as if from nowhere and stood pointing at the knight, His eyes burned with divine judgement. He had the appearance of a sainted prophet of old. The hall resounded with his grave voice. "Now you have proven, sir knight,that you are willing to die in the place of your own flesh and blood. But would you do it for the least of God's children? Greater love hath no man....!"

The distraught knight awoke from his dream in a cold sweat. It was still several hours before the dawn. He needed time to think and pray. He arose and went quickly to find Father Brennan.

The drowsy-eyed priest opened the door to the rectory. Squinting into the darkness, he said, "Sir Leofred? What brings you to my door at such an hour?"

"I beg your forgiveness, good father, but I must make use of the village chapel. I need a place to pray, for I am greatly disquieted in my spirit."

"Very well then, sir knight," the priest said, rubbing his eyes and fumbling in his pocket, but finding nothing. Please, give me only a moment. I must find the key. The chapel is locked for fear of thieves."

The priest went back inside the rectory and returned with a set of skeleton keys. He beckoned to the paladin, who followed him next door to the small village chapel. The furnishings were meager, consisting only of six pews, a small pulpit and an altar of the same size. Several candle stubs with untrimmed wicks, which plainly had been used for previous prayers, were placed at intervals upon the altar. Leofred felt closer to the Lord in that tiny sanctuary than he did even in the massive cathedral near Castle Pallanon, with all their beautiful windows of bright stained glass. He did not need to be surrounded by precious works of holy art to be surrounded by the presence of the One Holy God.

Nodding his thanks to Father Brennan, Sir Leofred knelt at the altar. Seeing that the knight desired to be alone, the priest turned and left the chapel, quietly closing the door behind him.

"Merciful Father," Sir Leofred prayed, sweat beginning to bead on his brow, "I know my duty to liege lord and land. Yet your will is greater than that of any earthly king, and thus I readily surrender to it. It is true that I fear for my life and well-being.yet even more do I fear for the lives of my dear wife and son. I will that I would live to hold them again. But as it says in the holy tomes, not my will but yours be done. I pray that you would be glorified in this, whatever the outcome may be. If I am to be killed in your service I pray that you might send someone worthy to care for my family. For I know that if I go to ride among your heavenly host, I shall soon see them again at the trumpet call of your heralds at the ending of days. I beg of you, reveal to me what your will is for me to do. I humbly beseech you, O Lord my God. Amen."

The paladin listened a long time in the silence of the small sanctuary. Then in the quiet of his heart, the voice of the Lord spoke. Leofred stood, resolved to his heaven-ordained course. As the blue-gray rays of a new winter dawn illumined the sky overhead, the knight made his way back to the rectory.

"Father Brennan," he said as the priest opened the door, "please assemble everyone in the village square. I would have all hear what I am to say."

While the priest went about this work, Leofred donned his armor. Standing before the entire population of Drakinon, the pale rising sun gleaming on his mail, he raised his hands high and said, "People of Drakinon, last night the Lord God made plain to me my purpose in coming here. Six days from now, when the evil enchanter Kaermoth comes for his sacrificial tribute, I shall offer my life in exchange for the life of Mairead Wallace, daughter of Connor Wallace, the village leather worker."

Many of the villagers gasped at the knight's words, and a stunned silence followed. No one was more flabbergasted at the unexpected turn of events than Connor Wallace himself. For a long moment he stared at Sir Leofred, a tear trickling down his cheek.

Then he came forward and squeezed Leofred's mailed forearm tightly. "Words cannot express my gratitude, good sir knight. We are eternally in your debt. I pray that with your loving sacrifice, Kaermoth will be satisfied and will leave us in peace."

The paladin nodded his agreement but secretly held reservations as to whether such a miracle would occur.

Over the next six days, Sir Leofred went often to the village chapel to pray for his wife and son, whom he was sure he would never see again. One day bled into the next as he struggled with the torturous anticipation of what was to come.

Then the sixth day came. At dawn, as the pale sun rose into the sky, the dragon returned. And this time upon its crimson back rode a tall old man clad in a crimson robe, bearing a staff of black iron. His beard was gray and he was one-eyed.

When the red wyrm alighted on its pedestal, the enchanter dismounted and declared in a scratchy voice, "I, Kaermoth, have come for my tribute, which is the life of the girl Mairead."

Leofred came forth, and ceremoniously doffed his armor and laid down his sword and shield. "I, Sir Leofred, Paladin of King Jaerython, do hereby offer my life in exchange for that of the girl. Do you accept my offer?"

The wizard's lips curled in a wicked smile. The flesh of a strong knight would greatly increase his power.

"I accept your offer. Come."

Leofred gave his unsheathed sword to the leather worker saying, "My last request is that you send this to my wife and son, that my son might wield it after me."

The wizard led the unarmored knight to the altar and willingly Leofred laid himself down upon it. Kaermoth was so filled with glee that he did not bother to bind the paladin's hands and feet.

The enchanter took up his wicked dagger and raising it high above his head, he said, "Give me thy power," and plunged it into the knight's breast. Then something strange occurred.

There was a snapping sound. With the speed of lightning Leofred ascertained what had happened. The evil dagger had struck the shard of the sword of Baerynthine, which the Knight always wore over his chest. The sturdiness of the angelic steel had broken the wicked blade.

Thinking quickly and acting before the wizard could react, Leofred bellowed, "Sword!"

Understanding, Connor Wallace hurled Sir Leofred's blade through the air. It sailed toward the altar, turning over in two revolutions, gleaming in the pale sunlight. The knight leapt up and caught it and turned, swinging it in an upward motion. The good steel flashed up and clove off the dragon's head. The headless corpse tottered from side to side and fell to the snowy ground with a crash.

"NO!" screamed the vile enchanter as he, now drained of all his power, wisped away like smoke and was no more.

For a moment, the village square was silent. Then a great cry of "Huzzah!" rent the cold morning air.

Father Brennan and Connor Wallace came forward, tears streaming down their cheeks. "Thank you, noble Sir Leofred," the aging priest said. "Your great act of love has saved our village. We are forever in your debt."

"Even more so am I," the leather worker added. "Rest assured, you and yours will always have a home here."

That night there was a feast in Sir Leofred's honor. The next day the skilled leather worker presented the paladin with a gambeson made of the dragon's skin, which no ordinary weapon could pierce. Satisfied that his service to God in that village was done, the knight bid his new friends farewell, and rode north, coming in time to Baerynthine's Wall.

4.   The Sword on the Fen

Sir Hersker rode northeast from Castle Pallanon. He was clad in his bright golden tabard emblazoned with the rearing grey stallion that was his insignia. He wore a coat of shining mail, and a padded conical spangenhelm with a built-in spider or leather skull cap instead of the usual arming cap and mail coif. Coming down his neck under the conical helmet, his flowing golden locks danced in the cold wind. He wore also a pair of golden leather gloves, and bore a buckler of sturdy ash painted gold. He had inherited the shield from his father, Allegran, who had taken it as a trophy of battle from a slain Vaering barbarian raider.

He was the youngest and spriest paladin of Kyngesrelm, but barely come into his nineteenth year. His eyes were alive with merriment and unrelenting cheer despite the cold gale. Often he would sing aloud with gusto as he rode through his small shire. And often the children of the village would hear his horse coming at a distance, and run to wave to him, singing along with whatever joyous ballad he happened to be crooning that day. He was nearly always merry, with times of sadness being as brief as a breeze among flowers. In fact, when he was born, the midwife thought him to be under some strange enchantment, for his birth cries had lasted only a moment, and then they had given way to soul-warming giggling and cooing.

The plump lady smiled at the display and said, "Blimey, me boy! You would chase the scowl from the face of a coffin bearer, you would, and no mistake!" When he became his father's page at the age of seven, his father would always find him singing a child's ballad of a humorous nature as he kicked the chainmail barrel to remove the rust from his papa's hauberk. Often the old knight found it necessary to intervene when the cleaning task turned into a game of dwarven foot ball with the other pages.

When he became his father's squire, he rode to war alongside the old knight, and together they fulfilled the days of military service to their lord for the year, as is a just requirement in all knightly realms. Though these times of duty by combat were often long and laborious, the young squire was quick to make a kind-hearted jest or whistle a merry tune, and it made his father's heart glad.

After he was knighted and later rose in rank to become the youngest of the Nine Peers, he acted as both jester and bard. Even after a hard fought battle in one the frequent campaigns against the trolls and goblins, Hersker would cheer his comrades with his jolly songs and poems. The other knights found that, when he had finished, such great joy was burning in their hearts that their wounds no longer bothered them.

"Ho, Hersker my lad," Leofred chuckled one night around the open fire, his face beaming with a ruddy flame of joy. "Sing to us again of Inglamour and the taking of the topaz tower."

"Sing it anew, young Hersker," begged the kind-hearted Sir Cedric, whipping back his Vaering style braid from the diamond-shaped mop of chestnut hair on top of his head. (None of his comrades knew why the knight Cedric had chosen to model his hairstyle upon one popular with the pagan barbarians, but then again, this wealthy lord of Gelden Hill was a rather free –spirited chap.) "Sing it once more," Cedric repeated, "though as likely we have heard it over a thousand times tonight."

"Give us the tune, Hersker, my old chap," cajoled Godfrey, whetting his poniard on a stone.

"Only when you feel ready, and only if you be willing," added Liddegond, who was dabbing a spot of gruel from his chin.

"Very well, my lords, if you do so desire." The youth cleared his throat and began to croon.

"The topaz knight, Sir Inglamour, he rode out one day,

For to take back his topaz tower, over the hills and far away..."

When he had finished singing the ridiculous ballad, the silly song awarded the young knight the usual raucous laughter from his fellow paladins.

As he relived this fond memory from the previous summer, the thought occurred to him that a joyous verse would help pass the time on his journey to the north. And so, a song bubbled up in his spirit as he rode across the plain that day, and he sang it with great cheer.

"O'er the fields of snow and ice,

Verily doth my cheer suffice.

King Jaer commands and we obey

Into the north and far away."

The song served to heighten his spirits all the more, and brought joy to all who heard it as it echoed across the snow-laden hills, its joyful noise rebounding up to the very heavens.

He rode on for hours, whistling merry tunes and lays as they entered into his flaxen head. As he entered the gray fen country of central northeastern Kyngesrelm, which was called Delven Fen, the young man looked up at the sky, and saw the sun was blotted out by giant, dark and ominous clouds. They seemed almost to have personas unto themselves, bastions of despair seeking to blot out the light. So oppressive was their aura that young Sir Hersker purposefully set his mind and lips on reciting a canticle, a lorica of his own composition. He sang a canticle, for he knew that no nursery rhyme would steel his joyous heart against their oppression. For young Hersker understood that the true source of joy for the hearts of all men was found in heart-felt praise of the Lord their God.

"I bind unto myself this day

The name of the holy God my Father

Who gives strength to my sword arm

And joy into my heart.

I bind unto myself today

The cheer of the sun shining golden in the sky,

The mirth of the lightning,

Laughing as it flicks from cloud to cloud.

I bind unto myself today also

The beauty of the lily of the field,

Lovely and joyous,

Mirroring the brazen gold light of the sun.

I bind unto myself my sure salvation in the Lord

Against all evil powers

That walk upon or beneath this midden-realm.

I bind unto myself today,

By invocation of the name of the Lord,

My joy and my salvation."

Thus the joyous, flaxen-haired Sir Hersker rode on, his spirit heartened by this hymn of invocation.

As he rode on, the air of his surroundings became more despondent. Even his roan stallion began to tread at a slower gait, his head bowed low, as he plodded through the icy sludge. Far off in the distance, the knight heard the low rumbling of thunder, and saw flashes of pale light between the clouds.

As he rode up upon a small islet in the icy mud, he saw on the horizon, a large white lump sitting atop the fen. This feature seemed inconsistent with the surrounding geography. Perhaps it was the ruins of an ancient stone building where the young knight could seek shelter from the coming storm. Hersker rode toward it.

Coming closer, Sir Hersker saw that the white hemisphere he had seen in the distance was a small domed mausoleum of marble that appeared to be surprisingly white despite the climate and location.

There was a rumble of thunder in the distance as the young knight reined his steed to a halt. It did not appear to be a very comfortable shelter. But a storm was brewing, and so it would have to suffice.

Dismounting and leading the horse inside, the golden-haired paladin saw that what he had first guessed was true: the building was a mausoleum, and moreover a pagan one.

Inside there was a sarcophagus of marble set a on a large dais of the same kind of stone. The sides were carved in the runic language of the tawny-bearded Vaering barbarians, who would suddenly burst out of the north to raid monasteries and priories.

On the lid of the sarcophagus was carved the life-size image of a sleeping Vaering raider king. His arms were folded over his mail-clad breast and clasped between them was a rune-marked single-handed broadsword. It was doubtlessly a Vaering sword, for the hilt consisted of a short crossguard and lobed pommel divided into three sections, both characteristic of the hilts of the Northmen.

There was a flash of lightning. After it had passed, the young knight saw that the blade of the dead chieftain's sword was glowing whitely in the dark, almost burning with a white fire within the blade itself. *Could it be enchanted with black magic?* Sir Hersker breathed a prayer of protection.

Hersker waited for the storm to abate, all the while staring at the sword. His father, who had fought the Vaering raiders on many occasions, had taught young Hersker a little of their runic language. Slowly, the young paladin was able to decipher that the runic inscription on the blade read thus: "To unleash the true power of this weapon, look to the sky."

Every time there was a flash of lightning, the sword glowed white in response. Sir Hersker did not know if he should be amazed or fearful.

As soon as the storm had abated, Hersker prepared to leave the mausoleum. A still small voice spoke in his mind. "Take the sword with you."

"But it belonged to a pagan, and is evil."

"What pagan kings, and other enemies of God intend for evil, the True King uses for the good of those who love and serve him. Be not afraid to take the sword."

Hersker slid the sword out of the stone arms of the sleeping Vaering king, and stowing it in his saddle bag, struck out again across the fen. He did not know why the Lord God had told him to take up a sword previously used by a pagan barbarian king, but he had learned despite his relatively few years to obey the voice of God even when it made no sense at all to his human mind.

5.   The Mist of Darkimot

As the young knight continued north across the fen, he could feel the mist growing darker and heavier all around him. He looked up and saw what appeared to be a dot on the horizon. Perhaps it was a small castle or village where he could buy provisions; for he had been so zealous for his quest he had not brought much food. He was famished. High in the sky above the spot was a swirling dark cloud, like the eye of a storm. It filled young Hersker with a sense of foreboding yet he felt drawn toward it. As he drew nearer, the sword of the dead Vaering king began to glow within the saddlebag, but the young knight did not see it.

Hersker saw upon arrival that the place was a small village surrounded by a palisade of stakes. This was strange for there appeared to be no town militia. A strange mist rose from the icy ground, and despite his usually cheery demeanor, the young Sir Hersker began to feel somewhat depressed. As he rode through the dirty streets, he saw many townspeople, and though he often smiled and waved to them, they paid him no heed. They quickly shuffled out of the way, keeping their heads concealed in tattered black shawls and cloaks. Needless to say, Hersker found their behavior very odd. As he came near the center of the town, he thought he would cheer himself with a song. He began crooning a nursery rhyme his nurse had sung to him when he was a child.

"Old Father Giles

Ran twenty-six miles

Upon a summer's day.

And then when he was through with that

He danced for joy on the fresh-cut hay…"

His voice trailed off as he saw the pedestrians in the street staring at him curiously, eyes wide with shock. He had not noticed it, but as he sang the child's ditty, the oppressive mist surrounding him had dissipated ever so slightly.

He smiled sheepishly, once again receiving strange looks in return. He was growing hungrier with each passing minute, and, seeing a tavern, tied his stallion to a hitching post and went inside to buy supper. The tavern keeper did not even look up when Sir Hersker entered.

"Good even, my good man," boomed the smiling Hersker.

The man did not reply but kept his eyes on his sweeping.

"What ye be wanting?" he muttered at last in an almost inaudible voice.

"Might I have some stew, if you please?"

The man ladled some indiscernible concoction into a small wooden bowl and slowly slid it across the counter. The young paladin picked up the bowl and examined the contents. He could not recognize all the ingredients, but he was certain he saw something that looked like earth worm or centipede. The unpleasant sight stole his ravenous appetite. Frowning, he laid the bowl down, took out his purse and flipped a copper piece on the counter. "On second thought, I am not all that hungry. Thank you anyway, good sir." The tavern keeper grunted as Sir Hersker left his dingy establishment.

As the knight was unhitching his horse, he heard a sharp whistle behind him. He looked up to see a wiry youth with a tangled mop of dark hair staring at him. The lad cocked his head to the side, and disappeared around the side of the building. His curiosity aroused, Hersker followed. As Hersker passed out of view from the street, the wiry young man grabbed him by the scruff of his golden tabard, then pulled him in barely an inch away from his face.

"What is going on?" the bewildered Hersker demand. "What are you-"

"Quiet, please, good sir knight," the boy whispered, "lest Durving should magically hear you. I am Joderick of Darkimot, called "Jody". Long have I prayed for someone impervious to the curse to come to Darkimot."

"Curse? What curse? What do you mean?"

"Do you not see it? Look around the village. Everywhere there is an air of despondency and woe. But it was not always thus. There was a time when the village of Darkimot, was a place of light and joy. But then Durving the troll came across the fen, coveting the wealth of this town. When he saw he could not obtain it by deception, he cast a terrible curse on it, weaving an enchanted mist around the village that saps the joy from our hearts. One by one, the people of this place succumbed to despair. Only I, who was once known by the title of Jody the Jolly Jumper, the merry village fool, have held on to the last scraps of remaining cheer. Long have I beseeched the Lord for someone immune to the curse to come and save us. When you came and started to sing your little nursery rhyme, and I saw the mist of despair fleeing before your joyous tune, I knew that you would be the one who could slay Durving and end the curse and restore our joy. Please, will you help us, joyous paladin?"

Hersker silently praised the Lord God for making his purpose in this place clear to him. "I will. Where may I find my new enemy, this troll Durving?"

"He wanders the gray fen to the north of the village. The area of his patrol is very broad, but he is quite easy to spot, for a magical mist of despair surrounds him. And it is a mist even darker than the one that surrounds this village."

"Thank you, sir," the paladin said, nodding. "Rest assured, friend Jody, that I, Sir Hersker, son of Sir Allegran of Kyngesrelm, shall free you from this oppression or die in the effort. Please pray for me as I set out to accomplish this, and trust ever in the Lord, our God. Farewell."

Hersker unhitched his stallion and rode north from the despondent village of Darkimot, his course set. He would give his last breath to bring joy back to Darkimot. It was for that purpose the Lord had brought him to the grief-stricken village. This was his heaven-ordained mission. Of that the young paladin was certain.

The knight continued north, eyes scanning for a darker wisp of mist or cloud, anything that would hint of the troll Durving's current whereabouts. Strangely, as the surrounding mist began to darken, he felt a strong heat emanating from the saddlebag. There was a rumble of thunder in the distance and a flash of lightning. And even as the branch of pure energy flashed forth its white tongue, the inner white fire of the sword within the saddlebag flared.

Although Hersker knew he had precious little time to waste, he thought it best to discover what was causing the searing pain. He dismounted, his dark green leather riding boots sinking into the mire. He opened the saddlebag, and saw that the ancient Vaering sword was glowing with a strange white light, the barbarian runes illumined and traced in a sparkling gold sheen. The blade seemed almost to speak to the paladin in that moment.

"Take me up." Amazed, yet sensing a ghostly presence that chilled the life blood in his veins, Sir Hersker obeyed.

Placing his own sword into the saddlebag, the young knight mounted again. He clicked his tongue to his stallion and rode on.

After several minutes of searching the fen to no avail, Hersker saw in the distance what appeared to be a strange cloud, darker and more ominous than those laden with rain. It was very peculiar, for this cloud was very low to the ground, and seemed to be advancing at a slow gait, rather than billowing forward in the sky.

Riding closer, young Hersker saw that it was no ordinary cloud but rather a billowing insubstantial mass, surrounding a massive human-like creature. The creature was almost ten feet tall. It was broader than a team of oxen, and its entire body was bald, like the head of a vulture, and its skin was almost as gray as the mist surrounding it. Its hide appeared to be more compactly woven together than king's mail, so that no mere blade could pierce it. Two large, milk-white orbs were set above its bulbous nose and large maw. It carried a crude yet massive battle axe. A troll. Surely it was Durving.

Hersker dismounted, took up his round shield, and brandished his sword, declaring, "Here, in the sight of Almighty God, I have taken the war road against you." Durving grunted in response.

Uttering his battle cry, the young paladin charged forward. As soon as he reached the magic mist surrounding Durving, he could almost feel it take hold of him. His movements became slower as he felt despondency upon his soul.

Shaking the feeling from his mind he began to follow his mother's advice and to shout aloud thanksgiving for his blessings.

"I sing my thanks unto the Lord,

Who has given me a strong sword arm with which to fight the powers of darkness.

He has given me also a noble lord to serve

And through serving my liege lord,

I serve the Lord God himself!
I praise the Lord for my Godly father and mother,

Who have raised me in awestruck wonder of the Lord.

I praise him for his holy tomes of wisdom

And for the joy he has given to my heart.

I praise him!"

During this time, the troll had been raining down heavy blows with his axe that Hersker was able to parry only by the grace of the Lord. Blows that surely would have cloven him in two if it were not for his agile sword arm. What was more, another sword would have broken under such stress. But the blade Hersker now wielded was forged for a king and moreover was wrought with magic. Most importantly, it seemed that as Sir Hersker's joy grew so too did his power. And so too did the light emanating from the sword.

Lightning flashed overhead, and it was at that moment, that the young knight forced the troll slightly off balance. A voice spoke to Sir Hersker's mind in that brief moment. "Lift the blade to the sky."

Hersker obeyed. An arm of lightning blazed down out of the sky and struck the sword. Amazingly, the force of the strike neither killed Hersker nor in any way damaged the sword. Rather the lightning stayed within the sword! The skyward sword glowed all the more as the lightning crackled forth from the tip. Immediately, the young knight knew what to do.

He shouted at the top of his lungs, "I shall sing to the Lord for joy FOREVER!" With these words, the paladin plunged his blade deep into the fell troll's breast. Durving gave voice to an earsplitting cry of pain, the lightning crackled inside his heart and then… the troll Durving burst asunder.

Hersker barely had time to fall behind his buckler before the debris of the kill rained down upon it. Standing up and surveying the carnage, the young knight saw that the troll's arm was lying close by. Hersker put away his weapons and picked it up. He then loaded it onto his stallion and started back toward Darkimot. The massive limb was a heavy burden for the poor beast, but it could sense its master's joy, which gave it strength. Arriving back at the village, the young knight saw that the mist of despair had fled. Even the storm clouds overhead were clearing and the sun beginning to shine joyously once more. The villagers were standing around with awkward expressions on their faces, not quite knowing what to do with themselves.

Hersker threw the massive troll arm down on the ground. "Your oppressor, the thief of your joy, is now dead. Let your joy return."

Joderick, or Jody the Jolly Jumper, as he could now again call himself, came forward carrying a lute. "It has been a long time since I have strummed a tune on this, but I think I may be of some help." He winked. Then he began strumming a merry tune and singing a ridiculous song of his own spontaneous composition.

"And now for grumpy trolls, the death bell tolls

'Tis no idle tooshmclaver.

Let us sing a song of joy,

For this noble knight, our savior.

A tool of the Lord

With his buckler and sword,

More joyous than pipe or lute.

To that troll scum

That puddenum,

He gave the troll the boot.

And without your arm

And despondent charm

How will you blow kisses?

We know too well

That in the bowels of hell

Oh, how much you'll miss us.

But all you'll hear,

Is one great cheer

And many boos and hisses."

Joderick repeated the refrain several times. The villagers felt something strange bubbling up inside them, as they heard his song, a feeling long lost and now finally returning. True joy. Slowly, the lips of the townspeople began to crack open into smiles, and one by one they began to laugh and sing along.

There was much dancing and merry-making in Darkimot that night. With the coming of dawn, Hersker rode on to Baerynthine's wall, taking the magic Vaering lightning sword with him.

6.   Ofermod

Sir Fréalást rode directly east from Castle Pallanon. He was clad in heavy mail that sparkled despite the snow that clung to it. Not all of the flakes were noticeable, for most were well hidden by his rich purple surcoat emblazoned with the gold-hilted sword in a matching golden sheath that was his insignia. On his hands he wore violet leather gloves that his vassals would often see, usually raised to halt an argument between his serfs. Hidden by a great helm, his green eyes methodically searched the snow-chilled landscape. He had slung his pentagonal shield, also emblazoned with his heraldry, over his right shoulder, and his hand-and-a-half sword was sharp though he preferred not to use it if its use could be avoided.

He urged his horse on gently, and kept riding at a fast pace. He knew that it was important to arrive at Baerynthine's Wall on schedule, but he did not share his King's fatalistic urgency. He knew not how, but in the quiet of his heart he believed that this upstart Skrael would be defeated by heaven's providence and in the Lord's perfect time.

Quietly, he began to softly croon a hymn often sung in the city cathedrals at the turning of the week.

"It all shall come to pass,

All shall come to pass

Dunna race against the hourglass

For it all shall come to pass."

He spoke to his white stallion Grannock, though he was actually musing aloud to himself. "I do not know why my Liege King Jaerython believes that there is a possibility that our enemy, the shadow-raiser will succeed. My mind is at rest and my soul likewise within me, that the promises of God shall hold true in the end. Men are fools to doubt. All shall be accomplished, brother beast, all shall be accomplished."

He chuckled then and patted the white stallion's neck comfortingly.

He continued east, riding slightly to the North, through the firm land between the villages of Veylandin and Darkimot. He came to the eastern edge of Kyngesrelm and the village of Ofermod, where many dwarves and elves had dwelt together for centuries. His plan was to stop there for the night, purchase a fresh store of supplies, and continue northwest at first light, eventually making it to the Gateway to Varluckhuld in the center of Baerynthine's Wall where he would meet his fellow paladins. But something happened at Ofermod that delayed him and tested his mettle more than any battle he had yet fought.

While he was still about half a league away from the town, he came upon an engraved boulder that read: "Here begin the boundaries of the town of Ofermod, proud home of the elven house of Aelfwyr, master cattle herders, and the dwarven house of Feormund, foremost line of bladesmiths."

Strangely, below the human speech engraving, under the names of the respective houses, were several lines of elvish and dwarvish. Below the name of House Feormund were written Elvish glyphs with words such as thief and liar in the common tongue of men. Similar words that were slightly less decipherable to the knight were written in Dwarvish runes below the name of House Aelfwyr.

The paladin was pondering the meaning of the graffiti, when he heard on the wind a sound like the terrified bellow of a cow. Suddenly out of the driving snow, a brown dun cow charged toward him. The poor heifer was being pursued by a great black wolf, larger than any the knight had ever seen. Thinking quickly, Sir Fréalást withdrew his crossbow from the baldric on his back, and with the deftness of a true marksman, shot a heavy bolt past the frightened young cow, striking the wolf squarely in its yellow, bloodshot eye. The wolf snarled in pain and fell to the ground with a thud.

Fréalást dismounted and laid a comforting hand on the young heifer's shoulder, and began crooning softly to it until it had calmed itself.

Seeing that the cow wore a frayed rope lead, Sir Fréalást decided to take the heifer to Ofermod to see if he could locate the owner. But first, the knight took one of the wolf's paws as a souvenir. It would make a fine gift for his nephew, Brand.

Fréalást continued down the snowy road to Ofermod township. The first thing he noticed was that on one side of the road were buildings of dwarven stone architecture, and on the other side were high wooden edifices of the elves of southern Kyngesrelm. If elves and dwarves had lived together here for centuries, he would have thought to find the two architectures alongside one another and mixed together.

He was passing by a dwarven smithy from which wafted the oppressive heat and burning smell of a forge fire, when suddenly he heard a gruff voice call out, "Hold there, paladin, sir!"

A dwarf in the garb of an armorer ran out of the forge to accost Sir Fréalást. He had a dark brownish red beard that was forked. The bottom of the beard was divided in halves and each half twisted into a braid in a style common among all dwarves of the kingdom. His thick mane was bound up in a topknot.

"My name's Norron, chief weapon smith and elder father of House Feormund. If you please, sir knight, I need that cow to use for her leather. Brigandines, you see. What are you asking for her?"

"Well, you see, master dwarf, I am not sure..." Fréalást began.

"You must not sell that beast to him," cried an eloquent voice, cutting off Sir Fréalást's answer. A tall elf with braided golden locks ran up on the other side of the road and stood glaring at Norron.

"Back off, Reinil," the dwarf said through clenched teeth. "It's just like your family to prevent us from obtaining meat or leather. I saw him first."

The elf cast up his eyes, "Aaghh! While you and your family, O Patriarch of House Feormund, are busy stuffing your faces and clanking your hammers around, not to mention stealing cattle, we are working hard driving our herds to Dwarversdunn and Drakinon. But oh, I forgot. You are too lazy to work. Once a thief, always a thief." The elf spat.

"You!" Norron growled, his hand moving to the shaft of his hammer.

"Hold!" bellowed Sir Fréalást, holding up both hands. He removed his cylindrical helm, revealing his dark mustachios and goatee. He fixed both the elf and the dwarf with a stern gaze. "Obviously there is a great dispute between your houses. I am Sir Fréalást de Pacem, a paladin of King Jaerython, one of the Nine Peers, and I am thus able to pass judgment on disputes within the realm. I will hear both your cases tomorrow, when I have filled my belly and am prepared to arbitrate. But now I must rest, for your squabbling has caused my head to ache."

7.   Gem-Locks

"Now," said the raven-haired knight curtly, "I will leave the heifer here in plain sight. I hold you both to your honor that neither of you will take it. If I have cause to believe that either of you has done otherwise, I shall use my authority of as one of the Nine Peers to deal out severe judgment. That said, if one of you gentlemen will be so kind as to direct me to the inn, I shall take my leave to rest and think. Neither of you will be thought of more highly than the other for the sake of your information."

"Well, er, you see, sir knight,'" the elf Reinil began, somewhat stumbling over the words, "there has been no inn in this town for generations, not since the feud between our houses began long ago. You will have to stay with one of the families of House Aelfwyr, or, and I would be dead before I saw it happen, with a sniveling family of the accursed House Feormund. If I were you, Sir Fréalást, I would choose the former."

Norron's eyes bulged in anger, and he opened his mouth to pour forth an equally wrathful protest, but before he could give voice to his objections, Fréalást raised his gauntleted hand. "For simple reasons, namely the probable size of the guest bed in your house, I will pass the night in the house of Provost Reinil." Seeing Reinil's eyes glisten with triumph, the paladin quickly added. "But I will take my supper at your house tonight, Master Norron."

For almost an entire minute, the elf and dwarf patriarchs considered Sir Fréalást's decision, glaring at each other all the while. Finally they looked back at the knight. "Very well," they declared in a stony tone, and almost in unison. Another silent moment passed. Norron produced a small pipe etched with dwarvish runes, and lit it. Unlike men and dwarves, the elves of Pallanon were characteristically no lovers of smoke, so Provost

Reinil began to shift uncomfortably from one foot to the other. Perhaps this was the dwarf patriarch's intention all along. Finally the elf ceased his slight movements, and muttered, "Come with me, Sir Fréalást." Reinil turned and led Fréalást into the elven district. Norron gave voice to a loud "harrumph", turned, and walked back to his forge, puffing smoke rings in his wake.

Reinil led Grannock at a slow walk through the streets and alleys of the Elven district of Ofermod. It was said in ancient legends and tales that the first of the elves, who were the first free people created by God, and the ancestors of all the fair folk in Pallanon, could sing their dwellings out of the branches of trees when first they awoke in the vast forests of the young world. These homes, though probably made with axe and adze, still reflected an ancient, magical art.

Many of the mansions were built with high pillars supporting the high roofs. Many of these pillars had lenticular elven designs and images of beasts, primarily horses and cattle, crawling up and down their surfaces. There were also lightly-carved sketches of flowers and trees, showing the universal Elven value of nature.

Beside nearly every one of the grand dwellings was a stable, from each of which flowed a ceaseless melody of the lowing of cattle mixed with the neighing of drivers' steeds. Fair little elflings ran to and fro before the stables, armed with switching rods, yawing and clicking as they drove their wheeled toy cattle to market. If the mansions were any indication, Fréalást doubted not that the coffers of the fair folk of the town were filled to bursting.

The grandest of the mansions was near the center of the Elven district. It was a tall house painted forest green with a pearl white roof in the center of which was a tower in the shape of an unopened alabaster rose. There were five long steps leading up to a set of gilded mahogany double doors. In front of the doors stood two Elven warriors clad in leather breastplates with spiked steel spaulders on their shoulders and long capes of dark blue satin falling down their backs. Both of the warriors' right hands were on the pear-shaped pommels of the falchions that they wore belted at their waists. They appeared to be twins, and their hair was the color of ebony. Neither elf warrior wore a helm.

The one on the left raised a leather-gloved hand in greeting as Provost Reinil approached. "Well met, my lord. What are your orders?"

"Well met, Vendel. Go and tell your mistress that we will have a highly honored guest staying the night with us."

The dark-haired elf saluted, turned and went into the house.

Turning to his other retainer, the Elven Provost said, "Gondel, while your brother is otherwise engaged, take this good knight's mount to the stable and tend to the noble beast."

Sir Fréalást dismounted and Reinil handed Gondel the reins. Then Reinil walked briskly up the steps, opened the massive double doors with apparent ease, and both he and his guest entered the house.

The interior of the house was vast and ornately decorated. Divans and chairs, upholstered with what appeared to be moss, were arranged to form a sort of drawing room. Beyond this was a feasting table spread with a dark green cloth and set with silver dishes, goblets and a decanter of spiced cider. Still beyond the table was a winding stair leading up to the second level of the house.

"I do apologize," the elf was saying as Sir Fréalást was surveying his new surroundings. "I can never keep track of lady of the house, you see."

He walked hurriedly to the foot of the winding stair. "Elania!" he called. "We do not wish to keep our guest waiting, do we? After all, it is not every day that one of the Nine Peers of the King of all Kyngesrelm comes to our door, you know!"

Soon afterwards, a tall stately elf lady came down the stairs. She was clad in a gown of forest green laced with silver. She had the ever youthful features found in all elven kind, and did not appear old, except for the far-off look in her eyes. She was like many of the beautiful elves that the knight had seen in illuminated manuscripts. But her hair! Her tresses were dark green and sparkled like an emerald.

"Oh, dear," Reinil said, taking note of the awestruck look in Fréalást's eyes. "You are staring at her hair. Permit me to explain. My wife Elania is of an ancient and noble Elven line. They are called Gem-Locks and have almost passed into legend these days. Their hair strongly resembles that of a jewel or other precious stone. Speaking of the subject...." He turned back to the stair. "Nora! Come down and meet our noble guest."

A short moment later a tall Elven maiden descended the winding stair. She was the most beautiful woman Sir Fréalást had ever seen. Her skin was pale and smooth like alabaster, and her eyes were the color of cinnamon. But, as with the Lady Elania, the most captivating of her qualities was her hair. It was like burnished rubies, and sparkled with a blood-red, fiery light.

"This is my eldest daughter, Nora. I wanted to name her Ruadana, which is the Alfanonian Elvish word for "red". The reasons for my preference should be quite obvious. But her mother said that name was such a fuss to pronounce." The beautiful elf maid curtsied gracefully. And for a moment, the knight could not speak.

"Will you take refreshment, good sir knight?" The question from Provost Reinil jolted Sir Fréalást out of his enraptured trance.

"Uh, er, yes, my lord. Thank you," the knight stammered. He had resolved in that brief moment that if he and his brethren survived their quest and saved the kingdom, he would return to Ofermod.

8.   A Tale of Two Houses

It was now Fréalást's turn to shift awkwardly from one foot to the other. But he did so only a moment, and then, smiling at his host, joined the elf and his wife at the table. The knight was pleased though somewhat embarrassed that ruby-haired Nora took the seat next to him. Reinil clapped his hands and twice shouted, "Sveinil, Leyna, please bring the crumpets."

Two elves with golden hair and blue eyes, a he-elf and she-elf, both bearing a strong resemblance to one another, came downstairs, the girl carrying a huge platter of crumpets and jam. Sveinil, the male, filled three goblets with the decanter of spiced cider. Sir Fréalást turned to Reinil and said, "Now Provost Reinil, will you enlighten me as to the reason for the animosity you and your kin feel against Provost Norron and his house?"

The Elven Provost opened his mouth to answer but before he was able, the double doors swung open, slammed shut and in walked a sweaty giant of an elf. He was one of the gem locks and his long mane was ruby-hued like Nora's. Even beneath the leather riding jerkin the elf wore, Sir Fréalást could see that the he had the strength of a forest troll. He wore breeches of brown doe skin. Hung at his waist was a heavy hand-and-a-half sword with a hilt of white silver, a mark of the dwarven smiths of Dwarversdunn. A three-cornered shield hung in a baldric on his back. It was of steel, not of painted oak like the similarly shaped shield Fréalást carried. The Elven warrior's eyes burned with a cheery blue fire.

"Good, morrow, father," he boomed, his face beaming. "Old Gondel said we had a noble visitor. By the seed bull! He has the bearing of a knight, and one of no small importance at that. Will you not introduce me, father?"

"Ah, yes!" Reinil's face shone with pride. "Sir Fréalást, may I present to you my son and heir, Mennoth. He is the pride of House Aelfwyr. No finer champion has ever come from the line of the fair folk."

Mennoth gripped Fréalást's forearm in greeting and the poor knight felt as if it were in a vice. Sir Fréalást tried not to grimace. Once the elven youth released his hold, Sir Fréalást flexed his arm slightly to ease the soreness.

By this time, the golden-haired Sveinil had finished pouring the cider.

"Thank you," Reinil said to his servants. "You may go."

"Yes, me laird," they said with a distinct Alfanonian brogue. Then they left.

"Their father, Connall," Reinil explained, "is an Alfanonian clan chieftain. He wanted them to learn something of southern elven culture, so he gave them to me for a year as paid servants. Sveinil is good with a claymore and his sister is an excellent rider. They both have been teaching Mennoth the techniques their people use to fight trolls and goblins."

"You are one of the Nine Peers?" Mennoth asked.

Fréalást nodded.

A look of respect showed on Mennoth's countenance. "It is my dream to one day be a knight. But alas, I have no chance of proving my valor, for we live nowhere near Trillven Forest, so I have never even seen a troll or goblin. I must therefore content myself with great-wolf hunts. I am but just come from one."

"Pardon my ignorance, noble he-elf," Fréalást said. "I am not from this region of the kingdom. What is the difference between a great-wolf and an ordinary one?"

Fire entered the elf eyes as he spoke. "The old sages say the first great-wolves were pets of the Enemy, Skrael during the Everfrost War. Whatever the truth of that may be, great-wolves are still numerous in this region of the kingdom. They are nearly as large as ponies. Their paws are large and their claws and teeth long and sharp. An evil yellow-red fire burns in their eyes. They are always hungry, ever thirsting for fresh blood."

The Paladin thought for a moment and said, "I believe I encountered a great-wolf near the boundary stone of this town." He then recounted how he had put a crossbow bolt through its eye and brought the frightened heifer back to town.

"You killed a great-wolf with one shot?" Mennoth gasped, his respect for Sir Fréalást deepening even more. "Truly, you have the best luck in the whole kingdom."

"No, friend Mennoth," Fréalást answered, smiling. "The Lord sent his angels to protect me. I believe he brought that young heifer across my path for a reason."

Turning to his host, the knight said, "Speaking of this matter, Provost Reinil, will you now explain to me, in the simplest possible terms, the dispute between House Aelfwyr and House Feormund?"

"Ah, yes." Turning to Mennoth, the older elf said, "Son, let me borrow your back shield." The ruby-haired elf youth leaned forward, unslung the shield from its baldric and handed it to his father. Fréalást saw that it was emblazoned with a huge golden image of a bull.

"This is the ancient seed bull of house Aelfwyr. It is also the seed of our dispute with those of accursed house Feormund. My great grandfather, the honorable Provost Caradoc had ownership of him. Oh the great cattle that he could have sired! But alas, it was not to be. For a week before breeding season began, that pitiful lying worm, Provost Thunar of House Feormund, came and offered to buy the bull from my sire for a puny sum. He craved its beef and good hide. Being ever wise, my great grandsire refused. Old Thunar flew into a rage and stormed out, muttering odious threats under his breath."

"That night, as my great grandfather slept, Thunar and his male kin sneaked into the pen and murdered our seed bull, greatly mutilating the body.

"The next morning, after discovering the crime, Caradoc confronted Thunar and his sons, but they, being the sniveling liars common to House Feormund, pretended to be shocked and denied knowledge of the foul deed. They accused my honorable great grandfather of contriving the whole story in order to seize their great wealth. Since then there has been a feud of enmity between the elves of house Aelfwyr and the dwarves of House Feormund."

"Though, by God's grace, it has not yet come to bloodshed," Mennoth interjected.

Reinil nodded, acknowledging the truth of his son's statement, then continued. "That is why we import all of our weapons and armor from Dwarversdunn, not wishing to deal with these dishonest rogues who bang their hammers incessantly here in Ofermod. So now you see why I first admonished you and still so admonish you not to sell your heifer to the dishonest Provost Norron of thieving House Feormund."

"Here, here!" proclaimed Mennoth, raising his goblet high.

After the impromptu toast, the raven-haired knight took up his coif and cylindrical helmet, and took his leave, saying, "Now I must take supper with these thus-named 'seventh sons' of earth and see if they are of the caliber you claim them to be. Until curfew. " Raising his hand in farewell, he went to the stables, saddled Grannock, and departed for the house of Provost Norron.

Upon crossing the road that divided the two districts, the dark-haired warrior immediately noted a stark change in the architecture. Gone were the tall, sky-piercing mansions of the introspective fair folk, their careful reflections of God's natural masterpieces replaced by bastions wrought of the spine of his creation: adamant, unbending stone. The sons and daughters of earth preferred its touch to that of wood. Small wonder. For it was from the stone, the skeleton of all creation, that these small master craftsmen, obtained the ore from which they made their renowned articles of war.

There was a weapon forge on nearly every corner, marked by the images of beautiful crossed hammers or double-bladed battle axes. Ever—rising clouds of smoke puffed forth like rings from a troll's pipe, turning the winter sky all the more sullen, And yet merry, flowing words in the hard dwarvish language poured forth in battle-themed ballads as the short, scruffy smiths plied their trade at the forge fires.

"Ho, there, good fellow!" Fréalást said, stopping a fire-haired dwarf who was walking in toward him, gobbling an over-sized leg of mutton. "Where is the house of Provost Norron?"

"Between those two taverns," the dwarf belched, pointing.

"My thanks," said Sir Fréalást, somewhat disgusted.

The two taverns between which the gluttonous dwarf had pointed both bore plaques of bronze over their small doors which read: *"The Rook's Beak*, where Thunar Thunder Hammer, honorable Provost of House Feormund took his ale" and *"The Mad Raven*, where honorable Provost Thunar Thunder Hammer always ate the feast of Everfrost's Vanquishing."

Guiding Grannock between these two noteworthy establishments, the paladin came upon a curious, unmistakably dwarven dwelling. There was a smooth boulder, which was very massive, in the middle of the cobblestone street. A large hole had been chiseled out of its top and a meat scented stream of smoke billowed skyward. There was only one window, circular like that of a cathedral, above the door, from which poured flickering light, as of a great roaring fire upon the hearth. Both the window and door were of special blue dwarven steel. The small door was embossed and engraved with dwarven letters and images of dwarf warriors, battles, and battle gear. The knocker in the center of the door was crafted in the image of a huge dwarf forging hammer striking an embossed anvil, surrounded by blue flames. Sir Fréalást guessed that this was the heraldry of House Feormund.

Dismounting his horse and tying it to a hitching post, Fréalást took off his helmet and coif, drew back the small hammer with his free hand, and rapped on the door three times. He was somewhat taken aback, for the striking resounded with a great *boom! boom! boom!*

A muffled dwarven voice came from within the house. "I be comin'! I be comin'!"

Once the door opened, the knight looked down, and if he had not known better, would have thought that an oversized poppet belonging to his niece had answered the door. It was a dwarf maiden, with hair the color of blazing fire. Her hair was somewhat short and straight and her eyes were auburn. Her figure was rounded, and she stood just barely above three feet in height and wore a dress of rich black silk. The long skirt fell nearly passed her hairy feet. She did not have a hairy chin, as one of the many man-made myths held. She was quite pretty and charming, and the knight envisioned his niece waltzing up, as if she were in a toy shop, picking up the dwarf maid and purchasing her for a tea party.

"May I help ye?"

"Good evening. Is your father home? I am expected."

"Ah, yes. Ye are that knight fellow. Excuse my rudeness, Sir Knight. I am Una, Provost Norron's daughter, please come in. Papa be waitin' for ye."

The knight stooped through the door and went inside the house.

The walls were decorated with finely-crafted silvered axes, warhammers and round dwarf shields. Blue steel busts of Norron's ancestors filled small enclaves hollowed out at intervals along the wall. A large, steel-braced open hearth was built in the center of the room, over which great jowls of venison roasted over roaring flames. (Dwarven diet consisted mainly of meat, while the elves of southern Kyngesrelm ate it sparingly for health reasons.)A tun of dwarf honey beer was set against the far wall beside a long planked table. Here, a flaxen-haired dwarf with his mane tied in a long braid sat whittling and sipping from a drinking horn. Fire-haired Una smiled and said, "Sir knight, I present to ye me older brother, Skarden, Chief Huscarl of House Feormund. No one be handier with an axe and buckler than he."

The dwarf Skarden thudded onto the floor, marched over and reached up to pump Sir Fréalást's arm up and down in a stone-hard grip. "Ah, yes! Ye be the paladin fella me papa mentioned. He went into the store room to get seasonin' for the venison. He should be back shortly. Oh, where are me manners? Long life and health to ye! Have a spot o' mead!"

He picked up another drinking horn from the table (this one braced with ornate silver designs), filled it from the tap, and handed it up to the paladin. Normally, Fréalást would have preferred not to drink dwarven brew, for he thought it too strong. But he did not wish to offend Skarden. So, he put the horn to his lips and took a small sip. The dwarf smiled and Fréalást tried his best to return the gesture.

Once Fréalást returned the drinking horn, Norron entered. He was carrying a miniature spice rack in one hand and had a cleaned deer carcass over his other shoulder. "Clara, I have your special blend of parsley, sage, rosemary and thyme, ye true love of mine. That be the blend ye said ye wanted to use to flavor the venison, wasn't it, dear? I almost spilled it on me good camaric shirt, the one ye made me for our anniversary. Prepare the spit. The one that looks somewhat like a sickle of leather....What?! He be here! Right behind...? Oh, hello, Sir Fréalást. Have you met me children? You have? Good. Yes, very good. As soon as me lovely wife, Clara, fetches the spit, we shall have this here hart, prancing by way of the hearth, *he, he,* into your belly." He began feeling around in his pocket for something, saying, "Let's see. Where did I put that old... Ah, here it is. Care for a twist of dwarven leaf?"

In his experience at court, Sir Fréalást had smelled dwarven vintage tobacco, a recipe that was known to all dwarves in Kyngesrelm, one for which they were famous, and the crushed leaves gave off a pungent yet wonderful aroma when smoked. However, the peace-loving knight also valued peace of body, and from his talks with certain alchemists and apothecaries, had come to hold reservations that smoking and even excessive drinking, of which the dwarves are also fond, adversely affect each of the humors which make up the body.

"Hmm... I am still winded from riding. But thank you. All the more for you, I suppose." He wisely kept his reservations on wellness to himself, for he did not want to offend his host, who showed by his habits that he was a true son of earth.

While the Dwarven Provost was still lighting his pipe, an older dwarf woman with graying black hair walked in carrying spit her husband had requested.

"Clara, this is Sir Fréalást," began Norron. "He is a man of no small importance. He is one of those Nine Peer Paladin fellows of King Jaer. Mayhap he can finally bring justice to these pointy-eared malicious liars next to which we are accursed to live." Provost Norron spoke in a slightly seething tone. The knight could easily see that Norron's mounting anger would soon reach a boiling point.

Endeavoring to calm the dwarf, Fréalást said, "Before you start affixing uncomplimentary names to your neighbors, please tell me the dwarven side of this confusing and sordid tale. I have already heard an elven summary of the feud's origins from Provost Reinil and his family. Now I am prepared to hear, with an impartial mind, the case of House Feormund."

The dwarf patriarch took a deep breath and cleared his throat. "Well I can tell you one thing for sure, Sir Knight. Whatever that serpent-tongued money-monger told you was a lie. There was not a speck of truth in the whole yarn. This is the heaven-writ truth of the matter. Excuse me for a moment, if you please. I will be back in just a moment. When I return, I will bring with the *true* source of this festering dispute, and you will see that it be no stupid piece of elvish bovine, but something of much greater value. Excuse me now."

He left the room and returned a moment later carrying a large silvered warhammer of dwarf make, the finest Fréalást had ever seen. The shaft was three feet in length, three quarters of the height of dwarf, and was wrapped in golden cloth, wire-wrapped at intervals. Even more impressive was the octagonal head, which was as large as an Alfanonian hurling stone. Fréalást had the fleeting thought that if swung by a dwarf as powerful as Skarden, it could almost turn the paladin's great helm to mere steel shavings in one blow. It was etched along its whole diameter with dwarvish runes, and it no doubt requiring immense strength to wield. But the knight knew well that the strength of the sons of earth was unmatched among all the free peoples of the kingdom.

"This hammer is called 'Hilgrahond'." (Historiical note: Hilgrahond means *holy hand* in the language of the dwarves. The common language among the dwarves of Pallanon is very similar to that of the Vaering barbarians; there is some conjecture among scholars that the two peoples are distantly related, but that is another matter entirely). "It was forged by the first Smith of my line, Sterkwulf, passed down from one Provost to the next, a sacred heirloom of House Feormund. Hear this now, sir knight. I do not jest when I say that if sold at its proper value, it could purchase Castle Pallanon, nay, all the castles in the kingdom. Long has Caradoc and all other patriarchs of reeking House

Aelfwyr after him desired its wealth, and long have their thoughts been bent on obtaining it, but they will never have it, as long as my descendents are in their right minds. Therefore it needs no telling that Caradoc and his sons slew their seed bull, and then tried to blame it on my forebears, all on the avaricious pretext of seizing this beautiful hammer in a settlement of law and then selling it, as if it was no more than a child's wooden toy. Then they would live like kings the rest of their days, as if they cannot do that now. Therefore, now that you are aware of the true story, I can be sure that you will champion the just cause of my house."

The rest of the evening passed pleasantly, in a typical dwarven fashion, with plenty of feasting on meat and drinking of ale (though this was done sparingly on the paladin's part). Finally, Fréalást departed for the house of the Elven Provost, and lay awake long that night musing on the dispute that lay at the heart of the tale of these two houses. He knew he would need to pray all the more, to meditate, and to gather more evidence if he was to justly bring peace between these two houses. He was at peace in his mind that the reconciliation of these feuding families was the good work that the Lord God had prepared for him to do even before the time he arrived. He was no longer concerned with the rendezvous at the Wall, for he knew in his heart that the Lord had called him to this very place and appointed a peace-making mission for him at this very time. Therefore, he would not let his mind stray from that God-ordained mission until he had accomplished his task.

9.   The Correct Form of Trial

Sir Fréalást de Pacem awoke early the next morning and made his way down the winding stair to the Elven breakfast table. Today would be a very eventful and hectic day for the peace-loving Paladin of Pallanon. Still, he noted with a tinge of disappointment that the beautiful Nora had not risen yet. Laying aside such thoughts from more peaceful time, Fréalást downed a bowl of Elven porridge.

Provost Reinil was moving beads back and forth on an abacus when the knight sat down to breakfast, but now looked up and fixed Fréalást with an intent gaze. "Good morning. Will you render a verdict today, good Sir Knight?"

"Mayhap yes, mayhap not," the paladin replied in his usual mellow tone. "But do calm yourself, Lord Provost. I will need to gather more information before I am able to rightly dispense justice."

Reinil's face fell at the Knight's reply but he did not put his disappointment into words.

"Where might I find your chief cattle hand?"

"Randlo has his lodgings by the stable."

"Thank you. Now if you will be so kind as to excuse me, I need to speak with him. We shall speak again soon. Good morning."

Fréalást donned his armor and walked out onto the grounds of Provost Reinil's estate. Even with his subdermalis, the Knight felt winter's chill clinging to him, pressing into his flesh like talons into the falconer's glove.

First, he went to the post where he had tied the stray heifer. After feeding it grain and giving it milk from his own personal store, he made sure it was warm enough and went back through the Elven district to Provost Reinil's estate to commence his investigation. He happened to see Mennoth and Leyna, coming back from Mennoth's morning horsemanship exercise. He noticed that both Elven youths were wearing cured wolf pelts over their mail, something he had never seen elf riders do, and he had been on diplomatic missions to the Alf-anon Plains on many occasions.

"Hail and well met, my Elven friends. Pardon my ignorance, but what is the occasion for such attire as you wear today?"

"Ah!" laughed Mennoth, baring his teeth in a wolfish grin. "You are not from these parts of the kingdom, so you would never have heard even in history books of the Great-Wolf Raids."

"The *Tain Cuana* as we Highland folk call 'em." Leyna interjected.

"Yes," the ruby-haired elf nodded. "These events occurred just before this blasted feud began. Great-wolves began mysteriously raiding Ofermod and the Alf-anon Plains. They came in the night, bloody corpses the only sign of their presence come the morning. My grandsire Orondur, son of Provost Caradoc slew one with his great falchion. That weapon is now an heirloom of my house. I hope to wield it in battle someday, if that be ever possible."

"And you said that the raids occurred right before the feud began?"

"Yes."

"I see. If you will please excuse me, I am gathering evidence with the careful examination of which I will pass a just verdict. But, come to think of it. We are both heading toward the stable. Very well. I shall walk with you. But do not spur faster, for your stallions will soon outrun me."

"Oh, we'd never be so cruel," smiled Mennoth.

"Besides," added Leyna. "Our mounts be fairly winded now, me laird knight. 'Twould be killin' 'em to even ride at a canter."

The winded horses started back for the stable, with Fréalást walking between them.

Upon reaching the stable, Fréalást asked for Randlo.

"I am Randlo," boomed a burly, sandy-haired elf. His torso was bare and he wore black, greasy pantaloons with thick black braces. "How may I help you?"

"I would like to see if you still happen to have the bones of the great seed bull that was found slain here, the impetus of this unholy feud."

"Well, I never thought a man would ask that question. Come with me."

The burly cattle hand led the knight to a large back stall that was devoid of hay. There, reassembled in meticulous Elven fashion was the skeleton of the seed bull of House Aelfwyr. Upon close examination, the Knight saw that the preserved chalk white bones had large deep indentations that looked like many scratches and bites. When Fréalást asked about the markings Randlo said, "Those are from the back spikes of the dwarven axes. That's what my Papa told me."

A hypothesis formed in the knight's mind. He withdrew from his pocket the paw he had taken from the great-wolf and began to insert its talons into the scratch marks.

Huzzah! At last! There was the answer, as plain as the nose on a troll's face.

Mennoth was still tending his horse in the stable. Fréalást went to him, laid a hand on his shoulder and exclaimed, "Mennoth! Go to your house and find your father. Tell him that he must meet me in the street separating the Elven district from the dwarven district within the hour. I am going to the dwarven district to find Provost Norron. I have decided how to judge this dispute. Hurry now. Run!"

Mennoth cast up his eyes but nevertheless sped out of the stable like a crossbow bolt. Fréalást untethered Grannock, swung up into the saddle and galloped off for the dwarven district. Instead of going to Provost Norron's house he went to his smithy, guessing the Provost's whereabouts correctly from a comment Norron made the night before about his work ethic. The dwarven Provost was in the process of binding the shaft of a battle hammer. But when he heard the reason for the Knight's coming, he let the hammer fall to the floor with a great crash, the binding still incomplete.

When they reached the main street, both elf and dwarf said in unison, "Have you decided to take my side?" Both their faces betrayed their eagerness. Norron was nearly jumping up and down with glee.

"I have gathered the proper evidence," the knight began, pacing back and forth between the two patriarchs, his gloved hands clasped behind his back, his thumb and index finger rubbing together. "Now I can only see one possible way of passing judgment in this situation."

A pair of dwarven eyes, along with a pair of Elven eyes, burned bright in anticipation of the paladin's next words. The very air seemed to crackle with the fire of their excitement. "The only way this dispute can be settled is… In a trial by combat."

"A what?!" both voices cried in unison.

"You heard what I said. A trial by combat, as our ancestors did in days of old. But there shall be no bloodshed. On this day next week, at the boundary stone of the town, we shall hold a tournament."

"Ye be gone bats!" cried Norron. "We are still in the dead of winter. Besides, Ofermod has no lists."

"As much as I hate to agree with a dwarf of House Feormund, he is right on this account," asserted Reinil.

"Then we shall build them. The southern elves are skilled in woodworking and all dwarves are handy with stone. You shall have the lists built in no time."

"I shall never work in common with an elf of House Aelfwyr. And I will not have one sitting in my handiwork either." Thus declared Norron stamping his foot.

"And I say the same for those dwarves," spat the Elven patriarch.

"Then you shall each build the seating for your own families, but under my direction. I shall oversee the tournament. All you have to do then, is select a representative from your family to serve as a Marshall of the lists. We begin construction this very day. Gather your building supplies and laborers and meet me at the town's boundary stone in one hour, and not a moment later. That is my decision. Farewell."

As he left their meeting place, Sir Fréalást could hear a smattering of both Elvish and dwarvish curses.

Sir Fréalást was neither a carpenter nor a stonemason. But he had been oftentimes to the tournament held by Sir Peter von Wulfbain on the field in front of his stronghold in the town of Veylandin. So he had some knowledge concerning how to construct jousting lists, pavilions for spectators, melee arenas, archery lists, and the like.

The elves of house Aelfwyr worked with axe and adze on one side of the site, while the dwarves of House Feormund worked on the other with hammer, chisel, and mattock. They began construction with the air of forced-labor serfs, perhaps because of having to work in close proximity to their sworn enemies. But slowly, the dour glances and profane insults ceased. As Norron and Reinil passed each others' building sites, Fréalást noticed them trying to hide their admiration for the handiwork of their enemies. Their hearts still boiled with jealousy and distrust, but Fréalást discerned that they were at last developing a mutual respect.

Since dwarves do not usually ride horses, preferring to fight on foot, the elves were in charge of constructing the jousting lists, while the dwarves built with stone to construct a circular melee arena that was low enough for the inside to be viewed from both stands. To avoid further argument, Sir Fréalást decided that both houses would provide their own herald, to announce the combatants from his house in each contest.

What would have taken unskilled humans several months, the fair folk and sons of earth accomplished within a week. Sir

Fréalást was greatly pleased, for though he did not speak of it, he knew that if he had given the task to workers of his race, he would never reach Baeryntine's Wall by the appointed time.

10.   The Tourney

The tournament grounds were completed the day before the tournament. The next day, the stands were filled to brimming with boisterous dwarves and anxious elves. On high perches that looked like turrets at the right end of either stands stood Orroth, brother of Provost Reinil and Grenden, nephew of Provost Norron, who had both been selected for their strong, clarion voices. In the middle of the tournament ground, were the shields bearing the heraldry of both houses. The Tourney was about to begin, though Sir Fréalást, who was to act as judge had not yet arrived. Both Provost Reinil and Provost Norron had the same secret thought and intention. *If that Paladin does not arrive soon. I shall act as judge. That is surely the way to gain a foot over deceitful old Provost in the opposite stands.*

Suddenly everyone heard the baling of a battle horn. Three short blasts, a short pause and then three more short blasts. Up rode Fréalást, in full battle armor, his tournament lance couched in a stirrup cup, a blunted hand-and-a-half tournament sword at his side. Even through the knight's helm, each warrior could feel Sir Fréalást's cold gaze boring through his bones. Fréalást rode to the center of the field, where the battle standards of both houses blew in the chill winter breeze.

"Good morrow, Sir Fréalást," began Reinil, somewhat taken aback by the paladin's stern, commanding presence. "Will you take your seat in the judge's box?"

The Knights voice rang out clear and commanding. "I do not come to judge. Truth and logic shall judge for me. I come to compete in this contest of arms."

Each set of eyes widened in astonishment and several spectators gasped.

"Which House shall you champion?" Queried Provost Norron. An air of expectancy hung about the grounds. Not a sound came from the stands, for the knight's next words could spell either long-awaited justice or doom for either house.

For a long moment the bold knight was silent. Far off in the distance, a black rook cawed. Finally he voiced his reply. "I shall champion…House de Pacem! For God and King Jaer!" So declaring, the Knight drew his sword and struck both standards with the flat of his blade.

"In-in which of the events will you compete?"

"All of them. If I am victorious in this tournament, I shall still serve the cause of justice. But you must first give ear to all that I have to say." Fréalást said no more, but rode off the field and took his place among the riders waiting to compete in the joust, which would be the first event of the day.

First, an elven cattle horn sounded, followed by an ancient dwarven battle horn. ""In honor of her indebtedness to House Aelfwyr," began Orroth the herald, "the first one to bear the lance in the name of House Aelfwyr shall be our honored guest, Leyna of Clan McPharron, Daughter of Connall McPharron, chieftain of clan McPharron and lord of Rath Griogar. The champion of this contest will earn the right to represent House Aelfwyr in the first melee. As the first combatant and our honored guest, she will have the honor of choosing which rider with whom she crosses lances." It was only then that the Paladin noticed Leyna among the riders, clad in Dwarversdunn mail over which she wore a makeshift tabard of rugged northern Elven sheepskin. Couched in her oversized stirrup cup, was a wooden lance the size of an Alfanonian cabor with a large, blunted wooden tip in the shape of an Alfanonian halberd blade. Surely, she could not have the strength to wield such a lance. What were they doing letting a female, one of the gentler sex, compete in the tournament? Hopefully, he would not have to cross lances with her.

A wily grin lit up the Golden-haired maiden's countenance. "I will ride against that knightly human fellow in the purple surcoat."

Sir Fréalást shifted uneasily in his saddle. Such a proposal was against the courtly behavior he had been taught. "Pardon me, madame but I do not think that is such a good idea. After all, you are…."

At these words, the Alfanonian rider flew into a rage. "Pah!" She leaned forward and spat on the snowy ground. "I ken what you were going to say. I'm a woman, and therefore you feel squeamish to bear your lance against me. Too dainty, am I? Sidhe Dubh! By Shalaileigh's shalaileigh, I shall show you the courtly behavior of an Alfanonian Princess!"

So saying she rode at a lightning pace over to her end of the jousting lists. Fréalást breathed a quick, "Forgive me, Lord," and took his place on the opposite end of the lists, dreading the outcome of the encounter, but not for his sake.

The Elven cattle horn sounded, and the two riders swung their lances level. As both steeds thundered forward, the flow of time seem to slow to a crawl. Sir Frealas could see the red fire burning in Leyna's blue eyes, could see the shaggy hair on the ankles of her Highland stallion. Closer, ever closer. Then, they met.

Surprisingly, the elf girl's lance shattered on impact, yet Fréalást was almost unhorsed, flailing backward, all the time thinking *must not fall. Must… Not… Fall.*

Finally regaining his center of gravity, the Knight circled around to the other side of the lists for another charge, taking up a spare lance handed to him by an attendant. Luckily for Fréalást, Leyna had only one troll-sized lance, so she took up a regular sized one from her assigned page.

Coming around again, Fréalást planned with dragon swiftness. Spurring his mount to a faster gallop, the Paladin in the blink of an eye hooked his lance on level with Leyna's shoulder, accomplishing a move right before impact. The quick action caused the Highland elf girl to cart wheel horizontally off the saddle and strike her head with a resounding smack on the wooden partition. She lay still as her horse thundered to the end of the line. The red of her cherry lips was now not the only red marking her face.

Mennoth, who had been watching intently alongside the other riders, gave voice to a gut-wrenching cry of "No!" He leaped over both partitions and immediately began reviving his fallen friend. The knight began to wonder with a sick heart if there was something more to this tale, and, if so, he had just put an end to it before it had a chance to burgeon and grow.

He was not heavy of heart for long because he heard a broguish female cry of "I live! I live, you fool! Get off me!" Yet there with a smile on her face. Leyna stood up shakily, and doused her wounds with snow. Fréalást ran to her, and laying a firm hand on her shoulder said. "Never again will I doubt the courage of the elven warrior maids of the Alf-anon Plains."

After a long discretionary silence, and reassuring the crowd of the girl's well-being, Orroth the herald declared in a still shaking voice, "The victor of this match is Sir Fréalást of House de Pacem!" To the knight's surprise, loud cheering erupted from both the Elven and dwarven stands.

Once the Paladin had caught his breath, he signaled herald Orroth to announce the next Elven combatant. "The next member of our noble house to bear the lance against Sir Fréalást of House de Pacem shall be none other than our very own Mennoth son of Provost Reinil of House Aelfwyr."

Sir Fréalást had not seen the impassioned young Elven rider gallop to the other end of the lists. But now the knight could see that the red fire of vengeance burned in Mennoth's eyes. He resembled the gigantic, blood-crazed bull that was emblazoned on his shield. Surely, his "horn" thirsted for Sir Fréalást's blood.

He was clad in his Dwarversdunn hauberk and a white tabard stitched with the insignia of his house. His helmet was round, silvered, with steel cheek plates and a pike topped with a horsehair tassel protruding from the center. His hands were encased in black leather gauntlets and he wore his sword by his side.

He is the champion of Elven vengeance, vengeance against me, no doubt, thought Fréalást.

At the signal for the charge, Mennoth lowered his lance, and Fréalást unwillingly thundered toward him, the Knight could almost see the wrath emanating from the fire-haired elf. His teeth were gritted until the very last second, when he bellowed "for Leyna!" and tried to bury his lance into Fréalást's abdomen. Fortunately the lance broke on the knight's coat of mail, doing little actual damage, but unfortunately, Reinil was too far away to see his son's blatantly aggressive act. Sir Fréalást wobbled back and forth like one of his nephew's bobbing wooden toys. Finally regaining his balance, the knight took up another lance in exchange for his now battered one and circled around to charge again.

To his shock and amazement, Sir Fréalást saw that Mennoth had cast down his broken lance and drawn his sword. And in a further breach of honorable tournament rules, the sword was not a blunted one but his regular sharp Dwarversdunn blade. For several minutes, Reinil was too taken aback at his son's dishonorable conduct to intervene. Sir Fréalást drew his tournament sword and prayed that Mennoth's mad strokes would not be forceful enough to severely damage it.

The swords flashed in the pale winter sunlight, ringing loudly. For a moment it seemed as though the wild eyed elven youth had the upper hand. But then the paladin saw an opening and struck his adversary hard a blow across the knee.

Mennoth wheezed and, clutching his knee in both hands, fell over to the left side, off of the saddle. His feet were still in the stirrups so his weight caused the saddle to hang lopsided on the horse's side, forcing them to hang upside down with his hair in the snow.

The Knight pointed the rounded tip of his blade down at the young elf's throat. "Hear me now. I am truly sorry for accidentally hurting Leyna. But you must understand. An act of vengeance will never bring justice. Only the Lord can bring true justice."

At last, Provost Reinil spoke. "I beg you to accept my sincerest apologies for my son's rash and dishonorable behavior. You now will disqualify him, banning him from further activity in the tournament, will you not?"

"No," the knight replied. "God is merciful, and desires us to be merciful in turn. Therefore, I shall also be merciful now. But first, take this boy to the leach to have his wound examined."

"How, then, shall the heralds judge your bout with the lance?" the Elven Provost asked. "It has degenerated into a blood-vengeance crossing of swords."

Sir Fréalást cleared his throat. "Honorable Provost. The commonly accepted rules of the joust, as I understand them make it very clear that if one combatant is unhorsed, the one atop his mount is declared the winner. You see that the young Mennoth is unhorsed and I am still astride my mount, I leave it to you to decide the winner."

"I shall never be a knight," young Mennoth moaned ruefully.

It took four Elven cattle hands to assist Mennoth to the home of House Aelfwyr's leech, and from the sound of their mutterings it was plain that they were none too happy at being forced to miss the rest of the tournament. And although he had shown himself to be as tough as carpenter's only a moment before, Mennoth now left the tournament grounds whimpering and blubbering pitiful things such as "Now I shall never be a Knight! Never!" and "I have soiled my family's good name! Soiled it!" From the looks on the cattle hands' faces, Sir Fréalást could see that were he not the son of their master, they would have been very much obliged to cuff him on the back of the head. Looking over at Leyna, the Paladin could see a similar look of disgust, but beneath this obvious tomboyish facade a deeper, underlying look of respect and admiration, as though she were both flattered and grateful that a brave warrior, whether he be a knight or no, should hold her in such high esteem as to champion her and avenge her honor in a contest of arms.

When Mennoth and his grumbling assistants had left the field, Orroth, the herald of House Aelfwyr declared in a baffled and shaky voice, "By deference of a final decision and lack of more conclusive evidence and stricter regulations, the victory of this unusual bout of the lance is hereby awarded to Sir Fréalást of House de Pacem." Immediately both stands, but particularly the stands of House Aelfwyr, erupted with the sounds of cheering, and the banging of wooden cider mugs on the railing of the statements. This noise was peppered with cries of "Huzzah for Sir Fréalást of House de Pacem!", "Sir Fréalást the Just, Sir Fréalást the Merciful!" And although dwarves of House Feormund cheered the Knight's name because he had just defeated the champion of House Aelfwyr and the son and heir of their sworn enemy, it was easy to see that Sir Fréalást of House de Pacem was becoming the favorite of all the crowd.

Apparently the favor of the Lord was with Sir Fréalást, for, as the joust progressed, it turned out that Leyna and Mennoth were his most challenging opponents. Many other riders entered the lists in their turn, all of whom the Paladin easily unhorsed. Unbeknownst to the knight, in both the dwarven and Elven stands, the spectators began to take bets on how easily and in what fashion Sir Fréalást would unhorse his next opponent.

"I be telling you, Undric," one dwarf said to another as he sipped a horn of mead, "that Sir Fréalást fellow is gonna unhorse that dark-haired pointy ear on the second encounter. On the first encounter, Sir Fréalást's lance will shatter, and then he will take up that iron-tipped lance and unhorse the sniveling elfling, causing them to fall over to the right side."

"Nah, Bendlin," said the other, nibbling a haunch of venison. "He'll unhorse that one on the first pass, causing the pointy ear to topple back all the way over the flanks of his mount, coming clean out of the stirrups."

"A bag of fifty coppers says you be wrong."

"I be willing to take that bet."

The two dwarves struck hands on the deal.

Even more complementary were the words voiced on the fair folk's side of the stands.

"Father, he is quite amazing, is he not?" asked the fair Nora.

"I must agree with you, my daughter, though, in truth,, he is putting our best riders to shame."

"Surely, papa, the woman he chooses to marry will be fortunate indeed," Nora said, her eyes shimmering. "She will be able to rest confident that he shall always champion her name."

Provost Reinil looked at his daughter, raising an eyebrow, but said no more.

At last, Sir Fréalást had unhorsed his last Elven opponent. At first unsure of what to say, Orroth the herald first had to confer with Provost Reinil. Then he climbed back upon his perch and announced, "Due to the strange circumstances in which House Aelfwyr won no bouts in the joust, the honor of representing our noble house first in the melee falls to our noble guest, Sveinil, son of Connall McPharron, Lord of Rath Griogar."

The Alfanonian youth brandished his massive claymore amid wild cheering from the Elven stands. Sir Fréalást groaned as he saw the same red fire of vengeance that he had espied in Mennoth's eyes. He could only imagine what burning blue and black wounds awaited him in the arena.

Grenden, herald of House Feormund, who had remained silent up until now, now called out in a deep blaring voice, "Noble Sir Fealast, as the victor of the first event, you have earned the right to select your first opponent in the melee arena. Whom do you choose?"

The thought immediately crossed the Paladin's mind to be thrifty in his decision, and select the least blood thirsty, shortest in stature, and least armed to the teeth of the dwarvish huscarls he could find. When comparing these attributes among the present dwarves, he saw that Skarden was the shortest, was armed with only a short dwarven sword, and was looking particularly aloof.

"I select Skarden, son of Provost Norron, and chief huscarl of House Feormund." At his announcement, the dwarven stands erupted with boisterous cheering and loud catcalls, and above it all, the Knight heard Provost Norron exclaim, "That be me boy, Skarden! Make your papa proud."

Skarden was clad in a shirt of dwarven mail that sparkled even in the pale winter sunlight. Over the mail shirt he wore a small vest of leather scales that gave the blond dwarf the look of a dragon hatchling. The lobed pommel of the dwarf's sword was lacquered bronze with a round silver-encrusted ruby in the center. He was crowned with a round dwarven helmet with a rune-marked nasal. His breeches were of brown leather, and his blackened leather boots were fur-lined. He wore a red satin cape with a square-lined pattern stitched in gold thread along the edges. His hands were bare but on his wrists he wore thick silvered bracers etched with the image of crossed battle hammers that was the insignia of House Feormund.

As was required in a fighter against fighter melee bout, Sir Fréalást entered through one side of the arena, while Skarden entered through the other. When he had walked to the center of the circle of hard, smooth loam, the Knight saw that another dwarf, who had the look of a squire, had followed Skarden into the arena. The squire was carrying a large pewter platter with a huge domed lid. The blond dwarf took off his sword in its baldric and slung it over the squire's shoulder. Then with a great flourish he took the lid off the platter, revealing the heirloom of his house, the dwarvish battle hammer Hilgrahond.

Fréalást gasped and his heart sank. But once again, the dwarven stands erupted in cheers. Skarden took up the silvered maul and swung it around his head in a great display of strength. Only then did Sir Frealasr venture to give voice to his uneasiness.

He cupped his hands over his mouth and shouted up to the dwarven stands, "Ah, Provost Norron, are you quite certain that such a choice of weaponry is in keeping with the chivalric code of the melee?"

"Why yes," the dwarven Provost smirked. "May I make so bold as to remind you that said chivalric code requires only that the weapons used in a tournament melee be blunted? You see for yourself that the great Warhammer Hilgrahond, as fine a weapon as it is, is not sharp. It has no edge."

Yes, but it will nonetheless shatter my head like an egg shell, the Knight retorted silently. "Very well then," was all he said audibly though his heart was not truly in the words.

Silently, Sir Fréalást de Pacem not only made his peace with God, but prepared to meet Him as well.

A dwarven battle horn sounded as a signal for combat to begin.

Instantly, the heavily armored son of earth charged the knight. Thinking quickly, Sir Fréalást sprinted forward a short distance as if to meet the charge head on, but at the last moment, leaped over the blonde dwarf just as Skarden swung the hammer in a broad, sweeping arc. Fréalást somersaulted over Skarden, but could nonetheless feel the swooshing wind of the stroke beneath him. Landing on his feet in regaining its footing, Sir Fréalást swung around to meet his adversary, sidling slightly.

The dwarf's mouth twisted upward in a sly half smile. "You be quick to be sure," he chuckled haughtily. "Well then, long legs, try to duck this."

Skarden charged forward with the speed of a blood-raged bull, and struck the knight a full-force blow in the lower abdomen. With the speed of a ballista bolt, Sir Fréalást hurtled toward the low stone wall. He could feel his rib cage quivering, and he knew that if he hit the wall, the bones of his back with snap like kindling sticks. Holding his sword close to his wounded chest, in the blink of an eye, he brought his arms and legs together close to his body, so that flash of time he looked rather like a trebuchet stone He opened from his cocooned position so that instead of hitting the wall force, he narrowly missed striking it. By sheer chance and his own quick wit, he skidded to a grinding halt, his tournament sword trailing along in his arms, the blade biting into the cold earth. For a mere second his booted heels barely touched the stone. In a fraction of a second the knight ground his heels into the stone, and launched himself into a forward roll along the earthen floor of the arena. The knight scooped up his now dented great helm and quickly set it upon his head endeavoring to put space between him and the hammer-wielding dwarven huscarl, who was trying, unsuccessfully (and the Paladin hoped that it would continue in that fashion), to tenderize Sir Fréalást's skull, as though he were a cannibal.

Let me measure what I know of my opponent, thought the knight, inwardly commentating on the match as he dodged blow after blow. *I could certainly not wield that troll's hammer for very long without tiring, so even so must Skarden, though he has far more strength and endurance than most of the unbreakable dwarves. Therein lies my key to victory.*

Sir Fréalást resolved then to break his code of courteous conduct on this one most desperate occasion.

Give me the strength to do what I have to do, O Lord, the Paladin prayed, his brow already drenched in sweat despite the cold winter morning becoming all the more cold as a flurry of snow began to lightly fall.

Fréalást summoned what little strength with left in his over-exerted muscles and began to dance around the slower, more heavily armed dwarf. "Hey Ho, son of earth, shall you squash me like a dung beetle, or underfoot like a roach?" He danced aside from one of the blond dwarf's mad stroke, the massive silver hammer head narrowly swooshing past the paladin's unarmored hip.

"If you are overly tired from swinging that great thing, I can send a falcon with a note to my grandmother and she can be here by tomorrow to fight me in your stead. Is that agreeable to you, young Skarden?"

The dwarf huscarl's irritated growl rose into a bellow, as he once again tried to flatten Fréalást's head into the ground as a fuller would flatten a pair of trousers with his wooden softening mace.

Slowly, the chief huscarl of House Feormund began to tire, having exerted far more energy than the combined force of a dozen of his race. He now began to lug the silvered maul Hilgrahond as an errand boy for a town mercantile would lug about a sack of potatoes. Fréalást allowed himself a moment to chuckle at the thought, and he did not pay at all for his distraction for avoiding Skarden's heavy strokes was becoming easier and easier as the bout dragged on and the blond dwarf tired all the more.

Sir Fréalást was now searching around in his mind, for the one insult, the one utterly demeaning gibe, that would push his adversary to rageful and reckless insanity. Finally, he hit upon it, and he silently said a quick prayer of thanks though he knew not if it were the Lord God or his own inner sense of humor that had brought the snobbish comment to the mind.

"I do not know if you will best me in this bout, O noble and courageous son of earth. But even if you are not successful, you will make it all the more easier for a swordsman of noble house Aelfwyr to claim the victory over me in the next bout of the day. Oh, and I do hear that Mennoth, champion of noble House Aelfwyr is much more handy with a sword then you are with that trinket heirloom cobbler's hammer you have there. Do you not think so, little Skarden?"

This was the final straw, much more insults then the Golden-bearded huscarl's dwarvish pride would allow to go unpunished. Howling a deep-throated yet mostly hoarse string of dwarvish curses, the red-faced and sweaty chief huscarl Skarden summoned what little strength was left in his overtaxed muscles and swung one final, rock hard blow at his desecrating taunter. Sir Fréalást easily leaped out of the way, causing the young dwarf to overextend his swing and topple down face first, his torso slamming hard against the shaft of the hammer. He lay there for a moment, face down in the cold ground, the breath finally knocked out of his lungs. The night walked over to where his humbled adversary lay. Poking the rounded tip of his tournament sword into the back of the dwarves' scaled leather vest he asked with a tone of finality, "Do you yield, O son of earth, my worthy opponent?"

"Uhm arhm" came the jumbled reply, for poor young Skarden's bloody mouth was also filled with frozen dirt. But no one doubted that he had just conceded defeat.

Sir Fréalást turned to the dwarven stands and shouted, "Someone must carry him to his house to rest for he has exerted himself beyond the sane and conceivable limits of strength."

The dwarvish attendant's even with their great strength had a difficult time carrying Skarden, for they had to transport his full weight, not only because he had no strength left, but because he had fallen asleep the moment after he had conceded defeat.

Provost Norron was not pleased to see his son and heir defeated, but he was still quite proud of him. Fortunately, he had not heard the exchange of words between his son and the night during their combat.

When the sleeping Skarden had been borne away from the field, Grenden the herald proclaimed, "The victor of the first bout in the melee arena is Sir Fréalást of House de Pacem."

Cheering again erupted from the stands. Surprisingly, the loudest cheering came from the stands of House Feormund.

When he and the rest of the dwarves were certain that Skarden was well, Grenden, the herald appointed to announce combatants for House Feormund called out. "Now, which one of the huscarls of our noble house is brave enough to challenge the noble, brave Sir Fréalást of House de Pacem in the next bout in the melee arena?"

"I shall!" bellowed a non-dwarven voice with a thick Alfanonian brogue. Each set of eyes turned to see Sveinil McPharron stalking toward the arena, eyes filled with the undying red fire of a vengeful hatred.

Provost Norron stood to his feet in the dwarven stands, fairly trembling with rage. "This is a breach of tournament rules. It is the right of the warriors of my house to compete first in the melee. We will not be upstaged by the lowly, treacherous, sniveling so-called swordsmen of lying House Aelfwyr. I will be dead before I see such treachery!"

Reinil stood, equally seething in venomous anger. "We have as much of a right to compete in all the events of this tournament when we please, as you do, dirt spewing son of earth!"

Loud grumblings and exclamations were loosed out of the stands like crossbow bolts.

"Hold everything! Silence!" roared Sir Fréalást despite his great weariness. Though he had not seen Sveinil, he had heard and recognized the Elven lad's voice. Though he was tired and about to collapse, he knew he must bring peace if he were to serve the cause of justice.

"Young Sveinil McPharron of the clan McPharron is one of the fair folk, that is true," Fréalást began in a firm but even tone. "But he is not of House Aelfwyr, though he fights for the honor of that House in this tournament. Therefore, I say that whether or not I accept his challenge, is of no concern to either of your houses. But," (and the knight wondered if, by saying his next words, he was hammering the first nail into his coffin), "for the sake of your mutual entertainment, I accept the challenge put forth to me by Sveinil McPharron of the clan McPharron of the Alf-anon Plains, son of the noble Lord of Rath Griogar."

The knight's proclamation was greeted by several gasps from both the Elven and Dwarven stands, for all the assembled spectators knew that his recent bout with the dwarf huscarl

Skarden had sapped much of his strength, and that young Sveinil was fresh and ready for combat.

When Sveinil entered the arena, he was swaggering and smirking, holding the flat of his huge claymore against the back of his thick neck. Even beneath his heavy hauberk and deerskin cloak, Sir Fréalást could see the lines of his defined, bulging chest muscles. Most of his long golden hair was hidden by the huge, conical helmet that he wore. The helmet had a mail skirting, and two half-U-shaped Alfanonian Highland cattle horns, one protruding from either side. Sir Fréalást did not doubt that if he was robbed of his great sword during the bout, the Highland the youth would try to make use of the horns to run his opponent through the body.

Sir Fréalást was well aware that the Elven youth he had a very good legal case if he committed murder on tournament grounds. For even if he could not claim that the killing was an accident, he could not be tried outside of his homeland, and as there was no single supreme ruler of the Alf-anon Plains, justice would have to be rendered by his father who would undoubtedly declare him innocent out of nepotism. All of these thoughts coursed like lightning through Sir Fréalást's mind in the blink of an eye as he surveyed his opponent and these facts did little to comfort him.

"I am sorry for what happened to Leyna," Fréalást ventured, endeavoring to soothe the anger the elf swordsmen obviously harbored toward the Paladin. "It was unfortunate, and as I told Mennoth after I unhorsed him that it was an accident and I regret what happened deeply. Please do not attack me in anger."

"Agh," the big highlander swordsman grunted softly and inaudibly to the spectators in the stands, as he leaned forward and spat on the frozen ground in front of the Knight's feet. "Here be the facts, Paladin. Ye have wounded me own flesh and blood, thereby insulting and bringin' disgrace upon my family. Nothing ye can say will ever do a thing to change that. Only I can change that, with my Highland blade. And I plan to do that. I plan to mark ye very well for your insult, Sir Knight. And if I mark ye too hard, well, then that shall be the end of it. That is all that is to be said. To your mark, noble Sir Fréalást of House de Pacem and may the Lord Himself decide which one of us be in the right and which one of us be in the grave. As I said, to your mark."

Having delivered his famous speech, which Sir Fréalást de Pacem would remember for the rest of his life, Sveinil McPharron spun on his heel and stalked over to his appointed mark shedding his cloak and tossing it aside.

The next twenty seconds seemed to the paladin like twenty hours. The Highland youth stared at him, unblinking, with a look of searing hatred. It was the look of a hunting hawk, Fréalást mused, honed in upon its prey. The down-turned quillions of the claymore were crafted to resemble the jagged talons of a hawk. Though they were made of brass, they could probably still cut bare flesh. The ricasso was an inch or so wider than a gauntleted hand just below the hilt. Though the sword had apparently been blunted for use in the arena, Sir Fréalást did not doubt that it still was still capable of a decapitating blow.

The paladin could feel the sweat beading upon and pouring down his brow. His breath came in labored huffs. Sveinil's lips curled into a wicked smile. Then, the Elvish cattle horn brayed.

Sveinil flew at the knight, swinging his massive brand with the swiftness and ferocity of a Highland hailstorm. Fréalást silently prayed that the elf's blows would not be heavy enough to break his narrower blade in shards.

Consciously forcing his tired muscles into action, Sir Fréalást came forward to meet Sveinil's onslaught. Knightly broadsword met highland claymore in a dancing whirlwind of steel. So ferocious were their strokes the red sparks flew. Sveinil endeavored to make a sweeping downward diagonal blow, and cut Fréalást's legs out from under him. But the knight was still spry on his feet, leaping up in the air, while the blade sliced under him, so that the vengeful Sveinil did not even cause so much as a flesh wound.

That battle-crazed elf lad must think he is invincible, the knight mused tiredly to himself as he landed back on the ground. *Perhaps I can use his disposition against him. I will just have to keep myself alive until the opportunity presents itself. And with the way he attacks, that shall prove to be a feat in itself, if I can manage it.*

Sveinil swung his massive sword in an overhead downward stroke, which Sir Fréalást caught on the edge of his blade. Sveinil pressed down hard, trying to drive the knight to the ground. Fréalást exerted his muscles to their last ounce of strength, and with a great grunt, forced his attacker back. Then he managed a heavy cut across Sveinil's torso, with such great force that the blunted blade sheared off several links of mail.

Sveinil sucked in a mouthful of air at the sharp pain, doubling over slightly. Leaping over to the side, Sir Fréalást rammed his mail-clad shoulder into that of the Elven youth. Sveinil lurched to the side, falling to his knees, his magnificent horned helmet falling off of his head. With a hoarse yell, Fréalást struck Sveinil a strong, heavy blow across the back of the head with the flat of his blade. Sveinil gave voice to a long, sighing groan and fell flat on his face in the dirt, knocked out cold, a large bluish black welt visibly forming beneath his golden locks. "I told you not to attack me in anger," the Knight said to his now unconscious foe. "You were right on one account, though. The Lord decided who was in the right, for he is never on the side of vengeance. You must remember this, my friend: vengeance belongs only to the Lord. Mere mortals such as we have no right to take it. Rest well, and when you awaken, I pray that you will think better of me."

Sir Fréalást turned to the crowd. In the sight of all, he feebly raised his blade in the air as a sign of victory. The crowd went mad with applause. "Now," he cried, his voice barely audible to those in the higher seats, for he was both out of breath and extremely hoarse. "I beg of you gentlemen and ladies to allow the tournament to be suspended until after the mid-day meal, for my bones are weary in mortal agony. I must rest." So saying, the Knight hobbled from the arena, using his blunted tournament sword as a crutch. Several exceptionally strong cattle hands had to go down to the arena and struggle to lift the massive elven swordsman and carry him away from the field.

Though Sir Fréalást had observed that Leyna was grateful to Mennoth for endeavoring to defend her honor, he saw that she was not at all pleased with her brother for trying to avenge her, for she scowled at his unconscious form when it was borne past her. It was ironic, the knight thought, for she had been one who suffered most for his mistake, both physically and emotionally, but she had taken the least offense at it. Perhaps that was the way of the northern elves.

The fair folk went to their houses to prepare their bread and porridge, while the sons of earth went to their hearths and their cook fires to prepare venison, boar, and bear steak. All the while, Fréalást was in the makeshift tourney stables, wrapped up in dozens of Elven saddle blankets to ward off the winter cold, sleeping like a dead man.

When Sir Fréalást de Pacem at last awoke and emerged from the makeshift stable, he saw both by the position of the bleak winter sun and the now restless crowd, that it was between two and three hours past mid-day.

In truth, the knight could have slept the entire remainder of the day, but his duties demanded otherwise, and the rest he had already taken would have to suffice. As it was, he felt that much of his strength had already returned. As the spectators saw him emerge, they filled the stands with boisterous applause. Fréalást smiled weakly and raised a gauntleted hand before replacing his coif and great helm back on his head.

"It is time for the final event of the tournament: archery and axe throwing," Fréalást declared. "Which projectile for projectile launching weapon will you use, sir knight, dwarven throwing axe or Elven longbow?" asked Orroth the herald.

"Neither," replied the Paladin, approaching his stallion. "I shall make use of my crossbow in this event."

Orroth raised an eyebrow. "Do you not think you are dooming yourself to fail, Sir Fréalást? An Elven Longbow has much greater accuracy over a long distance then does a crossbow."

"I would not say that necessarily," replied Sir Fréalást, smiling to himself. For he knew that his crossbow was no ordinary crossbow. It was a langen crossbow, able to shoot with the precision of an Elven longbow. The bolts were loaded through the stock, so the bow could be fired and reloaded faster than the ordinary crossbow, requiring no foothold and cranking of levers. And because of the inner gear system, the chamber could hold up to twenty quarrels. It was full, so the knight would have no need to worry, having enough supply in the bow for the whole match.

There were three sets of partitions set up for the match, providing space for three contestants to compete at one time, with the target set a specific distance from the loosing or throwing line. A burly dwarf with a bushy black beard ,all of his hair tied in a long black braid, carrying a baldric of throwing axes at his back, approached the right stall. Gondel, one of Reinil's retainers, approached the left, a longbow painted forest green in his right hand.
"The first contestant to represent House Aelfwyr in the target lists," began Orroth the herald, "is none other than our very own Gondel son of Arland, personal retainer of Provost Reinil." The elves cheered loudly.

"The first contestant to represent House Feormund in this event," shouted Grenden the herald, "is that true son of earth, Beldrick, son of Kelldin." The dwarves cheered and banged their tin mugs of ale on the backs of the stone seats in front of them.

"Also competing in the first round is Sir Fréalást of House de Pacem." At the calling of the Paladin's name, both stands erupted with boisterous applause.

"First target," both heralds cried in unison, "at three hundred paces."

Gondel loosed first, and his mark was a straight bull's-eye. Then the dwarf let fly his first throwing axe. Its edge was buried deep in the center of the target.

Last of all, the Paladin loosed a quarrel at his target, and with a great *shok*, it buried itself to the butt in the center of the bull's-eye. The crowd was amazed and when the judges inspected the placement of the projectiles, they found that Sir Fréalást's mark was the truest of all three.

"The winner of this round," both heralds said and in unison, "is Sir Fréalást of House de Pacem." The stands exploded in raucous applause with loud accolades voiced in both Elvish and dwarvish.

"Sir Fréalást, by virtue of his victory," shouted the heralds in one voice, "shall stay to compete against the next contestants."

The event began to pass very quickly for the knight, for he began a wild winning streak that outwitted all who believed in luck.

"Next target at five hundred paces." Sir Fréalást won once more.

"Next target at eight hundred paces." The Paladin won again.

"Final target of the match shall be at one thousand paces." Even then the bolt of the human knight's special langen crossbow flew true, finding its intended mark.

"The winner of this event is Sir Fréalást of House de Pacem," the heralds proclaimed, sounding not at all surprised, after the course the events of the tournament had taken. Nonetheless both the stands of House Feormund and the stands of House Aelfwyr went mad with applause.

Orroth and Grenden both declared, in one voice, "The winner of this tournament is the Paladin, Sir Fréalást of House de Pacem!" Sir Fréalást received a standing ovation as the crowd cheered loudly for their favorite contestant.

The knight held up his hands for silence. "Noble lords and ladies, my new friends, the only order of business for the tournament left for me to do is, as champion, to select the Queen of love and beauty." The hearts of both patriarch beat fast at the knight's last words. *It has to be my daughter,* they both thought, their minds racing. *If he chooses my daughter, it Is a sign that he has chosen to render the verdict in favor of my House's cause.*

"Herein lies the problem," Sir Fréalást continued. "How to justly choose the queen of love and beauty. But I know exactly how to solve the dilemma. Friend Gondel, will you be so kind as to lend me your sword?"

"Certainly, my lord," said the dark-haired elf, handing the knight his falchion.

Sir Fréalást took the crown of holly berries made for the Queen of Love and Beauty, and to the shock and amazement of the onlookers, cut the crown into two equal tiaras. He rode over to the Elven stands and called for Nora, placing one on her head. The Elven girl's eyes beamed. Just as Norron was beginning to feel slighted, Sir Fréalást rode over to the stands of House Feormund and crowned Una with the other tiara.

"Two Queens of Love and Beauty, from two equally noble houses," the knight said. "Hear this now! Provost Norron and Provost Reinil have asked me to pass judgment on the dispute between your two houses. There have been bitter words and bitter feelings between your two families for decades. Here is my judgment on your dispute, having weighed the evidence carefully. The dispute between your houses is based on imagined grievance." He produced and flourished the great-wolf paw. Neither of you know the true story of what happened to the seed bull of House Aelfwyr. While both of your families slept, a stray great-wolf from the Great-Wolf Raids broke into the stalls of

Provost Caradoc and slaughtered his prized seed bull. No dwarf or elf had anything to do with the killing. If representatives from both houses will go with me to the Elven stables of Provost Reinil, I will present proof of what I claim."

Each house elected representatives and went with their Provost and Sir Fréalást to the stable to inspect the bones of the seed bull. Upon seeing the cuts in the bone and seeing that they match the length of a great-wolf claw, all the representatives were put to shame and quietly made peace. They decided to mutually raise the heifer that Sir Fréalást had brought to the town as a sign of the ending of the hostility between their houses.

After the representatives had made peace, Sir Fréalást came back to the tournament grounds with the representatives and announced with grave authority, "Citizens of Ofermod, the feud is now over. My prayer for you is that you now apply the balm of forgiveness and brotherhood to your wounded hearts, and that you might live together in a wonderful peace that transcends all understanding from this day forth. But if you decide to let another burning dispute flare up that again disrupts the peace, and if you willingly fuel the raging, destructive fire of strife, then a curse be on both your houses." So declaring, Sir Fréalást de Pacem, Paladin of Kyngesrelm, turned on his heel and walked off the field. For the first time since the tournament began, the stands were deathly silent.

Sir Fréalást left Ofermod later that day, eventually coming to Baerynthine's Wall. But he left a note for Nora, daughter of Provost Reinil. It was a very short note, consisting only four simple words: "I shall be back."

11. The Lord of Veylandin

Sir Waldon rode directly East from Castle Pallanon, but followed a slightly different path than Sir Fréalást. He was clad in a burnished hauberk of Dwaversdunn make, for his castle was near that township. He often thought on the unseen Kingdom of Heaven, as was plainly visible from his heraldry. His blue surcoat was emblazoned with the image of a seraph herald with a sounding trumpet by his side. Much like the seraph herald on his surcoat, though Sir Waldon was eager for the avatar of God to come and bring an end to the Dark One's blight upon the land, he knew that it would happen in God's good time. So he prayed that the Lord's will would be done, not in the timing of man, but in the perfect timing of God, be that in five days or five thousand years.

He was the only Paladin to have inherited his position. His father, Olnen O'Dumphreys, had been the youngest, yet most distinguished Paladin to serve under King Gandrine, Jaerython's aged father. After Olnen died fighting the half-troll war chief Grabosh and his horde, Jaerython, now a middle-aged sole ruler, instead of regent, had brought Sir Olnen's infant son, Waldon, to Castle Pallanon, to raise him to one day take up his father's spurs. Because he was not old enough to remember his father, the young Waldon often longed for someone to love him as a son, as only a father is able.

He did not share King Jaerython's anxiety over the desperate nature of this quest, but instead patiently, slowly and steadily, made his way to the place appointed for the staging of the mission. He wore a matching fur-lined cape, also of blue satin, which was meticulously combed. He was not a vain man but always took the time to ensure that his raiment, both of battle and daily life were in good condition. In addition to these vestments, he also wore a sugarloaf style great helm painted a deep blue, and wore dark blue leather gloves, the palms of which were sewn with bits of mail, and the digits of which were backed with spiked metal plates. His fiery red hair, although cut in the circular human courtier fashion, indicated that he had some Alfanonian blood in his veins. His short red beard was curly, and he spent a good hour pruning it with a razor every morning, although he had no sweetheart to please. It was not his intention to attract attention to himself, but to care for his body as a service to God. For the body of one of the free races, as his mother had taught him, was a temple of the Spirit of God. His mind was not paranoid by any stretch of the imagination, but whatever he did, he did with the utmost care, as a service to the Lord. He performed every task with meticulous excellence, even if it was a task as mundane as sharpening his light hand-and-a-half sword or polishing the painted white boss of his dark blue three-cornered shield. With all these colorful accoutrements, his companions said more than once that he looked rather like a painted pewter chess piece.

The middle southeastern part of the kingdom, through which he was riding, was sparsely inhabited, with hardly any villages and only a scant farm scattered here and there along the muddy road. Many a wood dotted the countryside. It was said that bands of thieves and highwaymen dwelled in these woods, as well as goblin, troll and half-troll "colonists" from the forest of Trillven. Some of these foul folk bandits would use their crude black magic to disguise themselves as shady looking beggars, to fish for an easier try at a meal of human, elf or dwarf flesh. At any rate, many of these rogue bands, whether consisting of human or foul folk, fell upon many an unlucky traveler who found himself along the road near dusk. Needless to say none of these unfortunate sojourners were ever heard from again. So it was that the richer folk who traveled the road, either brought along their personal retainers, or went so far as to hire mercenaries, many times retired Vaering warriors who had drunk away all the spoils from their days with their war bands.

So it was that with the passage of time he came within a league of the Township of Veylandin. He began to pass carters, farmers and other such folk heading to the town to go to market.

Sir Waldon was well aware of these dangers as he rode the winding trail among the gnarled winter trees. Many times he would glance to the left or to the right, and detecting slight movement, though he knew not if it were of bird, beast, or man, he would shift his gauntleted hand to rest on the hilt of his sword. Very often, he would stop and wait, patting his stallion's neck to comfort the beast, waiting silently until he was certain there was no danger.

So it was that with the passage of time he came within a league of the Township of Veylandin. He began to pass carters, farmers and other such folk heading to the town to go to market.

Every time he found himself to be blocking the path, he sidled his stallion over to the side of the road and waved the traveler past. Normally, a traveler who had come so far would be eager to find the inn. But as he approached the gates of the Township, he thought that it would be prudent to give his stallion some grain. So, he dismounted several hundred yards from the gates of the Township and pulled the store of grain from his saddlebag.

While the horse was still eating, a band of short, stocky youths, with mud-stained faces and clothes, most of them wearing long, tattered cloaks, sidled up to the knight.

"I e' zay, Sir Knight," said the leader in a slightly guttural accent. He smiled slightly, flashing a set of jagged yellow teeth. The boy reached out a stubby gloved hand toward Sir Waldon. At this point, the Paladin, becoming greatly disturbed at this new turn of events, moved his hand to the hilt of his sword.

"Need 'e some 'elp with yer horsey there?"

In a flash, Waldon's eye caught the muted glint of a rusted dagger blade. His narrow knightly brand whirled up, lopping off several of the shady youth's fingers. Black blood, not red, stained Sir Waldon's blade. Goblin!

Instantly, the ruffians' faces transmogrified, shedding their disguising enchantment. Their faces took on a greenish brown hue, their eyes became completely black and their ears became hairy, the lobes the shape of lightning bolts.

"Kill 'im, boys! *Gool-garaz!*"

Sir Waldon began to parry with lightning speed, both with his sword and catching blows on his shield as the goblins attacked him en masse from all sides with rusted axes, short swords, and barbed, black-bladed spears. His slender blade weaved in and out, drinking the blood of the foul folk. The knight sang joyful songs of battle as he slew, for it was the holy vocation, unctioned by the Lord Himself, that a Paladin bring judgment to all minions of darkness.

One goblin swung downward at Waldon with a heavy mace. Unthinkingly, the Knight put his first inclination into action, and parried the full force of the blow. If the sword had been broader and thicker, the blade would have merely shivered on impact, but so great was the force of the goblin's swing, that the blade shattered into shards.

Waldon's heart sank, but he did not have time to mourn for his broken sword, so he stabbed the goblin through the heart with the hilt shard, and, with the skill and ferocity of an Alfanonian boxer, turned the spikes of his gauntlets against his foes, having cast aside his shield.

Accosting one goblin armed with a barbed sword, he shoved under the goblin's elbow in a powerful uppercut, causing the weapon to fly out of the foul creature's grip. Without giving him a time to react, Sir Waldon pumped his fists back and forth in and out of the goblin warrior's face, causing black blood to fly from the now mangled pig-like snout.

The greenish brown rogue was now teetering off balance, so the night grabbed the goblin's head in both hands, and jerked violently to the right with a resounding snap. The body went limp and fell to the ground.

Two of the remaining goblins now worked in unison. One of them ran and went into a slide, skidding into Sir Waldon and knocking him off his feet. The other one held a spear to the Paladin's neck. Just when Waldon thought that his time to meet the Lord had come, he heard the silvery call of a battle horn and a bear-like battle cry bellow forth: "Ho-hie! The Light of God! Ho-hie!"

A colossal rider, nearly six and a half feet tall, and wielding a sword broad enough to be wielded by a troll thundered into the small goblin horde. Emblazoned on the field of the silver on the three-cornered shield he bore was a magnificent golden lion rampart.

The knight's massive blade flashed up and down like a bolt of silver white lightning. And as the blade cut into their flesh the goblins began to give voice to anguished death cries as their skin sizzled and smoked. There was some powerful and holy fire, born in the heavens, that burned within the battle blade of the mysterious rider.

The goblin holding the spear to Sir Waldon's neck dropped the weapon and began to flee, and so also one did the one who had knocked the knight to the ground. But the holy warrior gave chase and cut them down as they fled. Clearly, though he was not one of Sir Waldon's number, this knight was more of a Paladin then any one of the Nine Peers.

The knight dismounted and helped Sir Waldon to his feet. This knight was clad in a fine hauberk and bright red cape, wearing a sugarloaf style helm with a visor. The mysterious horseman lifted his visor. To the Paladin's surprise, there were many gray and white patches peppered in the once dark beard. He had the body of a powerful warrior who could not have seen more than thirty winters, but the face of a grandfather. The rescuer Knight was surely almost sixty years of age.

"I am Sir Peter von Wulfbain, Lord of Veylandin. Whom do I have the honor of addressing?"

"I am Sir Waldon O'Dumpheys, Lord of Dwarversdunn Shire," Waldon said as he gathered up the shards of his sword and retrieved his shield.

"Oh dear," said Sir Peter, shaking his head and looking at the broken pieces of steel in Waldon's hands. "You need a new sword, or perhaps someone to reforge your blade for you. I know just the right man, or, that is to say, dwarf, for the job. Come with me, sir knight."

12.   Supper with Lord Peter

Sir Peter von Wulfbain rode with Sir Waldon up to the gates of the town. As they rode, Waldon remarked, "That is a mighty sword, Sir Peter. Truly, I have never seen its equal."

"Ah, yes," smiled the old knight. "This blade is called Ettin-Bane. Master Smith Dunnir and his friend the alchemist François de Conlois made it for me."

"Ettin-Bane? That is to say 'Troll's Bane', correct?"

"Er. Well…Yes. I was not meaning to tell you."

Waldon's eyes widened in awe. "You are telling me that you slew a troll with that sword?"

Sir Peter's face reddened. "Well, er. Yes. It is but a small matter for that was four decades in the past."

"You were strong enough to wield that gigantic sword and kill a troll when you were ten years younger than I am now?!"

Sir Peter held up his hand in an effort to calm the young man. "To wield the sword, yes. To slay the troll, no. The blessing of the Lord was upon the blade, and it was alchemically reinforced thanks to François. My only regret about the whole business is that I have become somewhat of a celebrity as my ever inflating legend spreads. Why, several years ago, there was even some ridiculous troubadour named Danton Morry Quicksilver, or "Merry Danny" as some of his listeners call him, who made up an entirely fictitious ballad about the event. I do not begrudge the minstrel the song, nor Sir Leofred his patron the merriment he and his guests gain from it. But I prefer to remain humble concerning the deeds of my youth. Still, no comment you can make will surprise me. I have heard every single one of them." The old knight chuckled.

Sir Waldon grinned. He was beginning to like the Lord of Veylandin more and more.

By this time they had come up to the gate of the town. Sir Peter shouted up to the man at the portcullis winch. "Open the gate, Joachim. I have an honored guest that will be staying at my house tonight."

"As you wish, my lord."

As the portcullis creaked upward, Sir Peter said, "Please, join me for dinner at my house. I have a guest room in which you may rest for the night. Tomorrow we will go call on old Dunnir."

Because of the urgency of his mission, Sir Waldon would have preferred to go see Master Smith Dunnir immediately, but he decided to forebear making such a remark. He did not want to spurn the old knight's hospitality.

Sir Peter rode his white charger down the cobblestone street while Waldon followed on his dappled gray. Veylandin was a town famous for its steelcraft, so Waldon was not surprised to see a sign with an anvil above nearly every door. Some of the forges had very small doors to afford easy entrance for the dwarves that worked there.

The walls of Veylandin and its buildings were white washed, and they were palely illumined by the setting winter sun. Sir Waldon did not doubt that in the summer, they shone like alabaster in the brilliant sunlight. If the proved mission successful, the Knight reflected, he would like to come back to the town just to see that sight. He winced as another thought came to his mind. If the mission failed and the shadow-raiser covered the kingdom in eternal darkness, Skrael's armies would sweep down from the North, raze the city to the ground, and undoubtedly rebuild the city as a grotesque fortress in the terrifying flanged architecture of Varluckhuld that Sir Waldon had seen depicted in the history books of the Everfrost War.

"Are you well, Sir Waldon?"

Sir Peter's question yanked the other knight's mind out of its dark ruminations.

"Er. Um. Yes, my Lord Peter," Waldon stammered with a sheepish grin. "I was just reflecting on the beauty of the walls of the city. Have they always been as white as opal?"

"No. I ordered them made so shortly after the slaying of the troll. The foul folk do not much care for sunlight, and I thought if the walls reflected it better, we would be safe from other such warmongers."

Sir Peter's manor house sat atop a high hill, and the road winded up across the breast of the seemingly miniature mountain. The walls surrounding the gate were braced with shining dwarf steel that seemed almost silver in the light of the waning sun. There were many great, decorated flanged causeways, which resembled the buttresses of a cathredal, shooting out from the bailey, from which Sir Peter and his retainers could survey the whole town. These causeways were fitted with plates to hold cauldrons of boiling pitch and alchemist fire in case of a siege by the foul folk. At the pinnacle of each watchtower was a battle standard of a field of blood crimson on which was emblazoned the black image of a great-wolf stabbed through its back with a massive white broadsword, the broad blade passing all the way through its torso, the sword point sticking out of it chest.

Sir Waldon pointed to the pennant. "Is that the battle standard of your house, my lord?" he asked.

"Yes," the old knight answered. "My ancestor, Sir Ulfius, the first von Wulfbain, slew a great-wolf while fighting under the Paladin King Baerynthine in the Everfrost War. It was for this feat that he derived his name, "Wolf Bane," and for this same feat he was knighted after the end of the war by King Baerythine himself. He was given lordship of this town, and the rest is a matter for the history books and needs no retelling."

Then another thought occurred to young Waldon. "If the slain great-wolf is the standard of your house, why does your battle shield sport the bearing of a lion rampart?"

"Ah," von Wulfbain chuckled. "You are about to uncover a mystery that has baffled many a knight and herald throughout these southern lands. I do not mean to boast but I have many a full coffer in my keep. That, and I *did* slay a troll. I have a love of the joust and melee, (for the enjoyment, not the battle glory or money). Now, think you a less famous knight would want to enter the lists against me? Right. Well, I was called the 'Lion of the South', and never gave my name with my challenge."

The manor house was extremely large, three stories tall, with white washed walls and a roof shingled in dwarf steel. A belfry was placed in the center of the triangular roof and through the stained-glass, Sir Waldon could see a massive bell, with a rope that was either laced in gold thread or in silver. Miniature circular turrets stood at the four cardinal points of the roof. And each of these turrets had a conical roof, from the top of which a minaret pierced the sky. Near the top of the minaret, wrought in silver, was a miniature of the great-wolf insignia of the house of von Wulfbain. Truly, Waldon reflected in his mind, the wealth of this manor could almost rival any one of the wealthy Sir Cedric's castles.

Sir Peter and his guest rode through the barbican of the manor house wall, and were greeted by a bald short man with bulging cheeks, and wearing a pair of padded breeches and a scarlet and black cloak.

"Good evening, Elkins. This is Sir Waldon O'Dumphreys, one of the nine paladins of the realm and our honored guest tonight. Tell Gertrude to prepare one of the guest rooms and set another place at the long table in the great hall."

Elkins bowed politely to Sir Waldon and, once the knight had dismounted, Elkins took the reins of his horse. The footman led the chargers to the stable. Opening the massive doors of the manor house himself, Sir Peter admitted Sir Waldon into his home. The doors led into a great tiled anteroom, lit by torches placed in braziers at intervals along the gilded wall. In the center of the room was a fountain decorated with images of flowers from which poured a crystal stream. And before the clear crystal fountain, was a marble statue of a young woman but barely come out of her teens. She was clothed in a long, flowing dress with ruffles at the sleeves and gossamer at the neck. She had long wavy tresses topped by a small lacy cap.

On the pedestal of the statue was an inscription written with the runes of the fair folk: Katya, fair lady of Veylandin, beloved wife of Lord Peter.

Suddenly, Sir Waldon realized that he had been staring at the statue. Blushing slightly, he turned back to Lord Peter, to see that he was also staring at the statue, a far-off look in his misting eyes. "Your wife?" Sir Waldon ventured at last.

"Aye. My Katya was my angel. And so, like all other angels, she now dwells in heaven with the Lord. Oh, the love we had together. She was my damsel in the tower, and I her knight in shining armor. We had only been married about a year when we found out she was with child. I would rather have had it be that my son had a body like unto hers." He began to speak rather hoarsely. "But he was born to be the colossal body of a man that I was, or rather, am. Even though he was a giant of a child, he could not live long without his mother. For a long time, I thought myself the slayer of both my wife and child, but, at last the Lord spoke to me and said that I should put an end to all this self-blaming and rest in His peaceful assurance that I would see them again one day, beside the avatar of God, God himself, and the Spirit of God. But not until I go to my rest in the halls of heaven. I have no heir, but even more than that, I have wanted a son to teach, to encourage, and to whom I can give my blessing. I have always thought that I would make a good father, but I suppose I shall never have a chance to find out.

"Ah, I should not make you listen to the piteous moaning of an old man. Come. Let me show you to your room."

Sir Peter turned to the left and led the way down a long corridor. The plastered walls were illumined by many candelabras placed in braziers at intervals. Many bright tapestries hung in between these light sources, giving the place a cheery, comfortable feel. The insignia of the von Wulfbains was carved in bas relief along the mahogany baseboards.

Lord Peter stopped before a large door near the center of the left wall, lifted up the links of his hauberk and produced a ring of skeleton keys. The old knight selected the key he needed. The lock thudded open and Sir Peter opened the door.

The room was very spacious. There was a large fourposter bed with a red velvet canopy against the north wall. Beside this was a pewter chamber pot and a wooden dummy on which to place armor. A large ottoman rug was in the center of the room. On the rug stood a large divan, well upholstered and covered with rich velvet cloth. A large washbasin filled with clear, clean water was placed on an end table by the bed. There was a large window overlooking the manor courtyard.

"I am always hosting warriors and knights from other parts the kingdom," the old knight began. "So you will find your needs adequately supplied. The basin is for washing. Do not worry, Sir Waldon. I'm not a mage, if that was what you were thinking. It is used for washing, not for scrying." Sir Peter chuckled.

"Now, if you will be so kind as to excuse me for a few moments, I am going to doff my armor and wash up for supper."

Sir Peter left to go to his own apartments and prepare for supper. For a time, Sir Waldon looked out the window and as he did, he felt and an ethereal chill course down his spine. The days were growing colder and darker despite the season, and if he did not arrive at Baerynthine's Wall soon, he would be too late to succeed in his quest. Shaking the dark thoughts from his mind, he resolved to let events run their course in God's time.

Waldon doffed his armor and, placing it on the dummy, made good use of the water basin. Then he put back on his blue jerkin, black pantaloons and "courtly" dagger. There was nothing courtly about this weapon however, for it was a dwarvish long-knife and could easily pass for a small sword in the hands of a goblin. Running the edge of the blade lightly over the edges of his now unkempt fiery beard, he waited for the return of his host.

Sir Peter returned a few moments later, clad in a heavy red jerkin emblazoned with his pierced great-wolf. He wore pantaloons of black leather and heavy boots of the same material. A long satin cape lined with beaver fur hung from his shoulders. Sir Waldon could see now that the backs of Sir Peter's large hands were quite hairy, yet his nails were trimmed in such a way that Sir Peter's hands did not quite look like the paws of a wild wose of the woods from the pages of heraldric legendrysaid to live in the forests of these regions.

Sir Peter's silvery black hair was long, coming down to his shoulders, so that he looked a bit like the portraits of a younger King Jaerython that hung on the walls of Castle Pallanon. "And now, my esteemed guest," said the old knight, "let us go to supper. Gertrude has prepared roast wildfowl in elderberry sauce, garnished in parsnips, with plenty of barley rolls and light ale to go around." Sir Peter breathed a contented sigh in anticipation of the meal. "We will talk of your business in my domain as we dine at my table tonight. I will show you the way to the great hall. Come with me."

The succulent aroma of roast wildfowl wafted through the halls, assailing Sir Waldon's nostril as he and Lord Peter made their way to the great hall. The red-haired knight could feel his senses sharpening as the pleasant bouquet grew stronger the nearer they came.

A small woman with a rounded figure and graying auburn hair appeared in a side doorway. She had small gray eyes that sparkled with motherly cheer. Smiling, she pulled a bench from under the oaken feasting table for Sir Peter. Once her master was comfortable, she pulled out a seat for Sir Waldon to

Sir Peter's right. Sir Waldon noted this last detail with more than a little surprise, for, at a courtly meal, that was the place reserved for the firstborn son. Bu Sir Peter said nothing of the matter so the young knight was left to wonder.

"It be sauced just the way ya like it, my lord," the lady twittered. "The skin has a crispy texture to it, as ya like it."

"Excellent, Madame Gertrude! Excellent!" said Lord Peter, clapping his hands once. The sound of the clap echoed through the great hall.

Gertrude poured the ale from a pewter decanter and left with a curtsy. Since it was his table, Sir Peter acted as the lord of the feast and served himself first. Then he handed Sir Waldon the other leg. The meat was juicy and tender, with a sweet and smoky flavor, easily tearing away from the bone. The skin had just the right texture, not too crisp, yet not too soft, swallowed down easily. There was not very much unwanted gristle or fat on the bird either. The parsnips were soft and well-seasoned, and the elderberry sauce was sweet. From the first sip, Sir Waldon thought that the light ale was distilled using honey, from its sweet taste. This was a famous signature dwarven practice, not surprising considering the many dwarf inhabits in the town. And the sons of earth were the foremost among all the free races of the kingdom to have a heavy appetite for strong drink. For this reason, most of the taverns in the kingdom were owned by dwarves.

In between bites, Lord Peter asked the question that Sir Waldon knew would eventually come but that he was dreading nevertheless. "Sir Waldon, if I may make so bold, besides the reforging of your sword, what business do you have in my domain?"

Sir Waldon remained silent for a long time, weighing the outcome of his response, before answering. "I am answerable only to King Jaerython, but suffice it to say that I must report to Marshall Roderick at the Wall. It is of utmost importance that I have my sword reforged as quickly as possible so I can make it to Baerynthine's Wall in good time. As Master Smith Dunnir is a dwarf, I trust he will work quickly."

In response to this last statement, Sir Peter sucked in his breath and his eyes widened. "I would not necessarily bet your fortune on that, sir knight. You see, Master Dunnir treats his work as an art. He is as much an artist as he is a blade smith. He may be the finest armorer of his generation, but such fine craftsmanship takes time. Only once have I seen him purposefully work in haste, and that was when he and the alchemist François de Conlois were crafting my own blade Ettin-Bane, and they did so because they were afraid that the troll would destroy the town and gruesomely murder all the inhabitants. What is more, Master Smith Dunnir is a black-skinned dwarf, and though other dwarves cannot match the quality of their steel, ebon dwarves have a deep underlying philosophy to their craft, almost magical and benevolently arcane, not present in their fair skinned cousin's workmanship. Their work is the best in the kingdom, but they do not turn out their products quickly, for they think it a sin to not give their works proper time to mature and evolve. I am not saying it is a given fact, but you may have to wait a good while if you want old Dunnir to reforge your blade."

Sir Waldon was crestfallen at these words, but he did not give voice to his disappointment.

The rest of the meal passed pleasantly, with no confrontation on the part of Lord Peter concerning Waldon's meeting at Baerynthine's Wall. Sir Waldon wisely did not press the issue of the reforging of his sword, but part of his mind wished that he could explain to his new friend has urgent need for a swift departure. Yet he knew he could not, for as wise as Sir Peter von Wulfbain apparently was in the ways of strategy and war, Waldon knew that he could not betray the trust placed upon him by his lord and King. He wished that his friend, Sir Vaelen, could be there to help them resist these urges, for Sir Vaelen was strongest of the Nine Peers in resisting senseless urges of the human heart. But Vaelen was not there, so Sir Waldon did not mention the subject for the remainder of the meal, and took his leave of Lord Peter after finishing.

Back in his room, once he was dressed in his sleeping garments, Sir Waldon looked out the window and sighed. Night had fallen and the stars were shining a little dimmer than the night before. Waldon knew also that the wind was growing colder with each passing hour. If he did not arrive at the Gateway to Varluckhuld in time, his fellow paladins would not possess all the shards of the holy seraph sword of King Baerynthine, and Waldon knew well that the blade of Baerynthine was the only weapon in the land that could defeat the shadow-raiser, Skrael. And without all the shards, the blade could not reach its former magical potency. Waldon knew he could not travel without a sword, much less aid in the assault on the Black Tower. And if the shadow-raiser could not be defeated, it would spell the doom of the entire kingdom. The entire success of the mission now hung on the reforging of Sir Waldon's sword. The entire fate of the Kingdom depended on the dwarven blade smith Dunnir and the speed of his crafting. Sir Waldon could not rush the smith, for if he did both Lord Peter and the dwarf would become suspicious and start asking questions, for the success of the mission also depended on secrecy. Sir Waldon O'Dumphrey's would have to exercise undying patience. He could do nothing else. The knight sighed once more and went to bed, to be haunted by dark dreams.

13.   The Smith and the Alchemist

When Sir Waldon awoke the next morning, he discovered a note on the end table by the side of the bed.

Sir Waldon, please come to training area near center of manor house before we dine. I must speak with you. Come clad in armor.

Yours sincerely,

Sir P

Sir Waldon would have preferred to simply eat a quick roll and gulp down a slosh of tea, then be off to Dunnir's forge, but he merely shrugged, donned his armor and went to find his host. He arrived to find the training room deserted, but even so, he was glad he had come, for the room would delight alchemist and warrior alike. There were what appeared to be statues and sculptures of gigantic proportions, wrought of strange alchemically derived metals. In between these peculiar works of art were weapon racks filled with swords, shields and all other types of weapons of varying shapes and sizes.

Having a knight's characteristic love of weapons, Sir Waldon was looking at a rack of lances when he heard for a split second a whirring sound. He looked over his shoulder just in time to see a huge spear hurdling towards him. With a fluid, but not concentrated motion, he jumped out of the missile's path. He caught it as it passed, twirling it around his head and torso, and finally coming to poise himself in a fighter's stance.

There must be an assassin in the house!

There came a thunderous clapping from an indeterminable area of the room, and a moment later, Sir Peter von Wulfbain emerged in full armor from behind one of the statues. He was carrying a massive maul over his shoulder.

"You could have killed me. Are you mad?" hollered Waldon.

"Welcome to my personal training room," said Lord Peter, ignoring Sir Waldon's question. "I have had it for almost forty years."

"I thought we might work up a better appetite for breakfast. Take up that hammer there, son."

"A war maul?" Sir Waldon asked raising an eyebrow. "Would not the sword be a more knightly choice?"

"This hammer would snap an ordinary sword like a twig. Besides, for a knight to have mastery over only one weapon is foolishness."

Sir Waldon placed the spear on an empty rack, picked up the giant hammer and tested his new weapon's balance. Satisfied, he assumed a fighting stance.

Sir Peter did not even give voice to a battle cry, but began swinging his hammer in a zigzag pattern, so that had weapon head met weapon head and haft with such swiftness that the room echoed and boomed like the open sky in a spring storm. With Waldon's head ringing from the clangor, the older knight easily slipped his foot behind the younger's, and Waldon fell to the floor in a heap of jingling mail.

Helping Sir Waldon up, Sir Peter said, "That I learned from the Vaerings, when my brother-in-arms, King Jaerython, and I captured some in battle during the time of their winter raids. The tawny-haired warriors call those fighting moves 'the strike of Mjolnir.' The name has something to do with their god of thunder. Well, I do not care much for pagan lore, but I must admit that their method of wielding the war maul is quite effective. Are you all right? Yes? Good. Let us continue. Perhaps something a little different...."

Sir Peter tossed Sir Waldon a hand-and-a-half thrusting sword with a long, broad blade that tapered to a fine point near the end of the blade. The cylindrical pommel was overbalanced, and Sir Waldon found it difficult to manage.

The old knight seized a flame-bladed pole arm and began to weave the zigzag blade in and out, aiming for the young Knight's chest. Waldon parried swiftly, sometimes with the flat of his blade, but then, as Sir Peter began to twirl the strange spear in a circular motion like a windmill, he easily knocked the borrowed sword to the floor.

"That will never do," grunted von Wulfbain. "Well... have you ever used a falchion?"

Sir Waldon shook his head. "I guess there is a first time for everything," said Lord Peter. "Look lively with your shield."

Sir Peter tossed Sir Waldon a single-handed falchion with down-turned quillions. Then the old knight hefted up a huge axe with a blade as big as those wielded by the muscular half trolls. He picked up a large buckler from a shield rack and struck the flat of his axe's head twice on the shield's metal rim. The clanging echoed through the room like a blast of lightning. Suddenly, the old knight charged with a low growl, and swung the axe in a heavy downward blow. Sir Waldon caught the blow on the boss of his shield and could feel the defensive weapons shivering beneath it. For a moment he thought the shield would burst into a hundred splinters. But the good Elven woodwork held up to the reputation of its crafters. Recovering almost instantly from the slight stun, Sir Waldon swung the single-edge blade in a horizontal cut toward Sir Peter's massive torso. The older knight swiftly jumped backwards, the mail links of his hauberk jingling into place as he came down.

"Bless my beard, this may work after all!" Peter von Wulfbain laughed with jubilation. But then he swung the haft of the axe at Waldon's sword arm, brushing him slightly on the wrist. The falchion clattered to the floor.

"Aaagh!" Sir Peter groaned, casting up his eyes. "Your grip is not well-balanced for that type of sword. That is the last. It will have to be enough. I took the shards of your sword last night and weighed them against several of my blades, trying to find the correct ratio of balance. I would have been able to give you a new sword so that you would not have to wait on old Dunnir. But, blasted beard of a Vaering, it be but a lost cause. Those were the most suitable swords in my collection. I suppose we will just have to wait on old Dunnir after all. At any rate, I am famished, as I do not doubt you are. Let us go to breakfast."

A very winded Sir Waldon followed von Wulfbain out of the armory training ground and through the winding halls toward the dining room. After they cleaned the sweat from their morning exercise and seated themselves, a smiling Gertrude set down a curious, life-size serving bowl in the shape of one of the new close helms. It apparently was very hot, for the aging cook had to open the visor with a damp towel. Sir Waldon saw that the inside was filled with steaming hard-boiled eggs, links of sausage and slices of ham steak. Sir Peter was quite proud of this serving dish, for he affectionately dubbed it Sir Egglamour.

After they had both eaten their fill, Sir Peter rose from the table and motioned to Sir Waldon saying, "And now, off to the forge of Master Smith Dunnir. Watch your tongue, my son, for old Dunnir is for the most part jolly, but there is a streak in him as volatile as the insides of a fire mountain."

Sir Peter and his guest left the manor house and made their way to the stable, where they found that Elkins had prepared their mounts.

By this time the sun was high in his climb through the sky, though far from the zenith of noon. As they rode down through the streets, many chattering dwarflings jogged for a few paces alongside Sir Peter's horse yelling up things like "Good day, my lord. Where be ye off to?" "May I see your mighty blade, Ettin-Bane." "Once again, Sir Knight, how many trolls did you slay with it?" "Will you put your signature on my illumination of you?"

Lord Peter, being the loving feudal lord that he was, was always kind to acquiesce to their requests in a patient, grandfatherly fashion. Accompanied by this great cacophony of compliments and childish questions, they soon found themselves before the doors of the large steel-braced forge of Master Smith Dunnir of Veylandin.

"Now if you will excuse me, my hairy little angels, my Paladin guest and I have business with Master Smith Dunnir inside the forge. And you know how grumpy he becomes if he can't concentrate on his work. So then, away home with you now, my darling dwarflings. Shoo, now." When the children had gone Sir Peter chuckled to himself and said, "They stole my heart long ago, God bless them. Well, now. Let us go see what masterpieces the master craftsman is forming on his anvil even as we speak." Sir Peter turned and opened the door to the forge.

Immediately, the young Waldon was met by three sensations. One was the enormous wave of heat that assailed his face. The second accosted his eyes. Every conceivable type of weapon from pole arm to Alfanonian boot dagger hung neatly on hooks and wall racks, neatly organized by typology. And every mail coat and coif seem to be of the most compact kingsmail yet had he been able at that moment to touch it, the red-haired Knight would have found it to be as light as gossamer. There were smith's apprentices and journeyman smiths working around the anvils, black and white-skinned dwarves mostly, but also a few human young men. The final sensation was one of sound, for not only did the wheezing of the bellows and the clangor of forging hammer upon hot iron meet his years, but he also heard a single deep, booming, baritone voice rise above the cacophony of laughter and talk, singing out in time with the beating of the hammers.

"I went with my brothers of earth,

To where the ore is given birth

I made hammer and fire sing

Forth a blade to give a king,

Forth a blade to give a king!"

Sucking in a deep breath, Sir Peter roared forth a loud greeting above the metallic din. "Good Morrow, old friend Dunnir. I have come with a most noble customer who needs to enlist your craftsmanship."

The bellows behind a large anvil ceased to wheeze and the hammer ceased to fall. Out from behind a high anvil came a black-skinned dwarf, clad all in black leather. The thick belt about his waist held forging hammers and tongs of all sizes. His bushy black beard and mane were flecked with gray. His black skin glistened as if it had been burnished with oil and his nose was bulbous and round. He was slightly taller than average for a dwarf, standing several inches above four feet in height. His forearms bulged like stuffed grain sacks, and the Paladin did not doubt that if the dwarven blade smith had been taller and in a fouler mood at the moment, he would have been able to knock Waldon or even von Wulfbain to the floor unconscious with one swift blow.

"How may I be of service to ye, young knight?" the dark dwarf asked.

Sir Waldon cleared his throat and said, "I am Sir Waldon O'Dumphreys, one of the Nine Peers, and was attacked by a band of goblins near the gates of the town yesterday, and your noble feudal lord came to my aid, but not before my sword blade had broken into shards during the fray. I am normally a very patient man, but I must make so bold as to request that you be swift with this task of reforging, for which I am able and willing to pay a very large amount. You see, Master Smith, I am needed by Marshall Roderick Goldenbeard at Baerynthine's Wall in slightly over a month."

"About the price, Dunnir," Lord Peter interjected. "Please do not charge my young friend anything for your services. I will be more than happy to pay all expenses incurred."

Before Sir Waldon could open his mouth to protest, Master Smith Dunnir said, "Well, good sir knights, you know the old adage among my people, 'a good blade is worth the wait, the best blade is worth a lifetime.' I may have to send for our old friend the alchemist François de Conlois. He has moved to the Township surrounding Castle Roldburg." Sir Peter handed the gruff dwarf weapon smith the shards of Sir Waldon's sword. The dwarf examined the steel shards for a long moment, squinting one eye and pursing his lips in thought. "As a matter of fact, I think I will call on the lanky ol' philosopher of an apothecary after all. Just in case the need arises for some alchemical or astrological touches. Oh, Alkimisa!"

Waldon listened to the dwarf adage with a sense of foreboding, for he knew the importance of expediency in this desperate time. But he did not want to alarm the dwarf or the other knight, or give cause for unwanted questions, so he merely resigned to wait patiently and forebear any outward signs of the anxiety rising within his heart.

Master Smith Dunnir went to the back of the forge and returned with a carrier pigeon, whom he had lovingly named Alkimisa in honor of his friend Francois' mysterious profession. Scribbling some message that Sir Waldon could not see onto a small scrap of paper, the dwarf weapon smith placed the paper in a small brass tube and tied it with a small length of cord to the carrier pigeon's foot. Then he whispered something to the bird and let it fly out through the open door. Dunnir watched it soar into the winter sky, and no one spoke until it had disappeared from sight.

"Master Dwarf," laughed von Wulfbain at length, "was that one of your secret couplet line stanza poem messages that you never let anyone see save yourself and François?"

"That was just such a one, my Lord Peter," the graying weapon Smith said, smiling.

Sir Waldon's initial impulse was to protest against Dunnir's methodical sluggishness, but then he remembered his nurse's often-quoted adage concerning dwarves: "Never judge the forging affairs of the sons of earth, for as their iron heats quickly, so do their tempers."

Lord Peter was still amused at the dwarf smith secretive poetry. "You are ever up to your old, abstruse tricks, friend Dunnir," he commented. "I have never been able to read the habits of weapon smiths, be they elf, dwarf or human, though I rely on their craft for my battle gear." Sir Peter smiled and shook his head.

"And now," the dark dwarf said. "If you will excuse me, I have some more pressing orders to fill. I will not be able to do anything with your steel bits until François arrives, and, as you both are well aware, it is quite a long ride from Castle Roldburg to this town." Seeing Sir Waldon's face cloud with an air of disappointment, the graying old smith began to mention creative ways in which the disheartened young knight could pass the time, with bits of advice such as "Young sir knight, there are many fine shops, with many goods of steel craft through which you may want to peruse of a morning. (Many of them sell some o' me finest works" and others like "if you need something to read or a place to pray, Abbot Grendbard, a very pious and worthy dwarf, will let you use the Green Chapel of the monastery."

Sir Waldon sighed inwardly. *I must not allow this to vex me,* he thought.

"Forget not, my young friend," the broad-chested older knight remarked with a soothing tone, "it is far better for a warrior to keep his body primed for battle. My training ground and jousting dummies will always be available to you. I suspect, God willing, that old François will be here within a week. But I do not want to fill you with a false hope, for as Dunnir has said, it is a long road from Castle Roldburg, and even longer when transporting star elixirs and philosopher's stones. Come, let us go back to the manor for tea and more exercise."

So Sir Waldon forced a smile and nod, and followed Sir Peter out of the forge.

Once Sir Waldon had remounted his horse, he turned to Lord Peter and said, "No doubt what you said of the dwarf smith was true. I suppose I will just have to wait. I relish your offer of continued trading bouts, but even I find this situation irritating. I am therefore going to go to the Green Chapel to pray and to seek advice from Abbot Grendbard. Will you be so kind as to give me directions? When I return, we can continue our practice at arms."

"As you wish, my son," von Wulfbain replied, smiling. He pointed a gauntleted hand to the West. "Do you see that spire sporting the double-bitted battle axe head painted forest green? That is the spire on the roof of the Green Chapel. Go down the main thoroughfare and turn to the left when you come to Doglend Steelbeard's Tavern. There is a hitching post outside the gate."

Sir Waldon thanked his host and turned his stallion, Gringolet, to the left and gently urged him down the main thoroughfare at a slow pace. He came to a Tavern with a grungy sign with a dwarf's bearded face, the beard colored dark gray in now chipping paint. Turning to the left again, he plodded down a narrower street and came in time to a domed building with green painted doors and emerald stained-glass windows set in triangularly arched frames painted the color of dew-covered moss. Upon the main door was inscribed, in dwarven runes, a dwarvish phrase -"*Urden unde varken*": "pray and work". The door handles were crafted in the likeness of a pair of stubby dwarf hands clasped in prayer.

Waldon hitched Gringolet to the post and opened the door. The interior was like that of any other chapel in the kingdom, except everything was green. The pews, the hymnals, even the altar. Everything was green. Forest green.

It was quiet. The only sound was a whirring, swooshing sound, the origin of which the Knight could not at first locate. Then he saw a dwarf clergyman twirling a halberd that was much taller than he was. He was twirling it and saying his prayers, though of course his eyes were open. The halberd had a single-bladed bearded axe head, like the axes used by the Vaering barbarians. Its head was painted green, and its shaft was wrapped in green leather. The dwarf churchman twirled it faster and faster, until Waldon was sure that the dwarf would drop the weapon. At first the knight was mesmerized by the dwarf cleric's deftness. But then he remembered why he had come and cleared his throat. The dwarf stopped twirling the pole arm, and turned toward Waldon stamping his foot and pounding the butt cap all at once.

It was then that Waldon saw the dwarf's face for the first time. He was clad in a clergyman's robe, forest green like his surroundings. He had grayish blue eyes that twinkled with liveliness and intelligence. His visage sported a great bulbous nose, very ruddy like the rest of his face, a full, long reddish-brown beard. His hair was cut in a tonsure, though it was not very normal for a tonsure. For beyond the large bald spot on his pate, his mane fell down to his shoulders.

"Oh," he said. "Ye startled me, Sir Knight. I am Abbot Grendbard of the Green Chapel. God's blessing be upon ye, my son. How may I help ye?"

"I am Sir Waldon O'Dumphreys, Paladin of the realm. I am on a mission to Baerynthine's Wall for King Jaerython." He went on to tell the story of all that had transpired in the past few days.

"And so," he concluded, "I am here to pray and seek counsel, to keep myself from becoming overly preoccupied with my plight."

"Well," said the Abbot. "There be nothing that some heartfelt prayer cannot help." Holding up the halberd he said, "This halberd belonged to Abbot Bardicus, the founder of this monastery and chapel. He was a warrior priest who fought against the goblins and trolls of Trillven Forest. He used the holy powers given to him by God to quell the raids of the foul folk. Every Abbot since him has been taught how to wield this weapon. Pray a while, my son. Here. This halberd may help you concentrate."

Waldon took the weapon and began twirling it faster and faster as he prayed, but images flitted through his head, visions of his quest, that blasted lazy dwarven smith Dunnir, that snail paced alchemist, Waldon's broken sword, Baerynthine's Wall; and the worst image yet of all: Skrael triumphant. All these images and more came crowding into his mind, blocking his prayers, taking his mind from the Lord God.

"Oi, lad! Ye be about to knock over the incense brazier!"

The dwarf Abbot's desperate cry jolted Sir Waldon out of his ruminations. He dropped the priestly weapon, and it clattered to the floor.

"Now just an axe-swinging minute, lad," began the Abbot. "I may not know much about warrior instinct or the heat of battle, but, clear as day, I know a heavy heart when I see one. What makes a man like ye be so desperate? Whatever it be, ye must yield it to the Lord. I am just one of the free folk like you, but my vocation is to see the spiritual needs of all free folk that cross me path. Are ye sure there be nothing ye be wanting to tell me?"

"I would, Abbot Grendbard," Sir Waldon panted. "But I cannot. I am bound by an oath of secrecy to my lord and king. And if I do not keep that oath, chaos is sure to ensue. Suffice to say that if I do not reach my destination within two months, the consequences will be dire. I cannot journey without my weapon. And I cannot have my weapon without Master Smith Dunnir." The knight thought for a moment. Then his mind lighted upon an idea and he said, "Father Abbot, if I may ask a favor of you, mayhap you could speak to Master Smith Dunnir. You are of the same race. He would be more likely to listen to you than to me."

The Abbot's eyes widened at the thought and he whistled through his teeth and said, "Were it any other smith or any other dwarf I would do it, but not that one.... I have a story about that one. Several years ago I ordered some embossed images for the altar. It took him over a year and a half to complete the order, and when I came back in the interim and requested the completion before that year's Avatar Mass, he nearly threw a hammer at me. Nay, my son, I cannot. Do not worry or grieve, noble knight. The Lord our God is faithful. I have never seen Him fail to provide for the needs of His children. Take courage, my son. I shall pray that you shall be filled with an assurance that everything for which you hope will come to pass in God's good time."

Over the next several days, Sir Waldon sparred and trained at arms with Sir Peter. Every day he would ride to old Dunnir's forge to see if the alchemist François had arrived during night, and he was always disappointed when the dwarf smith replied in the negative. The days grew colder, the sun paler. The young Knight heard malevolent voices echoing throughout his dreams and he often saw the town of Veylandin razed to the ground and rebuilt as a dark, vile bastion of terror for the twisted glory of Skrael. As these dreams became more frequent, young Waldon would go in the dead of the night to the battlements to look out for any sign of François de Conlois. How he longed to tell von Wulfbain, with his warm paternal caring, all the fears that deeply troubled the young Knight's heart. But yet he could not. For the sake of his vow to King Jaerython, he could never divulge the truth. He now had less than a fortnight to reach the Wall. And so he did the first thing that every warrior of God should do: pray. Every night in his room he buried his head into the pillow and prayed long and fervently, sometimes in a holy language of the soul known only to him and to the Lord. It was night time that everything he was connected and in an unbreakable bond, a Canticle kythe, with the heart of God, and there he found true peace. His long-suffering was bolstered anew. Then his prayers were answered by abstruse means.

One night, at the midnight hour, as he was completing his nightly vigil along the battlements, Waldon saw a strange light bobbing up out of the distance. He nudged the Captain of the guard on the shoulder. "Joachim!" He hissed, pointing a gauntleted finger in the direction of the approaching light. "What is that?"

Joachim von Dulern, a tall, whiskered man with unusually large fists squinted into the darkness and then turned, motioning to his second-in-command. "Auldron, what do your keen elf eyes see?"

The aging Alfanonian, who had been raised as a Highland hunter and scout, pierced the darkness with his blazing, hawklike gaze. "There be a wiry rider a-ridin' toward the gate like a madman. He must have been bitten by a foaming wolf." The elf withdrew one of his stag anter-handled throwing knives. "You want me to pick him off for you, sir?"

"No," replied the captain, raising his hand.

Cupping both hands around his mouth, old Joachim called out, "Halt! Who goes there and what is your business?"

A voice very soft, but loud enough to carry across the remaining distance called back in reply. "Joachim, you old lion. You know me well enough. I am François de Conlois, come from Castle Roldburg to help with one of friend Dunnir's orders. Said he was one of the Nine Peers, I think. Are you going to stand around like a bulged belly bear are you going to let me..." CREAK!

Joachim swung around to see that Sir Waldon was already cranking the winch to open the portcullis.

Once the gate was open and the small horse and his rider had entered, young Waldon bolted down the steps to meet the old alchemist.

François de Conlois was old but he didn't look it. His hair was still completely dark, that is what he still had on his head for was almost completely bald. A short goatee wrapped around his lips and he was wiry like a scarecrow and thin like a carpenter's nail. Yet it seemed that although most men of his trade led a sedentary lifestyle, he was as spry and quick of limb as he was of thought. The pack that his pony carried was filled with glasses and vials containing powders and tinctures with many various and sundry names. "I am insistent that old Dunnir and I begin tonight. I do apologize, Sir Knight, that he has tried your patience. But it is about to pay off. This is an alchemical blade we will be crafting, so we should be done with the work by sunrise, that is if I can force old Dunnir out of bed. Be thankful the slaying of dragons is up to you. It is much easier than rousing a son of earth from slumber. Now be careful with that silvery blue vial. It is the tears of a fallen star. And also the dark green goldish one; it's the blood of a bishop fish." The alchemist seemed very adamant, and yet even so, poor Waldon knew that he would almost have to kill his horse to reach the Wall in time.

As Dunnir and François were busy setting up François's makeshift laboratory, Lord Peter who had been roused at the news of François's coming, took the younger night aside and said, "Waldon my boy, you should rest while you can. I know this long unexpected delay has worn heavy on you, yet you have born it with more patience and forbearance than an Elven sage. I know you are loathe to talk about your business at Baerynthine's Wall, yet I pray for your great spirit of forbearance shall not fail you, and you shall rest assured that the Lord will make all things right in the end for those who serve him."

And so Waldon returned to von Wulfbain's manor, and collapsed into bed falling instantly into a dreamless sleep.

The next morning, instead of leaving his usual note concerning the schedule of the day, Lord Peter shook Sir Waldon awake. "It is finished, my boy. Old Dunnir and François have forged you an entirely new sword, a much better one. It is finished at last. Neither you nor I have ever seen the likes of it before. Come."

They rode to the forge, eating a meager breakfast of bread and apples on the journey. Dunnir may have been methodical, but when he forge something he was proud of, he flaunted it. "She be the best blade I have ever made. Behold!" Dunnir drew back the satin cloth covering the anvil, and did so with a great flourish.

Waldon gasped. The blade was twice as broad as his armored forearm and was fullered widely on both sides. It seemed to almost burn and glow with the righteous alchemical, aura of gold and pure pearl white light all at once, each one burning within and without the other. The sword was keen and could have cleaved an armored horse and half. The grip was wrapped in golden brown leather that was perfectly comfortable to the bare hand. The guard was thick and rectangular, yet on both ends was a spike in the shape of a wolf tooth. It's scabbard was of golden brown leather with silver furniture and a gold lion rampart was upon the chape. The pommel was pear-shaped yet somewhat shaped like a crown and could, according to Dunnir, who was an excellent judge of quality punch down through a helmet of any make. One would think that such a sword would be unwieldy and heavy, yet it was almost as light as a poniard, and could be wielded either one or two-handed. Waldon slowly took it up and found its balance to be flawless.

"Sir Knight," said François, winking at the dwarf, "do you remember the tales of the Everfrost War? Do you remember how they used narrower swords for a time?"

"Yes," Sir Waldon replied. "Skrael's armorers engineered armor made of riveted plates that a broadsword could not slice through, so they changed to narrower swords that could punch through the plate armor. Why?"

The dwarf smith stepped behind the anvil and returned with a blackened, grungy cuirass of goblin plate armor. "Take a swing at that. One of my ancestors picked it up off of a goblin officer." Waldon swung, though not very hard, for fear of damaging his new sword. To his surprise, it cleaved the goblin cuirass completely in half. Waldon stood staring at the blade in amazement and his heart was glad.

"The only way to truly test an alchemical blade," von Wulfbain grinned, "is in combat against another one. Look sharp, my son."

Lord Peter charged so quickly that Sir Waldon barely had time to strap on his shield. The mighty alchemical blades rained down on shields in a blood-firing frenzy of blows. Alchemical energy and lightning crackled between the edges as they met, sometimes shooting sparks in mismatched directions. The blades seemed almost to feet on the battle joy and surging strength of their wielders. It was an ever invigorating, endless cycle of combat. The more power the blades discharged the more the battle joy grew, and as the battle joy mounted, the blades, almost sentient yet subject to the will of their masters, the blades themselves increased their reservoirs of power. Suddenly the spell of battle ended as a cry rang out. "Ye be destroying me forge!"

The combatants fell to their knees panting.

"I apologize… Friend Dunnir…. in all my long days… I have never had a bout like that," panted Sir Peter.

"I should go," said Sir Waldon once he had caught his breath.

"I shall ride with you to the gates of the city," said Lord Peter.

Once they had ridden beyond the barbican, Sir Waldon said to Lord Peter. "You have been very good to me and I am forever in your debt. I hope that we will meet again someday under less urgent circumstances. I have thought of a name for the sword I shall call it Wolfsbane in your honor."

Grasping Sir Waldon's forearm, Sir Peter said, his eyes misting, "I hope to see you again someday as well. An old trick about these alchemical blades, raise it to the sky, and I, also being a wielder of an alchemical sword, shall see it. If you need to summon me to the wall, do this and I will come." He paused for a long moment and said hoarsely, "God's blessing be upon you. Goodbye…Myson." "Goodbye…My father."

Sir Waldon O'Dumphreys rode quickly north from the town of Veylandin bearing the alchemical sword Wolfsbane. He came on the very day of the rendezvous to Baerynthine's Wall, the last of his brother and to arrive. Yet he had no regrets, for his patience had won for him the mightiest sword in the land. And something even greater that he had never possessed: a father.

14. Reftkirk

Sir Cedric, Lord of Gelden Hill, rode northwest from Castle Pallanon. Some said that the chestnut haired knight had Vaering blood in his veins, for he wore his hair in a diamond-shaped shock, with a long braid coming down in the back, in a style common among the Vaering barbarians. One would think, as his companions often commented, that such a style would be cumbersome beneath a mail coif and helmet. But Cedric in all reality was not at all bothered.

He was clad this day in his resplendent gilded mail. On his hands he wore mail-backed gauntlets of rare Dragon skin leather sewn at intervals with silver mail. His mail shirt had been gilded with molten boullion and in several places encrusted with enameled pearls. The haubergeon was far from merely decorative, however, and could withstand the stab of a dragon's barbed tail. The knight's riding boots were of the best Alfanonian bovine leather. His surcoat sported his heraldry of the gauntleted hand holding the silver chalice. His shield was a three-cornered shield with embossed silver at the edges and his sword was magnificent to behold. The hilt was wrought of pure gold with a circular pommel, a sapphire encrusted in the center. On the fuller of the broad silvered blade was phrase inscribed in elven glyphs: "I am Westledon, Arm of Justice." He carried with him a silver-tipped lance with a grip wrapped in gossamer and velvet. It was highly ostentatious but very functional.

Sir Cedric also had armor that was of newer style and very rare. He wore one of the new model helmets, called close helms and wore a gorget to protect his clavicle. It tapered down to a point above the mail and right above that point was inlaid a large ruby. She also wore spaulders on his shoulders etched with Elvish knotwork.

He was engaged to be married to the niece of King Jaerython, the Lady Eliana Conchobar. As such, like Sir Leofred, more was at stake for him in the success of this venture.

Cedric was greatly blessed financially. He maintained no fewer than five castles, each with a garrison of two hundred fifty men. And the coffers of those keeps were overflowing with gold.

One would think that such wealth would make the chestnut maned knight as miserly as a dragon, ever guarding his vast hoard of gold and precious stones. However the good Cedric held his coin with an open palm rather than a closed fist. The reeve in charge of Sir Cedric's estate, a kindhearted man with curly dark locks and bulbous nose, named Ben-Yasson Hibbat, was always putting together deeds of credit with no repayment stipulation. "My master, he have generous chutzpah," the little man would say, smiling in amazement. Lord Cedric gave a large amount of his annual revenue to the local Chapel as well as to the Council of Bishops. And yet he did not use this as an excuse to shirk his annual stipend duties to the crown. Whereas many lesser Knights made gold their god, the Lord of Gelden Hill his heart had already been purified of avarice by the Golden hand of the true God. He knew that true prosperity was found in abiding in the will of God, not in great riches.

Any other experienced reeve or shrewd tax gatherer would no doubt think that such reckless generosity would quickly drain the wealthiest man's purse. Yet the coffers of Sir Cedric were always filled to the brim. Whenever a certain farm under his jurisdiction had had a poor harvest, and could not give their agreed portion of the crop, the good Paladin would forgive the debt and supply the needs of the family from his own storehouses.

And so as he journeyed forth from Castle Pallanon, Sir Cedric of Gelden Hill carried with him a bulging purse filled with gold pieces. Not because his expenses will be great on the strength, but because he was always searching for a way to generously show his great kindness to anyone who happened to cross his path.

His horse, Argonissa, whinnied with great joy as she carried forth on his journey. She was the best horse that money could buy and as loyal as a newborn babe. He hadridden the Highland Mare for the past five years, and she had served him well in both battle and tournament. Sir Cedric bore the lance far better than any other his fellow paladins. And although he kept very little of the prize money, he emerged victorious so frequently that the small percentage which he kept had only added to his already vast riches. He would always purchase food and drink for all of the spectators during a joust in which he was competing. So they knew that when the chalice bearing knight was competing, not only that the bout be well worth watching, but a complementary meal would be provided. "Huzzah for our man Cedric. May his sword ever be drawn to victory. And may God bless this knight of the kind heart! God bless Cedric, Lord of Gelden Hill, our noble champion." Sir Cedric heard these cries of encouragement and many other such acclamations whenever he entered the lists. But the knight always reminded himself to remain humble, for he knew pride came before a fall, and could cause him to trust in his riches, rather than in the Lord his God. He knew that just as soon as money could come, it would blow away like the wind. And so he put his trust in the eternal rather than the ephemeral.

As he rode his fine Alfanonian mare that bone-chilling day, he passed by many a cottage long abandoned by a serf in payment to a cruel feudal lord. This brought thoughts of his own vassals to his mind, and his heart was somewhat saddened that he could do nothing for the poor family. He had enough wealth both monetary and physical to purchase all the fiefs in the southern lands, and when it came between that and survival, and more important than survival was a heart bound to the Lord, loving friends, and a well-balanced mind. *Let it be said of me,* he thought, *the day when I pass at last into the realm of heaven that I had these latter things and not simply the former.*

"All these things shall come to dust

If in them, you place your trust.

All the wealth and richly things,

Even those of Dragon Kings

Shall melt in brazen fire

And only bring eternal ire

Bind your heart with fiery wire

Only as it must.

Rather, like the whitten dove,

Set your mind on things above

And store there treasures of love

In the Lord put your trust."

The burly Paladin smiled to himself after whispering these words. "Well, you know, Argonissa, he said to his charger, "I may compose that psalter Brother Wennedden was wanting after all."

As he continued through the cold breeze, he heard the Lord speak to him in the quiet of his heart. "Soon, I will require you to give much for my cause."

"I shall be wary and watchful, and have listening ears," Sir Cedric whispered.

Several minutes later, Lord Cedric heard the clip-clop of hooves, and saw what appeared at first to be a mounted Vaering warband coming up the road (though why they would be using a main road Cedric could not say).

Westledon flashed from her sheath. However, it was not a war band, but rather a troop of dwarven lads, side whiskers just beginning to grow into beards, but they were escorted by a single Vaering warrior who had the look of a mercenary.

Cedric hailed the man and asked, "Whither go you, warrior. And the why in the presence of dwarven youths?"

"These lads have taken up holy orders. They go to serve as altar boys at the Green Chapel. Their father, a very affluent dwarf, paid me to escort them. Don't worry. It's true I am a sword for hire, but I'm an honorable one at that. It is sad that my employer, Frori, did not have the money to hire an Elven Ranger instead.

Sir Cedric thought for a moment and said, "about a league from here is a Tavern known as *The Stag's Head*. They always have honest warriors looking for employment there." "I have no money to pay for that, you see."

"How much do you need?" Asked Cedric, gauntleted hand reaching inside his cloak for his purse.

"At least twenty gold pieces, Sir Knight."

Ample coins jingled in the barbarian warrior's callused hand. "There is ten extra for your time."

"But, my lord, are you sure…?"

Sir Cedric nodded holding up his hand for silence. "One of the five virtues of knighthood is generosity. I would be ashamed to not show as much. Do not worry about the cost to me. I'm more interested in eternal wealth than temporal. Godspeed to you, and guard these lads with your very life. Farewell."

Cedric rode on without another word, leaving the Vaering man speechless.

It did not vex the Lord of Gelden Hill in the least to give the Vaering mercenary most of his journeying money. Cedric held his purse with an open palm, not a tightly clenched fist as would a miser or a vile-hearted fire drake. And because of this generous, kindly nature, he never lacked any provision. All his needs were supplied by heaven.

Cedric began to whistle *The Lay of Amberene,* the epic ballad concerning the life of the Lady Amberene, the First of the Gemlocks, whose blessing and beauty came from the heaven-reflecting light of the Sun. She had swum down from the stars, the first elf to do so, given birth by the singing of a seraph maiden. She had carved for herself a tower of amber, the color of her hair, braced upon a white oak. The tower was called by the later elves Trael ar Aven, "Tower of the First Maid". (After the foul folk invaded and drove the elven inhabitants north to what would become the Town of Alfenton the foul folk took the name and slurred it to Trillven and applied the name to the whole forest once they had completed their sacrilege upon it." A hot-headed elven knight named Torreldell had fallen to his death after slipping from the turret of the tower when he climbed it to seek the Lady Amberene's hand in marriage. The Maid of the Tower was at first indignant but then had pity on the dead man and went back to the stars to comfort him. The full tale is recounted in the *Tolle-Amberuch-Tordellan, The Song of Amberene and Torreldell.* It was a shorter version, translated into the tongue of the humans that Sir Cedric now whistled.

As he was whistling, he heard a winter thrush cooing in a damp tree overhead, and to the knight its call sounded vaguely as if it were singing, "Soon again! Soon again!" Cedric felt another strong quickening in his spirit.

Strangely, the next sight he came upon was a most peculiar one. There was a black dwarf riding a large mountain goat. In his right hand he carried a ridiculous looking rusted lance with an uneven tip. Yet this dwarf did seem to have some knowledge of weapon and war craft. For he was clad in rusted mail over which he wore a greasy gambeson scratched with some weird insignia that resembled a war hammer. On his head he wore a pentagonal helmet with a visor crafted in the likeness of a sneering bearded dwarf visage. The toes of his boots were missing so that his hair-encrusted toenails showed through, and the thick nails were dotted with flakes of snow.

He hailed Lord Cedric, and exclaimed in his best herald's voice. "I am the self-knighted knight Don Jonnery Thonnery. I am sworn to a vow of celibacy. And thus I ride for the glory of my sainted sister, Casholona Thonnery. It is my aim on my ever knight-errant quest to unhorse a champion knight. And so do I hereby *shallange* (he said this word with a mock courtier accent) you." He removed his patched glove and threw it ceremoniously onto the ground between him and the Paladin.

He must fairly be chasing the Crusader's goose, thought the flabbergasted Lord Cedric. The idiom that he used was in reference to an event that happened several centuries past when a group of drunken dwarf "crusaders" thought they would follow a sainted goose to an unending stream of golden mead. The quest only served to create a phrase to be used of people who had lost their wits.

"Have at you!" The dwarf hollered, urging his mount into a swift yet seemingly drunken canter. Sir Cedric cast up his eyes but nevertheless withdrew his couched lance. Urging his steed into a very slow canter, for he did not wish to injure the dwarf, especially if Thonnery was, as Sir Cedric was beginning to suspect, quite mad. As he came upon the dwarf, Sir Cedric very gently swung his lance level. The tip of the lance barely touched Thonnery, but even this small amount of force was enough to unhorse him. The dwarf struggled for a moment and then barrel rolled onto his stomach and clambered to his feet. No sooner was he up then he produced a small, rusted flanged mace, which he proceeded to swing, with great ineptitude at the still-mounted Lord Cedric. Cedric dismounted, and, still not wishing to harm the dwarf, endeavored to pin the short warrior's arms down so he would drop the mace.

While Lord Cedric was successful managing to force Don Jonnery Thonnery to drop the mace, the dwarf broke free of the knight's grasp and began jabbing at the Knight with his toes. Sir Cedric soon found out, much to his chagrin, that a dwarf's toes can be very sharp, especially when filed down to a fine point. But Don Jonnery's grooming habits was the last thing on Sir Cedric's mind. Thinking quickly, the Lord of Gelden Hill snatched away Jonnery's helmet and grabbed him by the beard, (one of the most dishonorable things possible for a dwarf) and hoisted him up to his eye level. "You are without a doubt," he began, face sweaty and breast heaving, "without a doubt the feistiest son of earth I have met in all my days. Listen here," he said, giving the beard a little shake, (and adding all the more to the dishonor; but Don Jonnery Thonnery was in such shock that he did not think of it.) I am the paladin knight Lord Cedric of Gelden Hill. I am not boasting, but if you know of me, you will know that I am one of the Nine Peers of the kingdom of Kyngesrelm. Thus I am able to accept oaths of fealty from vassals, and bestow smaller, subordinate knighthoods. Even though you be not of noble birth, and as I can best surmise, not of great property, I am willing to bestow knighthood upon you if you will simply do one thing. Lord Cedric's tone took on a mock-honeyed flavor. "Do you know what that is, puny little son of earth?"

The dwarf shook his head as best he could.

"Let…me…pass!" Don Jonnery Thonerry had succeeded in doing something few people in the kingdom could. He had vexed even the kind spirit of Lord Cedric. Dropping the dwarf unceremoniously to the ground, he barked a single word command through gritted teeth. "Kneel."

The dwarf knelt, his eyes beginning to mist with tears. The paladin drew his sword. "In the sight of Almighty God, and in sight of my stallion, for there is no one else to stand as witness, I, Sir Cedric, Paladin of the realm and Lord of Gelden Hill, do hereby dub thee Sir Jonnery Thonnery, Knight of the realm in service of Gelden Hill." Next the paladin went back to his saddle and removing his purse emptied the last of its contents into the dwarf's hands. "Now 'noble' Sir Knight, take this money with you to Dwarversdunn and purchase knightly weapons and armor for yourself. Tell them I sent you. And if you say that you have bested me in single combat, I pray you be accursed. Now, be off with you!"

The bewildered black dwarf stumbled to his feet, and letting out a long laugh shouted, "Amen! Thank ye kindly, Lord Cedric, and no mistake." But Lord Cedric did not hear the dwarf's thanks, for he had had already ridden off, his mind a simmering stew pot of anti-dwarven thoughts and slurs. But after he had ridden a short distance away from his makeshift tourney ground, the Paladin stopped, lifted his visor, and, casting his face to the heavens, laughed with reckless abandon. He was so filled with uncontrollable mirth that he forgot that it should concern him that he had given the dwarf the rest of his traveling money. And so, Lord Cedric continued on, in a manner of speaking now destitute, but lacking nothing in good cheer.

The Knight continued on until he came into the vicinity of Reftkirkshire, and the village of Reftkirk. It was said, at least in Castle Pallanon and the land surrounding that the elderly Bishop Niels of Reftkirk, was not only highly wealthy, but highly generous, even beyond the normal expected generosity of the pontiffs of the church. It was said that he kept a ledger of the crops of the surrounding farmers, not so that he could tax them an exorbitant tithe, but if one of the farmers happened to be having a particularly bad harvest or hungry winter, he would open up his personal stores of money, not just from the poor box, and give liberally to any who needed it. Some of the bishops and legates of the church said he was mad and foolish to do such things, but Cedric although he had never met the Bishop of Reftkirk knew him to be his class of man. That is not to say simply by wealthy status but the status of being a truly selfless giver, for generosity is one of the principal five virtues of knighthood.

Yet, as Sir Cedric continued on into Reftkirk village proper, he saw that many of the inhabitants were somehow no longer benefiting from the family generosity of their Bishop. Sir

Cedric wondered even, if the Bishop had been taken up in a fit of avarice, as was common to happen among wealthy, high-ranking churchmen.

Many people that he passed looked gaunt and in want of food. *Alas that I have spent all my money,* thought Sir Cedric, *for alas I cannot hand out alms to these poor souls.* Then, the Holy Spirit of God, placed a revolutionary thought in Sir Cedric's mind and it seemed as though the dawn was breaking through the storm clouds of his sad thoughts. Do you really need all your rich armor and equipment, or could you spare a little? Surely such expensive armaments could buy food for the entire population of this town for the whole winter. Cedric struggled for a long time for he knew that a knight needed his equipment and he could not come to the Gateway to Varluckhuld unarmed. Yet he could not rid himself feeling, that this was his God ordained purpose to do in the village of Reftkirk. So he began to doff his armor, first handing his close helm to an elderly woman who was passing by, saying, "Good mother, take my helmet. It is worth a hundred gold pieces. Take it to the next town, and there sell it to buy food for your family." Next the knight doffed his gauntlets, and gave those to a starving boy hunting in the snow for a store of frozen sweat meats left by a squirrel. Cedric gave the lad the same instructions. Next he took off his gorget and gave it to a young woman scouring for firewood. Then came one of the greatest tests of all. He doffed and gave away his entire gilt-worked hauberk to a family with ten scrawny children. All looked at him with grateful faces and words of blessing. They had never been shown such kindness before, not even by their Bishop.

He came at last to the cathedral. All the gold, silver and pewter had been cut away from the statues. Once beautiful windows no longer held the expensive stained-glass. The cathedral itself appeared ghostly and forlorn, like a relic of a bygone age yearning for a renaissance of prosperity. A gaunt old man with a whitening gray beard stood out in front of the doors to the cathedral. He was clad in the red robes of a bishop and smiled kindly at Lord Cedric motioning him to dismount and come inside.

"Oho! You must be the noble Knight of whom everybody in the village has been talking. Oho, oho! Ho! I am the Bishop Niels of Reftkirk. Thank you for your kind generosity. We would have surely starve before the spring without your generous gifts."

"I am glad to be of service will, your eminence. But I must ask: normally you see to the needs of poor, for your personal fortune is by no means small, if what I have heard is true. Why could you not keep the townsfolk from starving."

"It is a tragedy but my fortune has been spent, along with all the wealth inside the cathedral, to pay Vaering danegeld, or raid ransome." Danegeld was the large fee that certain towns paid to Vaering raiders to avoid being ransacked. Typically, the prices inflated exponentially, and the people of the town were left penniless.

"I am going to Baerynthine's Wall and when I arrive there I shall tell Marshall Roderick of your plight, and have him send soldiers to protect your town."

The Bishop closed his eyes and breathed a sigh of relief. "Ah, ho ho! Your generous gifts will feed us until then. Thank you, from the bottom of my heart. But you are a knight and going through dangerous country, and will need protection." He leaned in close and whispered, "I am about tell and show you a secret, that because the Vaering you must divulge to no one. Understood?"

Cedric nodded.

Leading the knight into the sanctuary, he showed him a trap door behind the altar. It led to a flight of stairs which they descended, the Bishop now holding a torch he had lighted. "No one knows this save I, but the spot where this cathedral was built was once the burial mound of a Vaering king. I was afraid to use the treasure to feed my congregation, for the Vaerings would no doubt gain wind of it, and descend on this place like blood-crazed wolves." He took some ancient Vaering ring mail off of a treasure pile and gave it to Sir Cedric. He also gave him an ancient Vaering face mask helmet and a steel Vaering buckler, for Sir Cedric had given away his shield. But throughout it all he had thought it wise to keep his sword, Westledon.

"Thank you for everything you have done for us, Sir Knight. May the spirit of God watch over you. And take this blessing: may the Lord bless thee and keep thee. May the Lord make his face shine upon thee, turn his countenance toward the, and give thee peace." Bishop Niels was so overcome with gratitude that he embraced Sir Cedric. "This armor bears enchantment and can withstand a dragon's breath. Surely it will protect you on your journey to the Wall. Go, my son, and may God send angels to watch over you."

Sir Cedric took his leave of the generous bishop, and, wearing the armor of a Vaering king, rode North from Reftkirk, and came in time to Baerynthine's Wall.

15.   The Annals of Kyngesrelms

Here follow tales from the history of the land of Pallanon that Master Scribe Geoffrey de Dunnmouth of Kyngesrelm graciously included as anecdotes to this narrative to provide the necessary understanding of much that passed before.

The Topaz Knight

There are many variants of this Child's Ballad sung throughout the kingdom of Kyngesrelm. The version recorded here is slightly different than the one often sung by Sir Hersker. "Skree" is a child's pronunciation of Skrael.

The jolly, joyful Topaz knight, he rode out one day

To reclaim his shining Topaz tower

Over the Hills and far away.

Over the Hills and far away

Hurdy-gurdy sweetly play.

A dinga-derry deely-o

A sweet kenning.

A-ding a-dong a-dillio,

Lamb stew brimming.

The Topaz night met a knight of fright

High upon the road,

His helmet crowned with blackened horns.

Upon his shield a toad.

His black mad Steed,

He had six legs.

And oh, six legs had he.

Like the All-Pere steed of Vaering men.

A servant of old Skree

"Whither go ye, jeweled man,

"Whither now?" quothe he.

I go to reclaim my Topaz tower

Long 'fore stolen from me."
"In what Name of power

Cometh you? Of avatar or me?"

"Out on ye!"
Cried the Topaz Knight.

You do not frighten me,

For you are neither Lord nor Knight

You are but old Skree.

'Twas you who stole my tower,

Long ago from me.

To my Topaz tower

I take from you the key.

In the name of avatar

The blessed name of Me.

I banish you to your barren tower

In reaches wintery."

So my child the avatar shall soon come he

And take back this world from the likes of Skree

For by his Name's great power

He's taken back his Topaz tower

Over the Hills and far away

Over the Hills and far away

hurdy-gurdy sweetly play

Oh over the Hills and far away

Over the Hills and far away

Over the Hills and far away

Hurdy-gurdy sweetly play.

Sir Peter von Wulfbain and the Troll

Once upon a time, about two score years before the Everfrost Quest, the Township of Veylandin in southeastern Pallanon had a young lord with long raven hair named Peter, Peter von Wulfbain to be exact. Before Peter's father, Galway, had died, he had spoken an oracle over his son. "Our ancestor, Ulfius, slew a great-wolf in the Everfrost War, but I foresee, my son, that you will have an even greater victory."

At the time of this story, Peter was about eighteen years of age. Ever since he was old enough to ride out, he loved the five virtues of chivalry: faithfulness, honesty, courtesy, generosity, and prowess. Though he was very practiced in the first four, he longed to prove his prowess on the battlefield, his courage and bravery for the Lord God.

One day, in Midsummer, when the evenings were especially hot, there came a great troll to the walls of Veylandin. He cried out in a loud voice. "I shall do, by meat and crue, what the great-wolf failed to do. By my mace, and my small brain, I shall slay puny Wulfbain."

This continued day and night, until Sir Peter was very bothered. Finally he went to the young dwarven smith Dunnir and said to the ebon-skinned dwarf, "I need you to make me a sword, with a very broad and sharp blade, so sharp that it can pierce this wicked brother to the heart." Dunnir invited his friend from Roldburg Castle, the wiry bald human alchemist Francois de Conlois, to come help with the philosophy of forging the blade. Surely his powders and tinctures could avail much.

The two men worked long and hard at the forge; Dunnir beating with his hammer, François coating it with powders and tinctures, the properties of which only an alchemist could understand. And all the while, the troll spewed forth his tirade. At last the blade was finished. To test it, young Peter went up to one of the anvils and struck it lightly. It was such a good blade, that it cleaved the entire anvil in two from top to bottom. Peter was pleased. He named the blade Ettin-Bane.

He made his peace with God and went out to do battle with the troll the next day. He was clad in a hauberk and red cape. The bearing upon the silver field of his shield was of a golden lion rampart with a black great-wolf under its back paw. He wore a sugarloaf style great helm, unique in that it had a visor upon his head. When he came to the place of battle, he cried out in a loud voice, "With the host of heaven as my witnesses, I shall send you to the fiery caves below."

The troll merely laughed at him and began to rain down blows with his mace. Even with his alchemically reinforced blade, Peter had trouble parrying the mad strokes, and he found that with the troll's great strength, he could not counterstrike. But then he remembered that in battle, a knight of God must invoke the holy power of God when fighting creatures of darkness. He began to declare in a clarion voice, "A Knight is a warrior of light and truth, the power of God is manifest in his heart, he speaks forth the truth of God's holy books. He is faithful to the cause to which God has called him. He is not overcome by evil but overcomes evil with the goodness of God. Lord, to you be the glory of the victory."

He cut the troll across the chest in a great sweeping blow, and the cut sparkled with holy light. Then the troll fell to the ground with a great crash. Peter had proved his prowess.

News of Sir Peter's victory spread. So great was his fame that King Jaerython came on a royal visit to Veylandin and awarded Sir Peter with a gold chain to wear around his neck and silver spurs to put on his feet. Sir Galway's prophecy came true. His son had had a greater victory than even his sainted ancestor.

One day, when he was an old man, the troll-slaying lord of Veylandin would fight the vile spawn once more alongside another knight who also wore a sugarloaf great helm. Though his years were spent physically, the Lord God would constantly renew the strength and battle fury of his sword arm.

And oh, Dunnir and François' skills came to be quite in demand. But little did they know that Peter's sword was not their masterpiece, not by a long stretch. They would one day forge a masterpiece that would be remembered through all the ages of Pallanon. But that is another story.

Song of Dunnir (the message he sent by carrier pigeon to his friend Francois the alchemist at Roldburg village requesting help in reforging the broken blade of Sir Waldon's broadsword)

Hi-ho! The alchemist Francois,

The Knight's broken his blade in twa!

So let's now put twixt our brains

So it reforged we can gain!

The Elfin Knight of Pallanon

In the olden days of Pallanon, during the reign of the Paladin King Baerynthine (or, as the elves of the Alf-anon Plains say, in days of Auld Lang Syne), there lived a beautiful elf girl named Shalaileigh. Her true name was something that even her father could not remember. You see, he fashioned the poles for the pikes and grips for the claymores for the war band of Lord Griogar McPharron, the only Alfanonian war chief wealthy enough to build a castle. Though it was not even of stone, but rather more of a low, wooden circle fort built upon a high stone. Whatever the case Shalaileigh's father, who raised her after her mother died in childbirth, gave his daughter that name, because one day when she was about five years of age, after trying to play at hurling with some of the boys of the clan and they taunted her, she took up a fairly well sized log, and the outcome was that the lads eventually ran from her, sporting knots on their pates the size of dragon eggs. "Your God-given name shall be Shalaileigh, for no one can wield a club like you."

Now every year, the traders came from the South to barter for swift Alfanonian stallions and mares. They brought with them minstrels who had sung in the courts of the bravest knights of the kingdom, some even for the court of King Baerynthine himself. They would sing songs of great deeds, of the slaying of dragons by brave and courageous knights and the rescuing of damsels. There always arose a fire within Shalaileigh, a desire to meet one of these selfless heroes and have adventures of her own. She never spoke of any of these desires to anyone, not even her father. But one night, everything changed.

She dreamed that her spirit was flying through Trillven Forest, far beyond the dominion of the troll spawn. She saw a dashing elf with shining golden locks and eyes as forest green as her own. He was blowing a horn of silver crystal and its note mesmerized her. It seemed to have beckoned her. She was consumed with the desire to stay with him for all her days.

The next day, she said to her father, "Papa Murdo, last night I dreamed of a beautiful Elfin Knight who blew his horn both loud and shrill. I am sure that my true love I surely have found. I must go to him, Papa."

"But my dear," said her father, "you have never been beyond the Plains. Trillven Forest is fairly burgeoning with evil, has been since the rebellion of the Enemy. As your father who reared you and taught you, I beg you not to go. You are twenty years of age now and, as your first score of years is now past, I cannot force you to stay. But I beg you, as you love me, stay and preserve your life."

"Oh, Papa," she said, hefting her club, "did God not give me this strong arm, and this shalaileigh, from which I derive my name, for just such a time as this?" Then her father nodded and said no more.

Before leaving, she took her club to the blacksmith and had him wrap three thick bands of steel around the head of the club. As she was testing its new weight, a wondrous thing happened. The light of the setting sun fell upon the bands and they became gold, as the seraph steel of heaven. The elf girl knew this to be a sign of God's favor upon her journey. And she was well pleased.

The next day, she put on riding boots and a long shirt and pantaloons of brown leather. Bidding her father farewell, she struck out South, riding at a quick pace. She fetched quite a noble figure with her midnight black hair flying in the wind and her emerald eyes looking ever on to the unknown end of her quest.

As night fell, she reached that obstacle which her father had dreaded most: Trillven Forest. Beyond the earliest memory of the oldest elves, it had stood, a bastion of evil, the seldom-penetrated home of the vile spawn given life and breath by the canting of the Dark One and his minions. There was a small voice inside Shalaileigh's mind that urged her to turn and flee in utter revulsion. But she looked to the holy seraph metal bracing her cudgel, steeled her heart, and pressed on into the arcane darkness.

It seemed as though demons of the air and other things of dark magic born of the Dark One's malice were lurking behind every gnarled tree and shadowed stone. This supernatural paranoia bore an omen of death into the elf girl's brain. Death. Death was coming. On fleet hoofs. The shadow of the Dark One would envelop her and her silence was more soul-chilling than the most agonizing scream.

Then, when at last she did hear something, she wrenched to a halt, almost tripping over her own boot. It was a conversation between several voices, in the slurred, goblinoid common tongue of the foul natives of Trillven. The speakers, judging by the many civilized common words they used, were obviously raiders, such as those that occasionally raided the elven township of Alfenton, just south of the Alf-anon Plains. There were just enough civilized common words for Shalaileigh to piece together the flow of their conversation.

"Erk..Nardaz... I am war leader of this forest...OOK! And I say we don't find free flesh to eat soon, I'll crack open yer skull and eat the brains out of it."

"Good meat comes to those that wait, Lord Uddrok."

"KRUKEN! Well, Lord Uddrok, we may just have to eat your great-wolf, Vorgoonath. EEKZ!"

The elf girl whirled and saw that the party, two half-trolls and a goblin squire, all armed to the teeth and riding on great wolves, had come into her clearing. One half-troll was noticeably larger than the other, and wore a necklace of great-wolf teeth.

The larger one drew his barbed sword and grunted, "Now we shall have some sport and some sweet meat. The pretty dinner is mine."

He spurred his great-wolf mount forward. Shalaileigh, thinking fast, sprinted forward to meet the charge, but at the last second, barrel rolled beneath the steed's tall legs, rolled up behind its hind legs, and with the swiftness that only the fair folk possess, the elf girl leaped up over Lord Uddrok onto the mount's back. For a split second, she sat in front of the half-troll war chief. Before he had a chance to lift his sword, Shalaileigh, with all the might in her corded Alfanonian limbs, smote Lord Uddrok a sound blow across the chest. The blessed angelic steel added even more force of the blow and sent the evil war chief flying halfway across the clearing. He lay on his back for a moment, stunned. This afforded the Elven girl the opportunity she needed. She leapt off the great-wolf's back and he used her momentum to launch into a forward roll that carried her to the stunned war chief. Before he had a chance to lift his head, she rained down an iron-heavy blow upon his skull.

Had her weapon been an ordinary steel-braced cudgel, it would have been lucky to even bruise the skin of a Trillven war leader. But this was no ordinary steel. This was golden steel of seraph make, wrought in the halls of heaven itself. Therefore, the head of Lord Uddrok exploded. She could have easily dispatched the other half-troll and the goblin squire, but for the vile cunning of the now riderless great-wolf. It sprang forward with a low snarl. Before she could even turn, the venomous fangs of the great-wolf sank into her back. The effect of such a poison is instant.

A strange thing happened then. She saw her body with the eyes of her spirit, for it had departed. Just as she saw the two other members of the vile hunting party started toward it, a light flashed over her body, and it disappeared. It was safe from harm.

Then she found herself standing before the Elfin Knight from her dream. He smiled and spoke softly to her. "It was not chance that God sent me to you in your dreams. I have always been with you, though you have known it not. It was the will of the Lord Most High that you should go on a journey in search of me and pass through Trillven Forest. It was not chance that brought Lord Uddrok and his hunting band across your path. Yes. You see, that half-troll commander whom you slew tonight was none other than Lord Uddrok, leader of all the vile forces of Trillven Forest. He was planning a terrible raid on the town of Alfenton. He meant to raze it to the ground, and slaughter all the inhabitants, down to the last child. The feat that you accomplished tonight has saved hundreds of innocent lives. You sought after me to marry me, but this we cannot do. For I am a seraph of heaven. But come with me now. I will take you to your reward, and you shall dwell forever more with the Lord where there is no sorrow or pain. The very Angels shall spread word of this feat to the four corners of the kingdom. Come with me now to paradise."

He took her to heaven and made her a gown with seams of fine thread and gave her a garland of heavenly flowers to wear on her head. And God himself took Shalaileigh's war club and placed it in the heavens as a flying star. And even to this day, when they see the flying star sail through the night sky, the Elven riders of the Alf-anon Plains will point to it and tell their sons and daughters of one of their greatest heroes and of how Alfenton was saved by Shalaileigh's shalaileigh.

Two in the Tower

Night had fallen upon Delven Fen. Here, only about a league from the happy village of Darkimot, the full moon shone down, casting her adamantine light upon what appeared from a great distance to be a simple tor upon a muddy hill. Upon closer observation, however, one would see that it was not simply a standing stone but a tower, with a slight rudimentary turret "gracing" its summit. It was toward the small edifice that a tall figure moved deftly across the mist-enshrouded fen. The figure was clad in the leather jerkin and pantaloons common among the Alfanonian Rangers. There were two long-knife scabbards hanging from the Ranger's belt, one on each hip, that bounced rhythmically as the leather bound Ranger ran. Boots, also of leather, but fur-lined to protect the feet from swamp bilge, ran up past the shins. A boiled leather jerkin protected the figure's muscular but flexible torso. Long, blood crimson leather gauntlets protected middling-sized hands that were now clenched in fists for the sake of speed. A highland longbow hung in a baldric on the figure's back. About five hundred yards away from the small citadel, the figure paused and drew back the hood it was wearing. Long, silky turquoise hair cascaded down the leather bound shoulders. She was Vannalina Strongbow, on a desperate mission to filch the treasure of the now long-dead sorcerer Ralitrael, who was once a disciple of the Great Enemy, the shadow-raiser Skrael. However, she did not think of herself as a mere bandit or rogue, for she knew the dire circumstances that drove her to this end. For who was a ranger who did not guide those travelers who had lost their way? But, musing over the moonlit citadel, the elf Ranger wondered if she had lost hers, stealing from the long dead.

Her introspections were cut short however as a cry of "Hjol helki!" rent through the night. A huge metallic form rammed into her from the left. She fell onto her back and for a split second the wind was knocked from her lungs. She recovered almost instantly, rolled through the sludge, regained her feet, and to the naked eye, her long-knives simply appeared in her hands. She saw that her attacker was not a troll, but rather a man. He was clad in full mail but wore no helm. His eyes were as blue as the sky on a clear summer's day, and his locks were long and tawny, braided in many places with bits of mail. He held a huge battle hammer in front of him, his bulging arms poised to swing. A Vaering barbarian, no doubt. Most of them were pagan, worshiping bloody gods of thunder and war. Vannalinna had half a mind to split his gut without a word, but she doubted that she could slash through his fine Nordic mail. Though she could most likely pierce it with a shaft but did not have time to nock an arrow before he caved in her skull with his maul. Therefore, she decided to use the last result a man of his race would choose: diplomacy.

"Who are you, Vaering? What are you doing here?" "I could ask you the same thing, elf. I will not give you my name, for I don't owe my name to such a race as yours, that judges my kind prematurely. As to my business, I am bound for yon tower."

"To raid it, no doubt. I might have known. I too desire the treasures within, but not from my own glory or the drink it would buy. *My* intentions, unlike *yours*, happened to be honorable, *pagan*."

"Why, you…!"

Hammer clashed against knife and the ethereal silence was shattered by the ring of steel on steel. Swifter and swifter they clashed, neither gaining the upper hand. As the fight continued, sweat began to bead on the foreheads of the combatants. They began to wheeze and gasp as they swung their weapons. Finally, both tumbled down in the slosh, breasts heaving.

"How about this…, blue-hair?" the Vaering panted. "We scale the tower together… Take equal share of the loot. It's not to my liking, but it's better than wasting time like this, for we might as well face it, we are too evenly matched."

"Agreed, Vaering."

"My name is Kollskegg, ranger."

"I am Vannalina Strongbow."

The Vaering nodded curtly and produced two large iron spikes. "The door will most likely be locked from inside. Not only that, but the hinges are rusty. Climbing is the only and I have no rope. I don't see one with you. I will use my spikes. You have your own?"

Vanna nodded and produced two spikes no larger than knitting needles. Kollskegg inspected them and shook his head. "Those aren't strong enough."

Then Vanna blushed inadvertently as she felt his eyes surveying her. "You seem to be light enough. You won't like this. But all have to carry you up."

"Why, of all the…!"

"Take my offer or leave it."

Flushing red, she stalked through the muck toward the tower. When they had reached the base, Kollskegg placed his hammer in the baldric on his back and bade the elf hold onto his shoulders. Proceeding slowly so the hammer would not strike his passenger, the barbarian began climbing by shoving one spike after the other, higher and higher up the wall of the citadel.

Strangely, Vanna felt safe and warm next to the barbarian, a feeling akin to excitement welling up inside her as she felt his strong, corded muscles working in unison to climb the tower. She almost felt disappointed when they reached the battlement.

Kollskegg looked around awkwardly and fiddled with the scruff of his mail as the Ranger slipped off his back. Vanna at first wondered at this, but let it pass. Finding a stairway leading down from the turret, the two thieves made their way down into the interior of the tower.

Upon descending the stairs into the main chamber of the tower, the two were arrested by a vision of brazen light. Mountains and mountains of treasure filled the room almost to the ceiling. Gold pieces of an unknown minting, brooches, rubies, sapphires, opals even turquoise as blue as the Elven maid's hair. Every type of treasure ever wrought was there before their very eyes.

Yet it seemed to bother the barbarian. He back to the hallowed childhood tales of his people. He knew the tales of the sorcerer as well as any man of the region. And in the tales of his homeland, the monomythic trait of all the stories was that the treasure was... Cursed.

Vannalina reached down to grab a gigantic sapphire. "No, Elf!" The room shook. There was a deafening roar. And then Koll remembered the other monomythic trait in the tales of his people. Treasure hoards guarded by dragons.

A massive reptilian head rose up out of the hoard. It opened its maw. "Elf! Get down!" He leaped on top of his companion just as a crimson jet of flame shot out above them. The barbarian could feel the heat nearly searing his flesh.

Thinking quickly, the Elven Ranger dashed out just as the jet of flame stopped. Quickly nocking an arrow, she lap fly towards the dragon's yellow eye, but the Dragon unleashed another jet of flame, which reduced the shaft to a pile of ash.

Next, Vannalina rushed in with her long-knives and began slashing at the dragon's yellow underbelly, deftly jumping from side to side, to avoid the wyrm's massive, snapping jaws. But her blades did nothing to penetrate the red dragon's stone-hard hide. Suddenly, the barbarian's mind hit upon a daring stratagem. Running at his highest possible speed, he leaped over his companion and brought his great hammer down upon the Dragon's red head. It did not brain the creature as he had intended, but it forced the head down with such speed that as it came down upon one of the elven ranger's long-knives, it impaled itself upon the blade. The fire of life left the Dragon's eyes.

For a moment, neither fighter could speak. Then both launched into hysterical fits of laughter. "We did it, Friend Vanna! We did it!" Only then once they had both calmed themselves do they noticed that a large portion of the carcass was blocking the stairs. They could not go back the way they came. For hours, the Vaering tried to use his massive muscles to move it but to no avail. He banged upon the door with his hammer. But found it to be bound with spells. "Lord God in heaven, hear my prayer, save us by the power of the avatar!" he prayed at last.

Vannalina looked at him curiously. "You follow the true faith? I thought you were a pagan."

"I was until I heard the God inspired preaching of the Bishop of Reftkirk." I came here for some cursed treasure to prove my worth to Abbot Bardicus of Veylandin. He would exorcise the evil from the treasure and I would be accepted into the church of the avatar. But now I guess that won't happen."

"I came here for some treasure to pay a greedy alchemist for potions to save the life of my mother. She is a southern elf, one of the gem-locks, hence my hair. Without the treasure, she will be lost."

"Well, I don't know if we'll survive, but I do know, that I will die in the company of a friend and comrade in arms. She smiled.

"Aagh! I shall give it one last try. God on high... Save us!"
So saying he swung his hammer at the door, and as he did so, it flashed goldenly. With the blessing of God, the hammer broke through the entrenchments binding the door.

Kollskegg lifted his arms in praise and laughed aloud. "Grab all the treasure you can carry. What matters is that your mother is safe. Let moth and rust take the rest. Surely, if one of the fair folk vouches for me, the Abbot will not object to my joining the church. He will believe you if you recount the tale. I will meet you there after your mother recovers."

That day as the sun rose upon the fen, two adventurers who had come to the tower as enemies departed as friends.

A Psalm of the First Spring of Pallanon

A psalm, or in the High Elven tongue, a *shael'ando*. Origin unknown, but it appears in the oldest church canticle books

Sing to the Lord, oh my soul. Brandish your blades, you knights of God.

Praise him whether you be fair folk or hill folk, half-blood or wudawasa, daughters of the stars

Or sons of earth.

Echo praise in dwarven hall and elvendom. Knight, Thrall, Cleric, paladin-king all, praise Him.

Again I say, praise Him!

The Demon Axe

The bearded hunter with a practiced swiftness slipped his hand into the confines of his traveling cloak. Drawing out one of his seven, Elven made knives, he wrapped his fingers (which were encased in the segmented steel backing of the letter gauntlets that he wore) around the short blade. He could fee its diamond-hard edge with his stubby thumb despite the strength of the cowhide. The hunter lay concealed on a ledge above an outlying half-troll settlement not far from Trillven Forest. The camp was alive with activity, though the clumsy foul folk moved sluggishly. The hunter saw a shadow raiser warlock, bearing the war axe which he had lost when knocked out cold by a large falling branch South of the forest of Trillven. He had quickly surmised from the footprints that the axe had been filched by half trolls and had spent the better part of three days tracing the tracks back to this settlement and laying out his plan of action. This was of course done after he had returned to the dwarf and village and received sanction for the quest to retrieve it. He, Bannon Tohar, an outcast one of the Dragonslayer dwarvish clans, knew for what purpose he had come to the hills to the west of Alfenton. The half troll bandits had stolen his father's Starsteel axe after all and it was only with this token of dwarven craftsmanship that he could buy back his tainted honor in the eyes of Volunstad, Jarl of the Thunderhammer clan. He knew that several warlocks of the half trolls used dark magics, and had he not stormed off so quickly he would have thought to go to an Elven settlement to seek the help of an Elven battle priest, for the fair folk were more generally excepting of half breeds, then were the pure-blooded dwarves with which he lived. However, the woodwose blood of his cleric mother, although it made him stoop somewhat, did make him much taller than the average dwarf. After his father had died, he had left the woods around avail around Veylandin and the protection of his wosen kin to try to live in peace with his father's old clan. The Dragon slayers had not taking kindly to him on account of his wood wose blood and what they deemed to be "questionable speech" of the church of the wild folk that lived in the woods near the town of Veylandin, so when his axe, for which Volunstad had always had a covetous eye, was stolen, the paunchy old dwarf had offered him the chance to gain equal rights among the clan, even though he was a hated half-breed. Though his father's acts was dear to him the only heirloom he had of his father, young Bannon was willing to give it up if it would earn him the one thing he had lacked after leaving his kin, the sons of the forest: acceptance, a place to call his home.

Bannon the hunter's father, Keldring, had been a traveling minstrel, who had one day gotten lost in a small forest near the village of Veylandin. Keldring had often heard tales, of the Woses and their somewhat unorthodox method of resurrecting the old tradition of speaking in languages of magic and universal song, but he decided to strike into the wood anyway. The woses who lived in these words spoke the unteachable language of the Spirit of God, supposedly taught to them by the elves before many of them replaced the Singing of Creation with an abstract philosophy. Many orthodox clerics were, as most still are, skeptical of this magic tongue, saying that this magic language comes from wraiths and other such dark spirits.

(Centuries later, it was said that the von Wulfbains had wosen blood in them, this would explain their hairy hands, and it was reported by a servant in the house of young Lord Peter of Veylandin that in his darkest hour when his beloved Katya died, the Lord of Veylandin was crying out to God in the strange yet beautiful and flowing language of his supposed ancestors).

There was a wild yet beautiful she-wose whom Keldring happened upon in the words. She was singing with words that could not be learned, yet were only given utterance through the unction of the Spirit of God. At first, Keldring's heart lurched within him and he was very afraid. But then the power of the unction fell upon him and he sang and danced with her. Their marriage was sealed in covenant by the Bard-priest of the Wosen Church, and act unthinkable to the Council of Bishops. (Though many years later many of the pontiffs began to look favorably upon both the sacred language and Church of the Woses. It was said and later verified as truth that the Elven Archbishop Thilvarnus, the tutor of St. Niels, the wealthy Bishop of Reftkirk, prayed to the Lord in the spiritual song of the Sons of the Forest up to eight hours a day. He would run up and down in front of the altar shouting forth phrases in unknown tongues at the top of his voice. Some said he was mad but others saw the true power residing in him.)

Bannon the hunter watched intently as a half-troll Shaman whispered fell words over his father's axe. Bannon's father had prayed with him to receive the unction of the Spirit of God when Bannon was very young, so it pained the half-wose to hear words blessed by the Enemy. The asked began to glow with a blackish purple fire. This gave the blade an acrid odor, and a demonic spume seemed to ooze from the blade, dripping off to burn the surrounding vegetation. Now Bannon realized how half trolls and those of like ilk were able to venture from the forest of Trillven with such power. They relied on demonic aid.

On the soft summer breeze, a sound came to the hunter's ear. It sounded somewhat like the cooing of a tree dove. In the blink of an eye, a slender hand shot over his mouth and pulled him back on his back. "Are you an Alfenton bounty hunter?" An eloquent female voice hissed.

An angular Elven face, discernibly female, though the forest green cowl hid most of the curly golden hair, shot down into his. "Ein ot effel un og ere olk, iye udd I beg a ownty unta?" Bannon muffled. (which is just clamped mouth gibberish for the sentence "I'm not even one of the fair folk, why would I be a bounty hunter?") The Elven maid did not understand this, so poor Bannon had to repeat his statement another time once the elf maid had released her hand from his mouth. The elven maid drew back her hood. She was exceptionally tall, even for an elf of Pallanon, standing several inches above seven feet in height. She was clad in the green cloak of an elven forest ranger and wore calf-length boots and breeches, both made of brown leather. Over the cloak she wore a segment breastplate of black leather. Her one weapon was a needle-thin, single-handed sword. Her eyes were aquamarine and held no pupils, a rare, prized mark among the fair folk. "Oh, terribly sorry old chap," the she-elf said. "I thought you would be one of the competition. The town council of Alfenton is paying up to three gold pieces for every pair of half troll ears any adventurer brings to the sergeant of arms. Oh how rude of me, my humble name is Lorenda Swiftrunner, Elven Ranger extraordinaire, what is yours, son of earth?"

In more words than a few, the dwarf Hunter explained to his new acquaintance his reason for coming to that place. Though for some reason, he neglected to mention, that the evil half troll magic user was now ensorcelling his lost weapon.

"All righty, friend B," Lorenda the Ranger said, coming up with a spry bounce, "I see how we can help one another. You use your inherent son of Earth fighting skills, to help me kill as many of those bugger boos as you possibly can, and I shall make sure your father's axe returns with you. Agreed?"

"Yes, but I…" he had remembered the enchanting of his father's axe.

Without letting the dwarf finish and uttering a southern Elvish battle cry of "Silva, silva, silva," invoking the Elven word for the forest home where the fair folk first awoke, Lorenda Swiftrunner leapt off the ledge, gracefully somersaulted in the air and landed with perfect poise in the middle of the half-troll settlement.

"*Urug Ghurluz! Therug Ghurluz zaf!*" cried one of the sentries in him surprise and endeavored to lift his crude iron war club. But before he had the chance, Lorenda's slender blade flickered in and out opening a black, blood-spewing gap in the sentry's throat.

Casting up his eyes at the Elven ranger's impetuous actions, and hoping none of the sentries or shamans would think to wield the ensorcelled axe, Bannon doe into the fray, clumsily somersaulting onto the ground, for the sons of earth are not as agile as the fair folk will. However he quickly recovered and was soon sending his daggers whistling through the air into the throats of hearts of the half trolls before they had proper time to react. When all of those were spent, the dwarf turned his metal-back fists upon the foul folk using a method frowned upon in free folk boxing circles of running around landing a javelin the back of the knee and then uppercut the back of the head as the adversary crippled. He began to feel the warrior spirit of his people bubbling up inside him like molten ore in the forge fire, he was doing what a son of earth was intended to do when God first fashioned their first ancestors out of the living stone: to fight. Fight hard. Fight foul folk. Until death.

Slowly the bloody haze, cleared from his eyes and he saw that he had crushed the skull of his final adversary.

We've done it, son of earth, we've done it." cried Lorenda the elf running up to the dwarf and impulsively bending down and planting a sloppy kiss on his forehead.

Let me retrieve back your acts, good ol' friend B."

"No, Lorenda. Do not touch it. It's ensor…"

But it was too late. She had already taken up the cursed axe. Her eyes flared green with evil demonic fire, and she gave voice to an ululation so terrible it must have come from the fiery pits beyond, for no one of a righteous soul could voice to cry like that. Suddenly a holy urge came upon Bannon the dwarf. He stretched out his hand toward Lorenda and he yielded his mind and tongue to the Holy Spirit of God fiery words of sanctified magic spring forth from his mouth and thundered like a stampede of Alfanonian cattle. He could feel a resistance building up the magic his God was wielding through him. And so he searched more deeply within the Spirit, yielding more of his mind and heart to the Holy Spirit of God. Slowly and dimly a white light began to shine forth from his outstretched palm and slowly it beat away the darkness and fell fire in his new friend's eyes. Suddenly she fell to the ground with a great tremor and the fire left her eyes and faded away from the axe, which she had dropped. He ran to her and held her face in his rough yet gentle hands. Slowly she stirred and her eyes fluttered open. "What?" She asked. "Friend Bannon, you saved me from the power of that awful magic, of that demon axe. You were singing magic, holy magic. What sort of magic is this that can drive demons back to the realm eternal fire?"

"Come," he said, lifting her to her feet and steadying her step, "and I shall tell you more about it. We may hang this quest of mine, for I know now that the Lord has called me to spread and preach the Message of this Magic, for that Quest gives honor that no other quest can match."

Tomnas Goldwhite, Highwayman

In the days when Sir Hersker the joyous was but a babe, there lived a very rich merchant who had a son with long chestnut hair. The boy most often wore his mane in a braid in the style of the Vaerings, but he did this purely for a fashion statement rather than to be posh toward his father. His father called him little Rick, no his name was not Richard. Rick always had the best of everything, and was never wanting for anything. And yet there seemed to be a huge gaping void in his soul. One night when he was about sixteen years of age, he lay in his featherbed and had a dream in which he was riding his favorite horse through the streets of a town that was very poor. His saddlebag had been split down the middle. And from it poured forth many gold coins. The people feebly took them up and whispered prayers for his blessing as he rode past.

The next morning at breakfast, Rick told his father of his dream. The man smiled and said, "Our great possessions do not exist for us my son. They exist so that we can be a conduit, a vessel as an alchemist's vile through which God pours His blessings out to others." A great joy rose up inside the boy and he said, "you have inspired me, father. And now I go out into the world not to make but to give away my fortune. Let it be to me as God desires."

He went into the small armory of the house and put on a jerkin and pantaloons of leather. Then we put on a black silk mask that covered his eyes but not his mouth then he put on a merchant stocking cap and took a broadsword and simple unadorned buckler and placed them in a baldric on his back. Then he saddled his trusty brown mare and rode out from his father's mansion. Leaving the name of Rick behind, he took for the time a highwayman's name: Tomnas Goldwhite, the hunter.

After going a little ways on, he came to a bridge upon which a coach was stopped, four gigantic men with bulging eyes appeared about to come to blows with the armed driver. "Goolz! You must pay the toll."

"I was just on this bridge last week and there was no toll. I think you are bluffing me, sir."

As he rode up, Highwayman Goldwhite sensed something about the gruff looking men that did not sit well with him. The passenger inside the coach stuck her head out letting her blonde curls dance in the wind. She wore a great Emerald Green traveling dress and her eyes were as blue as sapphires. Her somewhat angular face bespoke an Elven heritage and when she spoke, her northern indicated that heritage to brogue to be Alfanonian. She stretched out her hand toward the gruff man and was bird words of magic. Her hand shone with a holy light and by that light the gruff man's face transmogrified and became porcine and greenish blue. She was obviously a cleric. And he was obviously a disguised half troll.

Swooshunk! Tomnas' broadsword flashed forth from the scabbard and sent the half troll's head flying. The coachman was not at all slow to react and quickly employed his pikel axe to split the face of the other half troll standing hard by. Taking advantage of the confusion, Tomnas slashed across the third one's underbelly, spilling bluish black guts and intestines. The final half troll began to run away but the coachman threw his hand axe after the retreating monster and, after revolving to her three times in the air, the axe split open the back of the monster's skull. After he had recovered the coachman turned back to the young lady and said, "pardon me while I retrieve my weapon, marm."

While he was away the beautiful young lady stretched out her hand to Tomnas to be kissed. "Me thanks to ye, me fine gentleman, I am the Lady Eliana Devra Conchobar. I am on my way to my uncle's house. If you would accompany me and my escort, Sargeant Vilhelm Goetz, to see that we arrive safely, I will see to it that you are richly rewarded."

In accordance with his dream, young Tomnas had brought bags of gold with him. He gave her one of the bulging purses and said, "I do not desire a reward, for looking upon your face, and protecting your honor, is reward enough for me. But I will go with you to your uncle's house."

The further they progressed upon their journey the more familiar, as something from a history book, the terrain became. The Highwayman gaped in awe as he saw that her uncle's house was a castle, and not just a castle but Castle Pallanon itself. Eliana's uncle was none other than King Jaerython. They brought Tomnas the Highwayman who was by this time in a daze, before the King and he bade him take off his mask.

"What is your name, young sir?" The graying king asked.

"I was meaning not tell you but since you are the King I must tell the truth. I have adopted the man Tomnas Goldwhite the hunter, but my father is in truth one of the wealthiest men in the kingdom. He calls me Rick, but my name, in truth, is Cedric, son of the Lord of Gelden Hill Manor."

"I will run out of ink and parchment to complete the tales of the Paladins Nine at this time, therefore I will have to cut Geoffrey's tale short and begin the tale of Cadercyffel, Math Goth of Ar Memnu.,"

16.   Knights of Ar Nemnu

My name it is Cadercyffel

Call me Cadon, hear my tale

I am guardian of the star well

I am a Paladin of Ar Nemnu

Where before we came on the star-road

First there were the great Keimbold

Whose blood ran blue and cold

This was the will of Cael-Illu,

That we should come be here too

In this land of marble shales

From the land that once you named Cymru: Wales

I, the son of Goth-Curdion,

Do ever my armor don

With my adamantine bold,

This is the only metal we know

We make from it swords and spears to throw

And axes brave and bold

And we make much finer mail

Than what our fathers used in Wales

I have a story to tell in store

Of valiant deeds and times of war.

17.   Cadon's Command

The adamantine horn blared across the crystal-strewn marble landscape. Cadon Math-Goth swallowed hard. This would be his first battle in command of his own phalanx. He looked at his reflection in the adamant blade he held.

His long yellow hair was mostly obscured from view by the pikel-topped sallet he wore. The pikel had a long tassel of black hair taken from the tail of his Bulldron cavalry mount. The Bulldron were giant four-legged creatures the Arnemnuins had domesticated. His ancestors of a hundred thousand centuries past might have mistaken them for gargantuan bulls. Unlike many of his men, Cadon's steed, Pwyll by name, had elegant riding armor.

General Erethune, who had succeeded his father as high general of the Knights of Ar-Nemnu, rode back to the front line from the middle of the valley. He acknowledged Cadon with a brief nod and shouted loud enough for all the men of the 12th Battalion to hear. "I sent Rodrig to parlay with those overgrown horn-heads and this is all that came back of him." He brandished a red blood-soaked helm often worn by Rodrig. It was a strange thing that the blood of the Knights ran red when all other creatures on Ar Nemnu bled blue blood. "You know what they are after, though the reason why they seek it is perhaps the reason for their aggression against us. They want the Holy Book of Illu. Always they have thought of obtaining. But they must not take it from us, for it contains the sacred writings of Cael-Illu. And that is what gives the Knights of Ar Nemnu, nay, all men, women and children of Ar Nemnu the holy light. It is the soul of the people. It is the reason we survived when our ancestors followed the star-road from the mysterious land called Cymru. Though this war has lasted a thousand years, our enemies will not have victory. We, the chosen people of our God, shall reign victorious. Let us say the prayer of the offspring of Cael-Illu."

There was a deafening ring as each knight in the cavalry and infantry drew his sword and canted in one voice, both triumphant and beautiful.

"Our Father above the heavens, your name is sacred. We pray that you build your your kingdom in our hearts as you have built your kingdom above the stars. Sustain us for the fight and forgive us our many sins and help us to forgive. Keep us on the path of light and deliver us from the hand of evil. Your kingdom shall reign forever in our hearts, until it comes to this land. Amen."

Aelwyn, Cadon's best friend since training at the Monastery of the Light, leaned over and whispered in his ear, "Methinks I felt the ground rumble."

"Just wait for..."

THOOM THOOM! HOOM DOOM. DOOM-DO-DOOM DOOM DO-DOOM!

Both Cadon and Aelwyn knew well that sound. Keimbolden war drums. Aelwyn doffed his spangenhelm and wiped his hands through his sweat-drenched black hair. "You'll watch my back in battle, brother?" "As always, brother. Yours in life as well as in death". They struck hands. Though they had fought many battles together, the fire of their camaraderie had never ceased blazing.

DOOM DOOM! THOOM! DOOM DO-DOOM THOOM! The drums were nearing. The first standard bearers of the Keimbolden appeared over the horizon, marching into the valley below. They were as red as human blood, though theirs ran blue when spilled. They were twice the height of a human warrior. Three gigantic horns as black as a starless sky crowned each brow. They wore no armor, for their hides were oxen thick.

They wore only small kilts made of dirt and the purple fungi that spread over their homeland to the north. No one knew, not even the most experienced Lore Masters, why the Keimbolds bore the human inhabitants such enmity. Their hatred had something to do with the holy book of Illu. But the war has lasted so long that even the Bishop of Palantine, the capital city of the humans, did not know the reason. They hated humans and they hated the light. That was all the explanation the Knights of Ar Nemnu needed. For they were as devoted to their God, as their demonoid enemies were the hatred and chaos. Some say they follow a god, a princeling who was the originator of hate throughout the universe. And so with their maces and their axes and dark magics they destroyed everything in their path. The Knights had come to represent the saviors of the diminutive Nomegons, the winged Areoths, and the many other benevolent semi-humanoid inhabitants of Ar Nemnu. Often times they banded together in a multi-racial alliance, and partly because of this, the humans had won many of the noble creatures to the faith of their God. Once again the Keimbold marched toward Palantine City, the creatures ever intent on thieving the Book of Illu.

If the humans could hold them, an Areothan army, under the leadership of their warrior king Cole-Unden, would come to help secure the humans' victory. They alone, of all the other races, kept the secret of lightning fletching, able to loose bolts of blue energy from adamantine longbows. Though the entire army assembled numbered well over twenty thousand men, Cadon doubted they would live to see another day.

Sweat pouring down his brow, General Erethune drew his sword, and swung it level, giving the order to charge. With a universal cry of "For Cael-Illu!" the cavalry charged, followed by the infantry. Massive Bulldron hooves pawed the ground like thunder. All was silent in Cadon's mind. His adrenaline spiked and forced his heart into his throat. Then the force clashed in an explosion adamantine and demonoid fell-iron.

Cadon's blade flashed in the sunlight as he traded blows with a Keimbold armed with a large double-bladed axe. Black and silver sparks flew as both of the weapons clashed. Finding an opening, Cadon clove the Keimbold's arm off at the elbow. As thick, bright blue blood gushed forth from the wound, the creature's incapacitation afforded Cadon the chance he needed. Gripping the hand-and-a-half sword in both gauntleted hands, the Paladin sent the demon's head toppling from his shoulders.

Beside him, Aelwyn's Bulldron steed pummeled into a huge Keimbold The demon endeavored to skewer the dark-haired young man with the back pike of his massive war hammer. But the finely forged adamantine mail held true. Immediately countering with a blow from his single-edged war axe, Aelwyn brought the blade up backwards into the demon's forked chin. The demon gave a gurgled roar and began to fall backwards, the axe head still planted in his chin. Not wanting to lose his weapon in the midst of the fray, Aelwyn jerked the blade free, taking a good portion of blood-soaked demon flesh and bone with it.

The Knights of Ar Nemnu fought with vigor and passion, throwing all their might into butchering the enemy. But alas, the demonoids began to drive them back and back towards the hill from which they had charged. One of the Gladiator Elite, the exceptionally large elite soldiers of the demonoid legion, rammed his side into Cadon's Bulldron, knocking the warrior from the saddle. Planting a cloven hoof on Cadon's mail-clad chest, the doom lifted his barbed spear to plunge it into Cadon's neck....

BRAY-BRAY-BRAYOO! A familiar battle horn blared and the next second, the Keimbold's body burst into sizzling blue flame.

Golden-winged creatures with marble white skin and gem-colored eyes, their ears slanted back, flew over the battlefield, loosing lightning shafts from adamantine longbows. The Areothans had come, and in less than two minutes turned the battlefield into a raging blue inferno. The survivors brandish their weapons and shouted "Fwan-pwyll! Fwan-pwyll!" the victory cry of their ancestors.

Cole-Unden, a tall Areothan clad in a ruby-studded muscled cuirass, alighted on the ground in front of a sweat-drenched, bloody Erethune. The human general forced a weak smile. "Impeccable timing as always, Cole."

The Areothan removed his gold-crested helmet and nodded, his long amber hair flying in the wind, his sapphire eyes steady. "For our love of the Light of Cael-Illu, we will always fight beside you. Let us go back to Palantine so your men may dress their wounds and we may lay battle plans."

18. Cadon's Heart

The army leeches came, prepared the slain for burial, and gathered up the wounded onto stretchers. Cadon had known many of the dead, though fortunately, no one in his phalanx had died. The Army clerics led the soldiers in the saying of the benediction. Every man, woman and child in Palantine City, nurtured on the precepts of the book of Illu since birth, could recite it by heart. "Bwan fahn Yesule Brenithinen Ag Fanwyr Math." Which in the pidgin tongue of the Homeland was translated as "Now to you, Son of Illu, they come, a new Father for these Sons."

Cole-Unden himself added a token of goodwill and blew a long ululating blast on an adamantine carnyx, the mysteriously forward and backward curving battle horn of the Areoth. It was made by forging adamantine bands onto a Bulldron's horn. Cadon and Aelwyn had often remarked to each other that the sound the horn produced resembled the mooing of the Bulldron itself. But whatever their thoughts were on the subject, they were thankful but their brother in the Son of Cael-Illu honored their departed friends so.

The Areothans further assisted by flying the most grievously wounded warriors, Areothans, though lithe and thin, possess superhuman strength, so that the strongest among are able to lift a Bulldron without the slightest irritation.) So the two brothers in arms mounted their steeds and trudged back to the capital city sore and weary, but full of good cheer.

The city of Palantine was built into the side of and throughout, a massive mesa of marble shale. The tower where the Bishop of Palantine, Cadwyr, and King Rowend Starhammer had their residences, was built on top of the mesa. Streets and avenues wound circularly around and throughout the mesa, one side coming up to, and one side coming down from the tower keep. Being just a phalanx commander, Cadon did not have to go to the war rooms. So when they arrived at the city, Cadon said to Aelwyn. "Let's go and have a drink at the Well Wand shall we? I'm thirsty and some star well water would do my parched throat good, especially after all my exertions."

"Very well," smiled Aelwyn, already guessing the ulterior motive.

As Palantine was the capital of the Alliance-impetus humans, many dignitaries and travelers from other nations constantly came and went. Some even settled down to build a new life for themselves among the humans.

The Well Wand was a small yet respectable establishment where hardly any brawls ever took place. It was kept by a jovial old man by the name of Cadagon Cuthbert. He had a whitening red beard and small sapphire monocle through which he inspected his ledger. However, the aging man preferred to spend time with his grandchildren. So he left the running of the establishment to the chief barmaid Ara'Letza, who everyone called "Arletta".

She was one of the Areoth and was the chief reason why Cadon frequented the pub. Her hair was long and midnight black, her golden wings laced with sapphires and emeralds. Her eyes as her skin were as white as pearls. She wore long sapphire earrings at the base of her pointed ears. Though she had lived in Palantine for several years, she had never lost her rural Areothan accent.

"'Ello, jolly old chums! What'll ya 'ave today?"

A little kiss. This is what Cadon thought but with his mouth he said, "Star well grog, please, Arletta."

"Same for me," added Aelwyn.

They sat down at the aquamarine counter and waited as Arletta poured them their drinks. Star well water was an enigma unto itself. It was not at all intoxicating and could be used for a variety of purposes. The pilgrims from Cymru had first discovered the star well when they had journeyed over the star road. The star well was nothing short of miraculous. After the miracle of the book of Illu it had provided a magical conduit through which the book of Illu could channel its power. It was used for an endless variety of purposes throughout the human nation, from medicinal to functions of the church to simple consumption along with daily meals. It formed a large staple of the Arnemnuin diets. Not even the most skilled sages or philosophers could determine what gave the crystal blue water its magical properties, but as it had sustained them since coming from their world, the Arnemnuin s simply gave thanks to their God for it, and chose not to delve into its abstruse mysteries.

"How went the command of your men in battle today, love?" (Cadon did not take special note of the last word Arletta said, for he knew it to be a country Areoth term for a casual friend.)

"Thanks to Cael-Illu, no one under my command died in battle. Yet I mourn for those who went to be with our God this day."

"Well, I mourn them as well, but ya know what me people say best honors fallen warriors? A ballad recounting their brave deeds. Hold on a moment." She ducked behind the counter and resurfaced holding a lute made from Bulldron horn. She began to pluck the strings and croon.

"Red and blue blood spilled today

As the Knights of Illu rode to the fray.

To the demons they gave clash for clash,

Heads to roll and horns to smash.

Yet these men shall ride anew,

When comes the day of Cael-Illu.

When comes the day of Cael-Illu."

She repeated this refrain over and over more than a dozen times. And by the time she was finished, the other patrons of the tavern were clapping their hands and sing along with. She was perhaps not the most skilled Areoth bard, but nevertheless Cadon found himself enraptured and entranced by her song. "Um. I… Er. That was very beautiful, Arletta." *(It is almost as beautiful as you,)* he said in the deepest recesses of his mind, though, truly he would take his own life if he said that loud enough for her to hear. "Truly, at times I find that I have trouble falling asleep at the barracks. Perhaps in the near future, hmm, you could compose a lullaby and come sing it for me sometime. If *Umph!*" At that precise second Cadon felt Aelwyn's elbow jab into his side. Agh, Bulldron's teeth! Yet another faux pas in the presence of the woman who had his heart. The list was becoming a rather long one.

Arletta did not take umbrage at the rash statement, but instead gave Cadon a warm smile. "Mayhap I will, old chum," she laughed. "Mayhap I will." She winked. Cadon's face flushed red.

19. Cadon's Task

The illuminating crystals glowed blue the Council room of Rowend Starhammer, King of the humans of Ar Nemnu. The King appeared to be in his mid to late forties (that is, by human reckoning). He was clad in adamantine mail, which was for this purpose decorative but also more than functional. King Starhammer, holding his eponymous massive adamantine battle hammer, frowned over a map on the large octagonal dais before which he sat. He wore a short mane and beard the color found in the wet sand off the shores of long-forgotten Cymru, a caramel brown, only now beginning to speck with the gray and white "seashells" of old-age. Over the mail he wore a dark blue tabard emblazoned with his shining Golden Rood from the cover of the book of Illu, the standard of the paladins of Cael-Illu. This was a meeting of the King's cabinet, Bishop Cadwyr and several delegates from the two other principal races making up the sacred alliance. Of these, even less common to see in Pallantine than the Areoth were the Nomegons, the small hairy-footed humanoids of the emerald woods to the North. These never, unless caused by intermarriage, grew to be above four feet in height, the average height being three feet and six inches. King Boggelsby MacFuti was indisposed, but he had sent his most trusted general, the somewhat taller Kurti McErny. The graying commander had two curly-q mustachios and a circular-cut pile of dark hair. He carried his adamantine-braced, emerald wood club, Woodistock, on his back. Next to King Rowend was Cole-Unden, having meticulously polished the dust from his breastplate.

"Warriors, princes, friends," began King Rowend, stretching his arms out to his fellow potentates in acknowledgment. "Thanks to the speedy coming of the Areothans to our aid, we were able to stem the tide of the demonoids. But," the King continued, "it is in our best interest that we take precautions to protect the book of Cael-Illu from their grasp. I move therefore to elect a squadron of soldiers, with several from each of the free races, to take it in turns to guard the sanctum of Illu at all times."

"But Laddie," laughed Kurti McErny "who would be in command of this squadron. There cannot be one commander from each of the free races. Either of my sons Gurton or Annaky would be fine choices."

"I have already dispatched a missive to your realm requesting that Bogglesby relieve them of their duties at Caer Eliana. But, with all deference to you of course, we men brought the true faith to this lab and as such I think it should be a man with a true heart for all the free races to hold them together as sap does tree bark. I know he is the young, but if I had my way these things it would be a man like Cadercyffel, son of the late Goth-Curdion."

"As you say, Cadon is young," said Cole-Unden, running his hand through his hair, "but his phalanx did slay more enemies than those slain by any other company. I second the motion."

"Very well," the Nomegon general acquiesced. "In proxy for my King I support Starhammer's motion." A general murmuring of approval rose from all else assembled.

"Then we are agreed. I shall summon the boy at length. This Council is dismissed."

General MacErny stopped the Areothan king in the atrium of the Council chamber and asked. "I could see by your looks that something did not sit well with you." "Oh… It is but a small matter."

"Not as small as I," chuckled the Nomegon.

Cole smiled weakly at the jest.

"It's Leyenna, isn't it? You still wish to seek her out, don't you?"

"Aye. Truly that is why come so often to Pallantine. But... I did swear an oath to her mother. So she must know neither that woman's name, nor mine. Come."

20.   Arletta's Changing

"Ull bae turning in now, Master C," Arletta called back over her shoulder as she exited the Tavern through the back door. Once again she had been entertained by that sweet Cadon's antics. Ah, Humans. She never would completely understand them. She had long ago guessed his motives, and it had at first made her very uncomfortable. Yet she wondered why if he longed for her, he did not just come out and say it. She was acquainted, being a follower of the light, with the three tiers of love. The first tier, or degree, or house, depending on how you interpreted the book of Illu, was the love of brothers in arms, and was invoked at the taking of oaths. The second, more intimate was the love between a husband and wife. Arletta had at first suspected that this was the love Cadon had in heart for her, judging by his seemingly ridiculous behavior whenever he was in her presence. He had at first acted out of foppish infatuation. She was no apothecary, but she knew enough about the four humors to detect that. And now for almost 2 years, he had been trying to make up for that oversight . She wondered, the mouth of her mind standing agape, just then if it was the third tier of love, the highest degree that superseded all others. The deep love that Cael-Illu exuded for all the free races, whether they followed him or not, that *was* Cael-Illu. That love was unconditional. She did not know if humans could be capable ofthis love, for as Ar-Khena had said many times back at the orphanage in Yranthor: "Always doubt the heart of a human. It be treacherous."

Many of the little Areothan winglets had been abandoned due to illegitimacy, unplanned impregnation, or feelings of apathy on the part of their parents. Though she did not know who her parents were, Arletta did know that they had given her a parting gift, a small ruby set in silver. It had been her comfort item since she was a little winglet. Because of this she always dreamed that her parents were rich and important. Coming at last to her small apartment several blocks from the Tavern, she unlocked the door and went inside. The room was sparsely furnished yet comfortable, with a medium-sized looking glass in the center of one wall and the divan on which she slept against the other. A wash basin for evening ablutions stood in the center. There was a window next to the divan, on which sat a goblet of sleeping tonic. Arletta was prone to insomnia.

As she washed herself, she began to sing:

"I've ne'er kissed a warrior or sailor

Nor any children do I have

But by the great white eye o' Baelor! I'm guided by my Shepherd's Staff!"

She was so engrossed in her singing, that she did not see a shadowy hand come up over the windowsill and pour three drops of a clear liquid into her tonic goblet and then quickly vanish into the night. When the Areoth girl had finished her bath and dressed in her night clothes, she downed the tonic in one draught and immediately fell back on the bed, as cold as the grave itself.

The hooded figure hurried through the slums of Palantine. Coming upon a darkened doorway it knocked on the wall four times. A slender gauntleted hand pulled the other figure inside.

"The medicating was successful?" The gauntleted figure hissed.

"Aye. It should begin to work its magic as she sleeps."

"So, this Arletta is to come into her destiny," the figure invisibly smirked. "And when she does, rest assured. I shall be there."

Arletta awoke the next day feeling very strange. She was stunned when she looked in the mirror and saw that her skin was starting to take on the hew of human flesh. Not only that, but her wings were becoming as cloth. She frantically wracked her mind for some explanation. Anything. Such things as these had not been seen in thousands of years and were only told of in the legends of her people. "I'm devolving," she moaned. Such transformations took only a few days, and she was certain that when the transformation was complete, she would be cast out as an abomination, as many other Areothans were before her. *Why me? Oh, why me? Why am I the one? What did I do to deserve this?* She searched for a pointy reckoning with which to end the shame. The throbbing in her head must stop. And the rippling burning of her skin... Aagh! She must end it all now or she would explode like a sapper's bomb. But no. If she commited suicide she would be forever cut off from the Light of Cael-Illu. That was a fate worse than death in battle. There had to be some loophole, something that could save her from the life of a wretched outcast. The only thing that could save a devolved Areothan was expectancy of a child or marriage to a member of another of the free races. She was in neither situation. And who would take her once she had devolved? There was one, she thought. It was her only chance. Quickly bathing herself in face powder (white, the color of Areothan skin), she threw on a dark cloak and set out to find the one man who could help her: the human Paladin, Caddercyffel Math-Goth.

While the Areoth girl was this engaged in ruminations, the object of her "affection" was enjoying a bowl of Nomegon cinnamon root stew to break his fast when Baerleon, the captain of the tower guard laid a leather gauntleted hand on his shoulder. At first, Cadon thought that the salt-and-pepper whiskered soldier was coming to a challenge him to a rematch of Gampting, a sort of Golem-based chess popular among all the free races. The pieces were alchemically engineered so that when one piece was about to take another the back of both pieces would become viscous and allow the player to defend the piece using finger pressed wires in the pieces torso. Each piece was engineered to have specific move strengths and weaknesses. It became so engrossing to some that they almost came to blows. "Well, Baery," Cadon chuckled, eyes flashing merrily, "what shall we wager today?"

"My visit does not concern Gampting, as much as 'twould please me. King Rowend and Bishop Cadwyr have summoned you to the royal tower."

The youth's face flushed and he began to sweat. "Have I done something wrong? I assure you, my record is clear of insubordination."

"Well, lad, when the King gave me the missive, he did not seem upset. I believe they wished to bestow an honor upon you."

The pendulum of Cadon's emotions immediately swung in the opposite direction. With a broad smile on his face, he set out with the captain to the royal tower.

The interior of the royal tower was splendid to behold. The interior of the Council chamber and audience chamber of the King held walls carved with bas reliefs in marble and jet always encrusted with gold, and adamantine. Images of previous warrior Kings standing victorious over the bodies of slain Keimbold Champions, carved replicas of pages from the book of Illu as well as relics of past Kings, Rowend's ancestors as well as those of their favored champions, sat on pedestals, giving the room the appearance of a museum or mausoleum.

Rowend and Cadwyr sat before a game board set with a half finished game of Gampting. Cadwyr's spearman was set to unhorse one of Rowend's paladins. The battle was about to ensue. In truth, the Bishop and the King were reaching their hands and the backs of the game pieces when the great double doors boomed open and in walked Baerleon and Cadon. "Ah. Cadercyffel Math Goth. Just the man I wanted to see." "I was somewhat taken aback when I received your message. Nothing is wrong, I hope."

"No, quite the opposite. But first I must ask: are you ready to do your duty for your city?"

"Always, my King."

"I wish to bestow a great honor on you but remember: with honor comes responsibility. To put it plainly, the representatives of the free races and myself together with the good Bishop have decided that we must take new precautions to protect the book of Illu from the demonoid Keimbold. I am composing a new guard taken from the best warriors of all the free races. But they need a leader. You stood bravely in battle two days ago. Not only that but, you have the courage of your father, the noble Goth-Curdion. I see no one within the Paladin legions of Palantine more fit to take on this authority than you. So my lad, will you accept this new office, and make your King and Pontiff proud?"

For a moment, Cadon stood dumbfounded, too shocked to speak. Then he croaked, "I am unworthy of this honor, my Lord Starhammer but if this is indeed the will of the Council of the free races, I would be a fool not to accept. I feel very inadequate to the task. But by the will of Cael-Illu, I shall be able to rise to it."

"Very well."

The sandy-haired bishop came forward and put a golden necklace bearing the image of a great three cornered shield emblazoned with a rood, the symbol of the Offspring of Cael-Illu, around his neck, whispering the benediction at the consecration of generals: "May Cael-Illu ever watch over you with a ready sword and may your sword ever be ready to defend the cause of His Light."

Cadon Math Goth whispered his thanks to the potentates and tears still trailing down his cheeks, he made his way to the main thoroughfare of the city. But even the great shock and joy of his new good fortune did not prepare him for what happened next.

Arletta, reeking of an overabundance of Areothan perfume and dressed in a way that would make old Cadagon blush, fairly collided with Cadon in the street. She appeared quite cheery, but she didn't look well. "Cadon, Cadercyffel, me old chum. You be looking nice today."

She pulled him in close in a drawn-out embrace. Being so close to her, the poor young man half expected to smell the strong stench of spirits on her breath, and although through her perfumed and elaborate make-up, he caught a whiff of perspiration, she did not smell any the worse otherwise. Either the sun was playing tricks with her hair or she had dyed the roots golden with alchemist sand. He could not discern which was the case. She seemed slightly taller than when he had last seen her, though it could be due to her fur-stuffed boots.

"Arle- oomph!" (she had pulled him into another tight embrace.) "Are you, are you sick?"

"Yes I am. With the sickness that no apothecary can cure. Only matrimony can cure my ailment." Cadon's eyes bulged as she said this, and of course, he could not grasp the true irony of her statement.

"Long have you watched me. And though you have known it not, I have watched you. The fire of the third love of Cael-Illu burns in my heart for you. When I look at you, when I am with you, I am no longer a simple barmaid. I am one of the highborn of my people." (With this statement came irony that she herself did not yet understand. But she soon would.)

"Ar-I think this is going too-mmmffh!" She pulled him close and pressed her lips deeply into his. Now as any male of Cymru or Ar Nemnu can relate, when any man still in the flames of youth receives his first kiss, not only that but from the woman he loves, he melts like wax forming a seal.

"Oh, let's not wait for a long courtship. What better time to wed than the present? She seized both his hands and dragged him like a trained dog off to the monastery to find a priest.

Father Conwyth was just sitting down to a mug of Nomegon Greenleaf tea, when the Areothan girl, dragging her "betrothed" behind her. "I invoke the code of expedient matrimony."
"Oh," Conwyth gasped, "are you-?" He pointed to her abdomen.

"Yes, I am," she lied.

"Very well then. To save you from shame. In the sight of Cael-Illu, do you Ara'Letza of the Areoth, take Cadercyffel Math Goth to be your husband, now and forever?"

"'Course I do!"

"And do you, Cadercyffel, son of Goth-Curdion, take Ara'Letza of the Areoth, to be your wife, now and forever?"

"I-Um-I-I do!"

"Then by the power invested in me by this monastery, I pronounce you to be…"

"Hold!" All three turned to see Cole-Unden standing in the doorway, a look of triumph on his face. He was dressed in a white crystallite breastplate, the diadem of the Areothan kings upon his brow and the royal sword belted at his waist. "I claim the right to give the bride away."

"What?" Shouted all three in unison.

"By what denotation of kinship do you claim this right?" the priest asked. Only relatives could give away brides and pay dowries.

"I am her father."

"But you're the… how?" Arletta sputtered, staring at King Cole-Unden in wide-eyed shock. Both the priest and young Cadon also stared at the Areothan warrior king, mouths agape.

"Permit me to explain, my child." The Areoth girl bristled at the King's last two words, clearly taking umbrage. "As everyone knows, my Queen is now Tel'Peria but two decades ago, I was married briefly to the noble woman Leiniel of house Javarec. Your birth name is Leyenna, Princess of the Areoth.

When you were born, daughter, you were not only very sickly, but a very large babe. As such, your mother died shortly after your birth. The best apothecaries and alchemists live in Yranthor. I promised your mother on her deathbed that I would take you there, keeping your identity secret for fear of Keimbold assassins. However I did leave you with a token of remembrance from your mother, a ruby set in silver. I watched you from afar, swelling with pride as you grew into a headstrong young woman, waiting for the day when I could reveal to you your true heritage. Do not be afraid that you are devolving, for you are not devolving but metamorphosizing. You see, once every thousand years, a warrior noble woman is born of House Javarec and, once reaching proper age, she metamorphosizes into an oracle in the guise of a human woman with feathered wings. She is the Uberareoth, the Great Areothan. Normally initializing this metamorphosis would take a few more years. However, if you will excuse my eagerness, last night I had my royal alchemist slip a tincture into your nightcap that accelerated the stages. In a few days, you will resemble a beautiful golden-haired woman of the human race, the only sign of your Areothan heritage being your tapered ears and your wings. An oracle was spoken over you at birth, how you and your true love would save our world and many other worlds from destruction. Be careful how you react to this. For your reactions will become your outlook. Your outlook becomes your patterns of behavior, your patterns of behavior your habits, and your habits your destiny. You have an incredible destiny, my daughter. And though you probably wish nothing more than to send my head flying from my shoulders with my own sword, you must first rest, and recoup your thoughts. As your father, I claim the right to seal this union for I see no better human to protect my daughter than our young Cadon. Long have I known that his heart was for you. If you must lay blame on someone, lay blame on me, not upon him; for he loves you deeper than his own life, and I pray that by the will of Cael-Illu, you will come to love him in the same way. I pray that you will someday find it in your heart to forgive me, for I only did what I knew was best for you.

"Now, by the power invested in me as King of the Areoth, I pronounce you to be husband and wife. Perhaps you will be more comfortable kissing your bride later, Cadon. Now I give you her dowry. A position at court when your career here is finished, this gilded adamantine lightning bow, especially crafted for you by my master smiths, and my blessing. I hereby accept you as my son." With that, the King of the winged people of Ar Nemnu turned on his heel and walked briskly out of the priest's office, leaving all three staring after him in wonderment.

Half of Cadon's mind felt as if it had been crushed by a mangonel stone, and the other half felt exuberant. Whenever he tried to snake his arm around Arletta's, or, more correctly, Leyenna's waist, she would furtively yet noticeably sidestep. *That is rather odd,* he thought. *She is now my wife after all.*

When they arrived back at Leyenna's house, for Cadon spent most of his time at the barracks, they found that a bountiful wedding feast had been sent them by the Princess's estranged father.

"Wull, we might as well eat," the Princess sighed.

Truly, the young Paladin could think of a more creative way to spend the time, but he was hungry, and he did not want to rush his bride. The dinner consisted of luscious fruits and sweetmeats from the Nomegon forests and wisp of lightning, a rather strong Areothan vintage, roasted shale venison, and many dainty desserts. Strangely, when she had eaten all of her shank, she held on to the cleaver. "Let us set one thing straight, *dear husband.* If you ever, and I mean ever, even think of laying a finger on me I bleed you like a stuck Bulldron."

In truth, Cadon would have felt better if she had ran him in the gut with the blade and done just that.

Now, there were two goblets of wisp laying on the end table by the bed for the wedding, one was marked "Leyenna Reginente" and the other "Cadercyffel Princeps". Fortunately for Cadon, his new "wife" nor he, for he was too distraught with his grief, noticed a strange effervescence bubbling from the one intended for Leyenna.

"Well, er, um… if we are to have a monkish celibate marriage, can we at least drink to that?" asked the young man (with some slight hesitation, as he was still bewildered at his new wife's mercurial change of moods).

"I suppose, old chum, I suppose."

The glasses clinked and the draughts washed down the respective gullets. Then something very strange happened. The Areothan Princess became as if in a trance. Her head rolled from side to side and she closed her eyes. Then her eyes snapped open strangely glowing blue. She ran forward and embraced her husband with a deep, slow caress. And far-off in the diplomatic quarters of the tower of the Archbishop, Cole-Unden smiled, knowing that the Freyaric tonic had achieved its purpose.

And in another darker part of Ar Nemnu, a clawed red hand held a scrying crystal and malevolent eyes watched the unlikely couple. "Yesss," the beastling hissed. Sssoon we shall ssstrike. Very sssoon."

21.   Leyenna's Mistake

Cadon's eyes fluttered open and he found himself staring into half-closed, dazed eyes that were unmistakably human. It only registered that they belonged to his wife a second later, for they were pale blue and had pupils. He sat up and rubbed the sleep from his eyes, looking for the wash basin.

"Good morning, my children!" boomed a masculine Areothan voice coming from the darkened end of the room. "Waagh!" exclaimed both in unison, juming to their feet.

Cole-Unden walked out of the shadows, a broad grin on his face.

"There you are again, always poppin' up!" scoffed Leyenna.

"How does he do that?" Cadon whispered out of the corner of his mouth.

"I *am* a father after all, my boy, as I hope you will soon be."

Leyenna scowled at her father's last phrase, but she had to admit she now did not mind having her at first unwanted husband near her.

"And now my boy," King Cole said jovially. "It is time for you to meet the other guardians of the star well. "They arrived during the night. Clothe yourself quickly. I will be waiting outside.

Cadon, who was still somewhat taken aback by his new father-in-law's unexpected presence, dressed himself and girded on his armor and sword. Then he bid his new wife goodbye and met the King of the Areoth in the street. Putting his arm around the young man the winged potentate whispered, "I would do my best, if I were you to not vex Leyenna over the next few days for the Freyaric tonic my alchemist gave her last night will act as a mitigator of moods but, accelerated Uberareoth transformation is like unto female adolescent stages, so she will be very irritable over the next day or two." The King chuckled slightly to show his sympathy.

"Freyaric tonic… You mean to say that that's why… Oh, Bulldron's teeth! You and your confounded alchemy!"

"All for a good cause, my son. All for a good cause," the Areothan King returned, smiling.

The location of the star well was central to the city beneath the foundations of King Rowend's royal tower, and from the inner sanctum an azure mist constantly rose; for the magical energy of the book of Illu was blue, the color of holy wisdom. Truly it was this wisdom that kept the defenses of the city intact. Never had any Keimbold demon set foot in the sanctum of the book of Illu. And with the new precautions the Council of the free races was taking, Rowend, Cole–Unden and Bogglesby were certain that no enemy ever would. The only entrance to the sanctum afforded to anyone was a giant adamantine circular lift at the base of the tower of the King that employed four Nomegons, as their ancestors had built the contraption, who cranked four winches on chains to lower it down to the base of the mesa. From there, the guardians walked along a narrow, single file causeway which was also wrought of adamant, across a wide cavernous chasm to the cylindrical room which was the inner sanctum. And there in the center upon a dais, bound with the Symphonic chains of its own holy magical energy which it itself sang forth, was the book of Illu. Its pages were bound in gilded brown leather, but not grey, like that made from cured Bulldron's hide. And upon the front cover was the symbol of golden rood, also known more commonly as a cross, the symbol of the offspring of their God, and the symbol emblazoned on the tabards of the first warriors of the humans of Ar Nemnu, who had, over one hundred thousand centuries of the Areoth reckoning of years, crossed over from that peninsula of Cymru, on the western shores of the isle of the sea called Prydain by the children of Cymru. It was said in the sainted lore, that over eleven hundred years earlier by the original count of the children of Cymru, in a far-off land called Outremer, the offspring of Cael-Illu had died upon a cross of wood, hands and feet nailed to the tree of death, to redeem the children of that world from the wiles of the Demon Lord, who was said to also rule over the Keimbold. It was said that the Son of Cael-Illu would one day come to harmonize the world of the humans' ancestors with the world of Ar Nemnu. And it was for this blessed hope that the children of Cael-Illu waited and endured.

The book of Illu was also known for another miracle . For the humors of the bodies of the children of Cymru were unaccustomed to the rigors of Ar Nemnu. They surely would have died if it hadn't been for the grace of the holy magic worked by their God, through the holy book that they brought with them, which they had at first named the holy word of God. It was the call of the people of Cymru to be warriors so they soon began to call their God by the name of Cael-Illu, which means warrior of light in the tongue of the children of Cymru. But whether they called him Yahweh, Jehovah or Father of Christ, He was still the same God. The only difference was the language they chose to use.

The Areothan King led his new son-in-law along the causeway to the inner sanctum after descending on the Nomegon-powered lift. The young man could feel the very air tingling with holy magical energy as they neared the dais upon which the book of Illu rested. There was an honor guard of six warriors, consisting of two humans, including Cadon, the other being Aelwyn. Cadon's friend was armed with a pentagonal adamantine mace. He held it upside down by the half, keeping the head steady with his metal-braced boot. Two Areothan warriors bearing the winged crest of house Javarec upon their segmented adamantine cuirasses stood with spears clasped in flange-gauntleted hands, the undulating tips of the weapons pointing upward. They also bore broadswords with semispherical guards and pear-shaped pommels. Their pearl-white manes were partially hidden by high-crested rotund helmets with ambered nasals. Cadon had met them briefly before and he recalled that their names were Roxxar and Brendor, and that they were first cousins. Behind them were the sons of Nomegon General Kurti McErny, Gurton and Annaky. The almost four- foot tall warriors were twins and had the fiery hair of their mother, Eliana, and they also had round stubby goatees through which they hey had woven a small gold ring. They were exactly alike, from there emerald green eyes to the barrel-bowl pipes that stuck out of their crooked mouths (and were so kindred in spirit that they were known to often finish one another's sentences). They were identical in appearance, except that Annaky's nose had bashed askew in a long-past battle by a Keimbolden warhammer. The brothers were clad in bulldron-hide leather armor and bore emerald wood war clubs similar to their father's. On their curly heads they wore round adamantine helmets.

"This, my lad," Cole-Unden said ceremoniously, "is the free race Alliance coalition honor guard of the book of Illu, and these warriors are all at your command. Use your new authority wisely, and don't let it go to your head. Good day, Cadon." With that, Cole-Unden walked with swift steps out of the inner sanctum, leaving the young man baffled for lack of information.

"W-well," the flustered Paladin began. "I am Cadercyffel Math Goth, called Cadon by many. Cadon will do. Er, although I am your superior, we can usually dispense with the formalities. I am a simple man, um er, free being, as are you, and some of you, such as Aelwyn Pwyn Gwydyr here, know me very well already." (He almost wished that the aforementioned Aelwyn would do him a favor and brain his friend with his new mace to relieve him of the ironic embarrassment, for, in truth, Aelwyn was the only one of his new subordinate officers who knew him well.) "Now, um ah, I believe I know all of your names, but for the sake of, camaraderie and brotherhood..." (*Bulldron's teeth! This was beginning to sound more and more like a poor mimicry of one of general Erethune's well-rehearsed pre-battle speeches*).... "Let us introduce ourselves to one another." (*At long last, freedom! It was over.*) Gurton raised a ruddy, fur-backed hand. He said, "Let's not go..."

"...In order of height shall we?" Annaky finished the sentence.

"Very well then, my Nomegon brothers, the floor is yours."
"We thought it belonged to the alliance of free races." They said in unison, and burst into a fit of cacophonous laughter.

"Well put, wee fighters, well put." Cadon smiled, appreciating their efforts to lighten the mood and break the proverbial ice. Also, the warriors did not take umbrage at Cadon's referring to them as "wee fighters", for this was somewhat of a complimentary term of appreciation among warriors of their race.

They began talking in one voice. "We are Annaky and Gurton, stalwart fighters of the emerald wood. Ever we shall raise our shalaileighs in defense of Caer Eliana and of the light of Cael-Illu."

"Warriors of House Javarec…" Continued the new commander of the honor guard.

"It is as you say," intoned Raxxor with a stony air. "Ever do I, Raxxor, son of Anatheld fight for the glory of Cael-Illu and for the cause of my King and people, as does my cousin Brendor, Son of Arrannon, and I search for the coming of the next Uberareoth, as the stars show that her coming is soon to be upon us."

"There is nothing that I desire more," added Brendor, eyes facing ahead, past Cadon, "than to serve her that she may bring glory to our God and to our people."

Cadon mused on Brendor's statement and was slightly disquieted in his soul as he considered its irony. The Uberareoth was already in their midst, though hers was a destiny that she did not desire. Cadon wisely decided to keep these facts to himself.

Aelwyn stared for a while and at last said. "Well, I am not about to out-perform those introductions, so I will keep it short and simple. My name is Aelwyn son of Seamus and Caddercyffel Math Goth has been my best friend and brother in arms for a long as I can remember, so I am honored to serve under him in this new duty."

"Now what do we do?" chimed the McErny brothers, once again in one voice.

"Now, my little packs of Nomegon sapper's fire," said Aelwyn winking (this term was also complementary), "we wait and stand guard in case the Keimbold demons should create any sort of breech."

And wait they did. For they waited… And waited… And waited… And waited…

After a time, young Cadon could feel the blood beginning to pool in his legs. He had long since tired of counting forging lines in the edges of the inner sanctum. And so he was more than relieved when several novices from the monastery came with glasses of gramarye to measure the level of magic currently that the book of Illu was currently exuding. Several warriors of the Legion were trained to use these devices. It appeared to be an hourglass filled with red sand and the closer it got to an object exuding magical energy, the higher the sand rose. The holy magic was measured in how many demons it could kill. If the power exuded was capable of killing five demons the sand would register at five, and so on.

"Do you know how to use this instrument, human?" Asked a Nomegon novice with curly blonde hair as she was about to leave. She was directing her question at Aelwyn. "I know how to well enough," the raven-haired young man replied.

"Good, then I'll be leaving it here just in case you might need it."

Today was Leyenna's day off, even though she did not come into the Tavern the previous day. At any rate, old Cadagon Cuthbert had heard a jumbled up version of her wedding story, and had decided that it was best to leave sleeping bulldrons to lie. Probably due to her transformation, the Areoth princess was feeling very queasy, and was laying down while waiting for the kettle of Nomegon tea to brew, (she thought that might settle her stomach) when I read this time that look like sand of the red desert to the South blew in on a breeze through the open window and she inhaled some of it. The strangely bitter fragrance immediately caused her to drift off to sleep, sleep as deep as that of the dead. And as her eyes fluttered shut, she thought she could see herself, with a strange ruddy countenance that was slowly paling as she walked out the door.

Kullkreesa, demon witch of the Keimbol did not like her new semblance but she knew that Khraz'Zoon would not have given her this assignment if it would not succeed. She had long been studying this human, this Caddercyffel Math Goth and found him to be stalwart, but she knew his one weakness and she would exploit that weakness. The power of demondom would grow beyond reckoning.

Cadon looked over his shoulder and saw that the brothers McErny were perspiring like bulldrons in the midst of a hard-fought battle. And in front of them, the Areothan cousins were faring little better. Cadon looked to the side at his best friend, and saw that Aelwyn himself was by no means comfortable.

"All right," he barked at last. "I can easily see what's happening. It's barracks. I regret to have to do this but I'm issuing a directive, we each take ten laps back and forth along the Causeway.

"But the book…" began Brendor.

"Do you honestly think that Keimbold infiltrators will be able to waltz right in and take it up with us just fifty feet away?"

"I don't," a new voice slightly croaked, slightly sang. Everyone looked up and there in the doorway of the inner sanctum was Leyenna her hair had become more blonde since the previous night, yet it still had roots of almost ominous black.

"I shall stand watch. I can do this, for you are my husband now after all." This last statement solicited whistles of surprise from Aelwyn and the sons of the Nomegon general, who apparently had not been told or gained wind of Cadon and Leyenna's union.

"Well I do not know if that is exactly protocol, but we are practically dying in here. That suits me just fine."

As the free race alliance guardians of the book of Illu went out to stretch their legs, Kullkreesa returned to her hag like form and smirked malevolently.

Leyenna awoke wondering at the sight she had seen before falling into her deep sleep. She finally attributed it to the intricacies of her transformation and decided to take Cadon a lunch of Bulldron steak. She felt a very strange tugging in her spirit as she walked toward the King Rowend's tower that noonday. And she felt that with each step she took, another was taking the steps of doom.

Strangely, as he finished his ninth lap, the young Paladin commander saw a familiar figure coming toward him. He stopped short, catching his breath, as he saw with great consternation that it was his wife.

"My dear, whatever are you doing out here? I thought you were back…"

"I know I spent a long time sleeping today. And guess what?! Voila! Do you like my new hair color, Cadon? It be as golden as the sun now."

"Wait!" Cadon said in great shock. "You are right here now. And your hair is completely blonde when just a moment ago…"

"Not just a moment ago, husband. Since I woke up from my nap a few minutes ago."

"A few minutes ago you were in the house, you mean to say?"

"Yes. I only came here now because I thought you might want some lunch. It's Bulldron steak. I am trying to be a good wife after all."

"No that's not what I mean. You're supposed to be…"

CRASH! The thunderous sound came from the inner sanctum. "Bulldron teeth!" Cadon growled through a clenched set of his own as he bolted across the causeway back into the inner sanctum. There he found the magics of the book of Illu waning, for the dais was bare. The book of Illu had vanished.

"They've taken it!" Cadon moaned in despair. The Keimbold stole the book of Illu." By this time the other guardians and the real Leyenna had entered the sanctum behind him.

He turned to face his wife and companions shame plainly written on his face. "The demons stole the book of Illu." "They did WHAT?!" The Areoth princess screamed. The gramarye glass began to register. It was only then that young Cadon remembered what his father-in-law had told him about not vexing Leyenna during the remaining time of her transformation. A Golden magical energy began to surround Cadon's wife. She began to levitate, so tense was the magic surrounding her she crossed her arms and then asked for him in front of her and then drove them down to her sides, bringing them apart and screaming "Aaagh!" She continued screaming and screaming and screaming and all the while the magical energy grew until it threatened to crack through the center of the sanctum. "Aagh!" Magic winds blew and wrenched the weapons from the warrior's hands and began swirling in a magic whirlwind around the hyper-transforming princess. The ground shook, metal twisted and contorted in the trimmers were even felt by portly Cadagon Cuthbert in his rooms above his tavern. "Aagh!" The whirlwind grew in intensity and began pushing the warriors and the wall. Aelwyn peered through the gale at the gramarye glass and bellowed over the din to his friend. "She is creating enough magic to slay over nine thousand demons!"

"Over nine thousand?!" Cadon yelled back disbelievingly. "Leyenna, you'll kill us all! Stop!" And somehow the desperation of his love broke through the anger, the whirlwind and magical explosions ceased. And Cadon saw a wondrous sight standing before him. Leyenna had become extremely muscular so that the muscles of her arms, torso and legs rippled with strength. Her skin was completely the color of human flesh and the only traits remaining of herAreoth heritage were her pointed ears and her wings. But they were like the wings of the holy warriors depicted in the book of Illu: broad and white-feathered, soft yet powerful and her hair was Golden blonde shining with a radiant light of its own, and it fell at least halfway down her back.

"My name is Leyenna, princess of the Areoth," she intoned in a powerful, clarion voice. "And I am the Uberareoth."

Epilogue: The Quest

"This is an outrage!" Bellowed King Rowend, pacing back and forth in front of his throne. Cadon, Leyenna and the guardians of the star well, knelt before him awaiting further chastisement and the declaration of their punishment.

"Without the book of Illu we are defenseless. The demons will come and raise the city to the ground. We stand no chance in battle against the Keimbold without it and cannot make an assault on their land. It is not as if we can simply walk into fortress of our enemy to take it back."

An idea suddenly formed in the young Paladin's mind. "Majesty, I beg you hear me out. We may not be able to make a frontal assault upon our enemy. But what you said about walking in and taking it back may work. I offer my body as collateral and my life along with it, that I will go alone in secret to the Keimbold homeland to retrieve the book of Illu. The golden magic brought forth by my wife's transformation should hold our enemies at bay until then."

"But that is madness!"

"Madness or not, it must be done," said Brendor. "We will go. We are just as much to blame as he is."

"And we shall go too!" The brothers McErny declared in unison.

"Cadon's my blood brother. It would be the greatest dishonor for me not to go and watch his back."

"I am the most skilled in holy magic in the city by virtue of my heritage as the Uberareoth," Leyenna said gravely. "And also, he is my husband, whom I have grown to love. I shall go wherever he goes." Cadon's heart swelled with joy as she said this. His lifelong wish had at last come true.

"Well," said King Rowend at length, "you are, in my opinion all marching into an early grave. But if this is what you would do as penance, you have my blessing and I pray along with the Bishop that you have the blessing of our God as well.

Henceforth, you shall be the company of the Book of Illu."

"Now I am nearly run out of parchment and ink and will have to wait for another parchment to be delivered. I must at least begin the introduction of the adventures in the world of Veritia. It is the tale of Balladin, arch knight of Silvardrassil. But the tale does not begin with him or any of his companions. I shall only begin with the journey to the west and likely not even make it to Balladin's part in the tale."

22.   Knights of Silvardrassil

Prologue: In Search of Truth

Of all the gods of the Bovatu

There is none, none like You

For unlike the gods many false

That line our temples, city walls

You, Bright Star-Father, are true

The Tauromins, the bovine humanoids, have long held the reputation of being among the best alchemists and astrologers in the entire world of Veritia. The chronicler knight Balladin, son of Kergath, has only seen the city of Silvardrassil. And like one link in a coat of mail, Silvardrassil, as glorious as it is, is only, one small piece of the grandiose library of lands that is Veritia.

As Esulien, the Savior of Veritia, once indicated, there are those who have heard the name of the Radiant King his Father, though they know him not. Here follows the tale of such a one.

Sekanda Praveen, a great, muscular jet black Tauromin, had lived in the city of Bolra-Gol, the center of learning of the Indulon states his whole life. His fur was always clean and his horns were always polished, but he was by no means effeminate, for the blood of a warrior flowed in his veins. His father, Praveen Rajput, had been a warrior turned astrologer who was as wealthy as a nabob. He had taught Sekanda the way of the tulwar and the mace, and any other weapon that a humanoid bovine could deem necessary. If polytheism is the way of many of the peoples of Veritia, none surpass the Tauromin pantheon, which consists in excess of one billion deities, for every area of life imaginable. There is even Anujput, god of excrement. But above all others reigns the Queen Goddess, Kundi: creator, destroyer, regenerator. One day while searching in the library, Sekanda had come upon an ancient tome, *The Tome of the Lion*, in which an oracle claimed that one day a God, whose symbol was a lion, would come to conquer all the other gods, who were in reality demons, and restore tranquility to the lands of the Tauromin.

That night, Sekanda was restless, his dreams dark and disquieted. Suddenly through the darkness pierced a great Light, and he saw a man, a mystic, with the teeth and mane a lion. The man spoke, and his voice was like that of rushing waters. "I am He of whom you have read today. Rise up, leave the vile faith of your fathers, which is but trickery of the shadow king. Journey to the West until you hear the voice of a young human man. Where that young man's voice is, there I have prepared your destiny. Now, arise, arm yourself, and go." The dream abruptly ended. Immediately the bovine man began to don the armor of his father. He put on a shirt of fine disc mail and a piked helmet with a broad nasal for his maw, and two great holes in the forehead for his horns. He took up his father's gargaz mace and buckler and mounted upon his horse, Tadigiri.

It was still very late at night and he wanted to make it to the great oasis that separated the Centaurine desert from lush Indulon before midday. He did not know whether to cross into the Centaurine Desert or to go into Nazgool, of the Dragon-men. The half-horsemen, also being dark of skin, were on friendlier terms with the bull people than the motley colored humanoid lizards. But traveling through their arid homeland would not only be trying to both him and his steed, but traveling through Nazgool would save him several weeks of travel, and be slightly easier since the draconic language was very similar to that spoken by the bovine people. He would just have to steer clear of awesome Mount Najoola, which was reportedly the highest mountain in all the lands of Veritia.

Deciding that he would cross that proverbial bridge when he came to it, he set forth into the wilds of Indulon, following the unclear yet captivating path to which the lion man had called him. He wended his way through the fertile Vendhus Valley, past the many rice patties and small farms of the Tauromin people, steering away from the cities to avoid questioning. Those who did see him probably thought him just a messenger, delivering a missive for some local nabob. He did not slow his pace until he came to Yetuunar, village of the demon yeti men. The village consisted of what appeared to be dilapidated pagodas of the bull people's northern neighbors, but these were grimy and rain-soaked and smelled of yeti musk. The local potentates were also shamans, leading the people in rituals that would even turn a bull man's stomach. Endeavoring to skirt the village, as he urged his horse into a sidling position, Sekanda Praveen heard angry shouted words in a dialect he could not understand.

"Urunga ghoolz thara'hak! Kef'han thara'hak!"

Although he could not see very well through the foliage, the bull-man made out the colossal image of an Earth elemental, rising up out of the ground that was its home seemingly to devour an elf youth with ebon skin.

"Glasta thero-theinin!" Thero-laluth!" This plea for mercy came from the elf, his accent betraying him to be from the Elvenwood near the center of the continent. (Though in truth no one had been to the true center of the continent, for some unexplained magical hindrance blocked their way.) Although young Sekanda had no love for the monotheistic elves, he still shared with them a love for astrology, so the bull man decided to come to the hapless elf's rescue. Uttering a great cry of "Elppa sira Taurominu shupto!" (Northern Indulon dialect: 'I am a Tauromin Warrior!"), he charged into the yeti man throng, the globe-headed mace of his father flashing in the early morning sun.

The yetis as well as the elf were greatly taken aback at this unexpected challenge, and at first, no one lifted a white-furred paw to try to stop Sekanda. If there is one thing, and indeed, only one thing, bull men love more than the study of the stars and the five elements, it is cavalry .charging to war against draconic men and yeti men, bloodlust in their eyes, screaming the numbers of warriors they have killed.

Sekanda struck the first yeti on the back of the head with an underhanded blow from his mace. This caused a jet of black blood and pinkish white brains to spurt up into the air, tarnishing the nasal of the bull man's helmet. In reaction, the white wild man crashed into the one in front of him accidentally tearing a gash in the neck with his jagged paw. One more quickly thinking beast man leaped over the others, flint dagger poised for the bull man warrior's unprotected eye. But once again the bronze-colored steel mace swooshed forth and caved in the yeti man's chest cavity. As he flew backward from the blow, the beast man lost hold of his dagger which flew toward the altar.

Suddenly something occurred to Sekanda. If their god were to die, they would all flee in terror. Wading his horse by brute force, stamping a red swath through the white-furred beast men, the humanoid bull stood in the stirrups, leaped forward somersaulting through the air, toward the Earth elemental's massive head. Bringing down his Mace in a crushing blow, the bull man skidded down the crumbling body as if it were one of the landslides that commonly ravaged the mountains of the North of Indulon. As the Tauromin had suspected, the yetis broke into full retreat. Under normal circumstances, the Tauromin warrior would have given chase endeavoring to slay as many as possible. Yet he retrieved one of the flint knives and cut the elf youth's bonds. Through stunted common tongue, much poetry of which the bull man had studied, he came to realize that the elf was a scholar, somewhat of a naturalist, whose name was Verlien. While studying the flora and fauna of West Indulon he had been waylaid by a group of hunter gatherer yetis, and, as they did not take kindly to foreigners, they had decided to sacrifice him to their god, the Earth elemental. Now having someone of similar skin color to help him through the Centaurine Desert, Sekanda decided to take the easier yet longer route to the Western lands. So after several weeks of journeying through the land of the half-horse nomads, during which time they stopped at night, to haltingly discuss the paths of the stars with the seers of the various tribes, they came through other lands to the Elvenwood. Sekanda Praveen was just about to bid the elf lad goodbye, when he heard the voice of a young man carried on the wind, speaking some strange dialect of common tongue, which declared, "I for one shall go! Who shall go with me?"

And then it seemed as if over thousand human voices answered with a great resounding cry of "We shall go!" The bull man felt a quickening in his spirit as he and the elf set out in search of the voices. Surely this was the voice of which the lion man had spoken of in his dream. Surely this was where his destiny in the true God lay. He did not know what trials lay before him, but both he and the elf new that through that voice, they would write their own destinies.

***

In the Highland home of the barbarians, or the "Heelands" as the barbarians themselves name the place, there lived a warrior bard named Cunavol. In the barbarian culture, bards are very much akin to priests. These priests travel the Highlands and moors, carrying news from one clan chieftain to another, and in times when they were united under one ruler, as they wereunder Uilleam "The Hammer of the Bryttevulf" Mac Eollath, a very rare occurrence, bards would be in charge of relaying battle plans among the troops during a campaign, be it against the Giants to the north or an unlikely Bryttevulf resurgence. At any rate, the Hammer of the Bryttevulf was long dead, his bones crumbling to dust beneath the stone of Stan Wynn, the nation was a piecemeal hodge-podge of independent tribes, each suspicious of the other, and constantly degrading into blood feuds. So this Cunavol had no other duties than his local kirk, the attendance of which was dwindling for one reason or another, mostly illness and death among the parishioners. In fact, throughout the last month, he had officiated no fewer than five funerals. And so now in the despondency of his mud and thatch hut, he slept, his mind swimming in a sea of regret and unanswered questions. "Why, O Ard Ri," he cried into the blinding maelstrom of his dark dreams. "Why are you so far from me? Make your will known to me that I may follow it. Draw me near to you. Speak, oh, speak, I pray." Then a silvery white light filled his vision. The voice of the Ard Ri, the High King, his God, filled his mind. "Rise up," the High King said. "Rise up now and put your claymore and targe on your back. You must journey to the Southeast until you find an elf with skin as black as coal who travels with a companion who is both man and dun cow. Rise up, now."

Cunavol the bard immediately awoke in a hot sweat. Though he knew that to the Southeast lay the Wosenland, the dark forests of the heathen wild men, he put his trust in the word of his God, and set out that very night, taking his hairy-hoofed highland pony with him as a mount. He journeyed through snow, wind and rain. He would have become very lonely, but bards, in addition to being capable messengers and town criers, are also accomplished minstrels. Many bards make their living by the tunes they sing in the presence of noblemen and in the halls of wealthy chieftains. And so he began to sing this song in archaic Heeland speech:

"Ard Ri! Ard Ri, Rop tu mo baile

Rop tu mo baile, Ard Ri, Ard ri!

Ri Gealana, Ard ri Naofa! Naofa!

"Ard Ri! Ard Ri, Rop tu mo baile

Rop tu mo baile, Ard Ri, Ard ri!

"Ard Ri! Ard Ri, Rop tu mo baile

Rop tu mo baile, Ard Ri, Ard ri!

(Highland Speech: High King! High King, be thou my vision!

Be thou my vision, High King, High King!

King of Light, holy high King! Holy!

High King! High King, be thou my vision!

Be thou my vision, High King, High King!)

And so with the clip-clopping of the Highland mare's hairy hoofs, whittling away at the hours and days with as many merry songs sung for the glory of the High King, The bard Cunavol came to the dark forests were dwelt the wild men. Although Cunavol did not know it, the wild men were more united than the Highland men. They were one people, semi-simian, and golden furred, sporting maws of great yellow teeth dripping with mud and fowl water. They were led by their King John the Iron, or "Iron John" as both friend and foe called him.

And though Cunavol kenned it not being, he would soon meet face-to-face with the paunchy wose.

The bard could no longer see the sun overhead, for the canopy of the forest was too thick. Yet he felt as if malevolent eyes were watching him from above. To calm his nerves, he began to croon a song, stroking his Highland mare's mane.

"The Ard Ri is with me on the murk-ed heath,

Even underneath the shadow of deeth.

I will mack well when I mack maen,

Of your goodness to glorify your Name."

It was just then that the young bard heard a strange ululating call, that sounded like a mixture of rustling leaves and a crow cawing as its wings beat the air to take flight. Young Cunavol's hand shifted to the hilt of his claymore broadsword and his eyes darted from tree to tree and all the spaces in between.

"Gua graash!" This strange cry tore through the stillness of the forest as a dozen bent and stooping wild men crashed down on the forest floor from the trees above. Many were armed with great clubs, makeshift stone maces and knives and spears with flint points and blades. The woses may be slow of movement at times, but many of them, though their appearance would seem to indicate otherwise, can be very cunning.

As a matter of fact, many a hapless adventurer passing through the forests of the wild men lost their lives by underestimating the hairy men's capability in matters cerebral.

At any rate, one unarmed wild man leaped with the agility of a spider toward the horse's neck, latched on with his razor-sharp serrated yellow teeth, and burst the poor creature's jugular.

It immediately fell over dead, but the bard had thought quickly and jumped out of the saddle and stirrups.

Barrel-rolling back onto his feet, he drew his sword and unslung his shield "*Ard Ri gu bragh!*" he screamed (Highland speech: the High King forever.) Cunavol began swinging the Highland blade back and forth, landing brownish red cuts and gashes on his of his. Although, since the days of Adahan, the forefather of the barbarian people, they have known the true God who may have called the Ard Ri who is known in Silvardrassil as the Radiant King, a wild thirst for blood, which they name "Rhiastrad", burned with undying brilliance and blinding rage in the hearts of the Heeland Men. The music of bagpipes wailed in the warrior bard's ears, though there was no one there to play them. The songs of King Uilleam Mac Eollath and Domnaill McDarrin his friend, the banesmen of the bryttevulf, echoed in his mind. His heart pounded like a bodhran drum, the room making his feet almost dance a sword dance. Thus he slew. The metallurgy of the Highlanders is among the best in the west of Veritia, so the massive blade cut through head, foot, leg and torso with impartiality. He even caught one wild man skewered on his blade and flung him off the blade into the trees like the stone off of a hurling stick. Another of his blows consisted of a cutting of brain, skull bone and muscle tissue, and the wild man with the now even more grizzled visage crumpled with a groan.

Unbeknownst to the Highlander, a wild man who had slipped away from the battle hurled a rock at his head with a crude sling. The barbarian bard suddenly felt the impact on the back of his head and crumpled to the ground.

When young Cunavol came to, he was bound to a stake, in the center of a woodwose village, before him and thrown made of bones from human and other varied free folk, sat a great wild man with a rotund belly. His hair was matted and on his head he wore a crown in semblance of a Dragon skull. This was Iron John, potentate of all wild men.

"*Ecca Feron Herronjun. Errac esi dodt.*" A big, brawny wild man with a massive crude axe stepped forward. Though the young bard could not understand the language, he could easily ascertain that this was the executioner and he was about to die. Suddenly, he was filled with the Spirit of the High King and shouted out in a mighty voice "*Ecca serdi Esulinca, Dure emtagen! Dodt heilke vuash nin!*" (Wild man speech: I am a servant of Esulien your enemy! If you kill me, I will torment you for eternity.") Though Iron John did not know who this Esulien was, he must be a powerful chieftain or shaman to give a human the knowledge of the wild man language.

While the unintelligent Iron John was processing this in his feeble mind, a strange sound like the mooing of a dun cow mixed with an indiscernible battle cry rent the stillness of the forest. Iron John looked up, and what he saw, if the bazaar look on his face was any indication, both perplexed and terrified him. A cow, a black cow burst into the village. But he was not a cow that stood on four legs but rather two. And though his arms and chest were covered in black fur, they were those of a man, or humanoid, in any case. With him was an elf with skin nearly as black as coal. They were both armored and armed and were soon slaying all the inhabitants of the village. Cunavol felt as though he were a spectator at a Highland fair where a melee arena stood. But this was no game. This was real. He was too shocked to cry out, but the bard saw that iron John, "bold" chieftain of all wild men was slinking away through the trees. The fray was about to end, so the time to seek rescue was now.

"Help, help!" He cried out in his best common speech. Fortunately the elf understood him, and after he had run through the last wose with his slender blade, came and cut Cunavol's bonds. "I am Verlien of the Elvenwood. This is my traveling companion, Sekanda Praveen of the bull people. He is still perfecting his common speech." The Bull man nodded in acknowledgment. "I am Cunavol, a Heeland man. My God visited me in my dreams several weeks ago and told me to depart my homeland until I found a dun cow that looked like a man and an elf with skin as black as coal. I know now that he meant you and your companion. Do you wish to know of my God?"

"I have begun to doubt the astrological faith of my fathers, as has my friend Sekanda his polytheistic religion," the elf said. "I do not know much of your God but if he preserved you from the wild men to meet with us then so be it. Tell us of your God and join us in the quest to discover the lion man of your God."

So it was that Cunavol Mac Echu found new friends and the purpose for which the High King had called him out of his homeland. But far away, in another part of the forest, in his guttural speech, Iron John declared, "You have earned the wrath of the wild men. We wudawasa are not finished with you. You will never see the last of us."

***

The plan seemed simple enough. Cut through McFarogh lands to the Northeast and then head southwest to the origin of the voice that Verlien and Sekanda the Bull man had heard. However young Cunavol had not counted on the children of bloody Heimish to be raiding this soon after winter. For in truth, the snow and hoarfrost had but barely melted and the bard had counted on Heimish's men being preoccupied with fighting the woses in their yearly coming-of-age raids. And the young man would rather trade his sword to a sorcerer than return to the land of the wild men. And now the tale shall turn to the encounter between the sons of Red Heimish and our warriors three.

They were at this time very near to the plain of Arlagh (where a great battle would one day soon be fought between the forces of the bryttevulf and a glorious alliance of Heeland clans. But that story is for another volume of history.) Now the man Cunavol did have some reservations about killing warriors of his own race and species by the reflected that, in times past, when certain tribes had practiced sorcery, this was a necessary evil. Still he prayed that he would not cross paths with the MacHeimish clan. There was at that time a sub chieftain of the bloody clan by the name of Engis the white-eye. No one knew exactly where he came from, but he had just appeared one day at the Council fire of the MacHeimish Clan saying that he was a priest of the great god and if the sons of Heimish would grant him partial leadership, in conjunction with chieftain Murdoch, she would bring them more glory in blood than they had ever known. And so he led a party of fifty men as a vanguard to the MacHeimish, wreaking unspeakable travesties on the peaceful clans nearby.

The moon shone bright and full over the plain of Arlagh. "I see strange torches," whispered Sekanda Praveen, who due to his Tauromin heritage could see better in the dark than the elf or the man, they burn with a strange ghostly fire that feels from here like the etheral of devils. Only an arcane alchemist, and one deep in the black arts at that could conjure such things. There is more to this war leader than meets the eye.

"I hope and pray to my God that it is not White-Eyed Engis, he of one black eye and white. He has been raiding with men of the MacHeimish clan for several months now. They say he has much command over the dark powers, an alchemist of sorts, who infuses his warriors with the blood of goblins. I do not wish to fight but if these be goblinoid men we've no choice but to send them to their master in the dark realm. I pray that we survived to meet the lion man of our dreams one day but even if it is our fate to die this night, I know our sacrifice will please Him."

The arcane torches bobbed nearer and nearer, like ghost ships tossed on a sea of death. The first ranks of men, or rather, goblin men, came into view. In the midst of them there arose a figure as bone chilling as death itself. It was clad in a kilt of black leather and bore a sickle bladed ax on its back that was carved with strange runes. Its skin was as white as bone, its beard long and black, and the rumors were true, it had one eye as black as coal, and one as white as a skull. It seemed to be orchestrating the every move of its small Army with its arcane will.

"Wait for it!" Hold!" hissed the young barbarian, sliding his claymore free of it sheath. "On my word!...Now!"

Screaming a bloodcurdling cry of *"Cleadhe do McDarrin!"* (Heeland Tongue: The sword of McDarrin). The human led his two motley companions ramming into the demonic MacHeimish horde. The blade licked forward and back, tearing open a goblinoid throat in a spurt of demonic black blood. Then the fray turned into a wild foray on the part of all three, parrying halberds, dirks and claymores. Several fell to the weapons of the motley three warriors, but young Cunavol could tell that they would soon be overpowered. Then a wild strategem flew into his brain: strike down the leader. The only sure way was decapitation. Wounding a man superficially, he leaped onto the incapacitated man's shoulders, leapt up and somersaulted toward the white-eyed rider. Screaming a blood curdling cry, he gripped his weapon in both hands, and swung with every last ounce of his strength. The blanched head went flying, and as it did, strangely, it laughed. For this was not the first time that White-Eyed Engis had died by decapitation. A wave of dark energy dispersed over the small Army and they fled in fear. The three warriors were far too weary to give chase. But even as he sagged, leaning on his sword, young Cunavol felt in his heart of hearts that he had not seen the last of this "White-Eyed Engis."

**

"If you would have this great power, swear an oath upon your soul." The disembodied voice echoed through the gnarled wood. And Iron John, chieftain of the wild Men would have heard it if it were ten thousand miles away. He clutched a flint dagger stumpy hairy hand and ran the blade across the palm of the other. "Aeka gahar! We will die for Asteroth, we shall serve him for eternity if he will but give us the blood of our enemies." The stooping wild men surrounding the King followed his example by drawing their own blood. As soon as the blood hit the ground, wisp of smoke, nay, spirits, in the semblance of wolves trailed like slithering dragons into the nostrils of the wild men and the skin and hair of Iron John became as hard as the metal that gave him his name. His eyes became blood red and his fangs lengthened. With a newfound vigor born of his wolfish blood he looked up and baled at the moon and the name of the man the scent his dark swelling yearned to track came to his mind: Cunavol Mac Echu, the Highland man.

And this Asteroth kenned well. For he knew if the highlander met with Sir Balladin, Arch-Knight of the Knights of Silvardrassil, it would someday spell his end.

"Shall we go north from here, Sekanda?" Asked Cunavol the highlander, coming up behind the mail-clad Bull man and pausing to catch his breath. He looked back to where the usually spry Verlien, his hair tied back in a dreadlocked bun, his adamant katars, which it acquired from a Tauromin trader, ever on his wrists, was now lagging behind.

"My heart tells me suth, to the interior of Veritia."

"You're more of a scholar and cartographer than I am. South it is. I noticed the land is becoming greener. And you see, there are patches, as if the earth has been recently sealed up."

"My heart tells me we are very close to our destination. Yes, we are very close. Come on." He looked back over his shoulder and bellowed, "Come on, elf. Quickly!"

Then a howl rent the air. It sounded a bit like the howl of a wolf stirred in with the scream of a man gone mad. And this soup was not appetizing to the heart. Not at all.

Suddenly wild men with incredibly long claws and gray fur, they looked more like yeti men. He did not know if they were new species or begotten by some sorcery, but decided to guess the latter. The voice of the High King came to him in that moment and said, "Kill them, Cunavol son of Echu, kill them as Domnaill did of old."

He thought quickly. They would bite through their steel. The only thing that could kill bryttevulf, or maybe even, bryttevulf hybrids, as these appeared to be, was King's Steel, or adamant as some named it and they did not have... But wait...

"Verlien!" He shouted. "Lift your blades to the sky!"

The elf complied then lifted his bladed bracers skyward, forming them into an X above his head as he knelt down. Silver lightning flashed down from the sky onto the blades and from them to the weapons of his comrades. Then, their weapons still crackling with magical energy and thus adding to their holy strength, the three motley warriors charged. Asked rocket engineer it through sorcery so the "Vildevulf would be impenetrable to the mirror weapons, even at the neck, which was the bryttevulf's only weak spot. But he had not counted on the holy lightning a magic from his enemy, the Radiant king and so it was that when their weapons met the hides of their enemies, the bodies burst asunder like alchemist fire. But there was one larger than the others that managed to make his way unhindered to the young highlander. With one blow from his maul-like fist he could have sent Cunavol son of Echu to meet the he High King. But thinking quickly with heightened senses from his God, his single-handed claymore flashed forth and sent the wild man's head flying from his shoulders. By this time the bull man and the elf had dispatched the rest of the small Army. Coming up to the severed head and kicking it over, the Tauromin are saw that it was the head of Iron John. "Well done, Cunavol Ironbane." Tired from their exertions, the trio of warriors stumbled over the next rise of Hills and saw before them a city with silver-etched and gem-encrusted towers.

"I have fully run out of parchment now. Contrary to what I first suspected these tales will require another book for the library of the Nexus.Let me leave you now gentle reader with this thought. It is the heart, not the sword that makes the Paladin"

Your humble scribe of all universes,

Lamathrath

Bardic Insipiration: The Last Confession of Brother Lamathrath of the Nexus

"WOHW" In-Game Player Log I:

To my brother and caregiver, the Connorman. I love what Good taught me through ye. Forgive me for not seeing you. Your Reward this Quest: All I can do thank my brother and fellow adventurer is to write this, my greatest bard-song I've yet writ

Well-met, fellow adventurer! Huzzah, Holy Magic! When I was only five my mom and Dad and their buddy lead me through the process of creating a Player Account in the greatest MMORPG EVER: *Worlds of Holy Word-Craft: Battle for the Heartlands*! Yea Verily, Yea. Salutations and Blessings, Friend. Allow me to me my name. I am Marcellus of Capricornius. That is my Screen Name. I am a Bard and Fighter hybrid. Strange you say? According to the silly "benefits of player classes" section of the Quest Beginners it's recommended that bards "Compliment the feel of an Adventure." My Favorite Gamebook Footnote: The Game Is not intentionally frustrating We have received Emails from former players that during their Subscription, when Gaming AI Player Class Recommendations are free chosen, the gaming storyline is most realistic. Some other folks are trying to fix an auto-rep fighters that raid dragons say I infuse them with so much bardic inspiration it REALLY is as effective a Wizard Spell and helps them win the raid. It is said I am the Best Bard on the Server. Other bard are labelled useless with the Vile In-Game dinstinction "newbies." Yes well. In my heart, I desire to be a swordsman. I am only told I AFTER the raid while my mates and I revive our healthpoint ratings at an inn. Why could you not have said that *during* the final boss fight with High-Sorcerer Ancalogan. Yes… I was in the back of the cave by a pillar, by *Strumming the Heck (Literally) out of my Consecrated Crystalline Lute of High Divinity.* Divinity? Maybe I should just erase Marcellus and create a Battle-Priest character. They cast healing spells. Yeah... same kind of ability Some people say that only one character is allowed per player account. The Lute is my highest level and my most Valuable Item. Our Party Ranger, Jennar the Hunter picked it up as epic drop from Lack the Green Death Knight. The Ranger could not equip it. It was bard-specific. He was the only one in the party high-level enough to best a Dulhan. He found it when I was though. He said he had a feeling the Game Itself seemed to give me what had in his satchel, but only I could Bard Marcellus is Ridiculously High Level for a bard, whether hybrid or plain-class.

Player Log Update

I ended up strangely becoming co-leaders on multiman raids with a warrior named Jonan. He didn't say much and I at first...sigh... Thought that he kind of didn't like me. He used in-game slang that I at first found hurtful. Whenever we were fighting a boss, I could effectively use battle short-hand. The instance we were running together would of time out. I felt bad. I cou. I thought wrongly that Jonan didn't like and often blamed me. As bard, I'm kinda new to this fighter thing. It's not deleting a character. But I'm sending a chatbot request to In-Game respecting. We're an odd couple. Raid Match-Ups in this Roleplaying Game of Life. Hey, Hey, Hey AI tailored my special But if they are In-game, they may do similar things, but every time there is a New Player, they are New Character Class as only they can be. And each member of the AI-Led Guild of Light needs each as a sword needs its sheath.

Players like to win, don't we? The only real way to end in this game is to not. Wait, you say. Even greenhorns to the Game have seen "Bad Players" that kind of unintentionally make glitches. Glitches are what all players always used to call those user-code system fail a few updates ago.

While always intended be adventurous, the Great Game, designed by the Developer, nicknamed the AI, was always simply fun to fun. Imagine that, dudes. No latency, no need to repair items, no loading lag times.

What happened? That could sell like hot cakes. Sure, we players already know the Guy. With Perfect Coding in the Game, The Game Developer would have every online follower in the gamer fanbase. You remember I said I was trying to be a Fighter, when I knew all along, I should always be a bard? Think I know better the Great Original Developer? That is where we get going with the True Storyline.

I have heard that God had Assistant Developers, the Angel Team, I heard them called. There was a highly gifted secretary of sorts. His real name isn't in the official paperwork, now he's called the Hacker but originally he was in just in charge as Michael, the Angel Assistant that now keeps him outta development. Some of us think he can stop God. They thin God is threatened by him, as The Hacker is God's . Naw, he's Director Michael's bad version. There is no higher Developer, none like, No Greater Maker. That Patch. took this guy a long time to understand. He wanted to Make the entire game obey him alone. He was arrested in Development. He went into the Game when it was Just outta Beta and convinced those original subscribers to follow his way of gameplay. That was the introduction of the Great Virus There are many glitches, and many minor confused but well intended gamers find many minor game-coding patches that may work a bit, but for the greatest gameplay experience, you need to download the GREAT PATCH.

God always knew that HE was the One to Fix the Great Virus. He would the Greatest Patch. He Knew that he would insert himself into the RPG.

You know when you fight a huge bugbear, and he is lumbering toward your party. He is so huge, you kind of can't help being scared. We all have harvested the aggro at one time or another in our Quests. When the game was in pure BETA download and after the fall of the users. In God's Heart He said. "When we gamers download files to change our player's appearance, this downloable file is a skin". no offense to who do pay for the microtransaction. I don't really mind. This player did once desire to be a fighter. But I have always been very confident in my avatar's physical appearance. Ask my mom, Mama Nienna always my green forester suit shouldn't be seen outside the hamlet. The thing in question was not to be. Alas. God had wanted players to look their own avatar on the outside but have his soul on the inside. (the original development imaging file code. He is the most powerful guy. If he came in the game in his true form, they'd get scared. To be Developer updating the game during live gameplayer, he would download a skin and become a Player. His Account Abilities were beyond any character stats ever seen, before or since.

He played the game perfectly accordingly. He never used the magical Ability of Call Out truth to intentionally hurt anyone. It's sad, many Cleric Gamers think that they should say true words without checking Spell of Truth in the Official Guide, especially in Section II. I think there is a cleric who said we should ONLY speak the Truth in Love. Note to Clerics, and all of us, if you're feeling fatigue, before casting Word of Truth, Drink a Love Potion, even if it's your ninth today.

I never found the place the Developers Avatar (Jesus) was from... Nazareth... I can't find in map of the In-game world of Veritia...if HE comes from Nazareth, that must be town you heard of in the news.

Jesus played the game perfectly. But a raid party that thought were greatest players in the history game. They only to stop Jesus because keep power over loot from raiding dungeons. They called themselves "oracles". Long name and I'm Lazy. Orcs for shorts

The orcs finally decided to challenge Jesus to a PVP Battle. They found a coding glitch in the server so that if Jesus lost, he would be deleted. The storage memories Verita Gamers had of Jesus would be deleted.

And you know, what, guildies? He didn't move. Didn't speak. He let them win. And not just his current guild or players like me today. He wanted them kind seem they could boss him around so he could win to him. He felt the greatest and then he said. "Patch Update Complete and was banned.

Sometime later (3 days of Gameplay). There was for a second a static crackle and a Great BOOM!

There was a shock of light that all current players felt. The ones who knew Jesus got a direct message. "I am going now to make Development HQ Ready for y'all to have the Greatest LAN Party ever. Players in the future forget kinda forget this game of Life, When Played Well, it is called following Jesus Christ, is meant to be simply fu.

The Divine Purpose of Mankind, meaning God's Marcellus the Bard. Too long NAME again. Let me change my screenname here, Gentle Readers. Got sidetracked again. Maybe it's a gift once thought a curse. Marshal Myers. Storyteller and Bard for Jesus Christ. Many aliases I have had. My favorite one was "Lamathrath of the Nexus". I am supposed to follow Jesus in love, but I have heard in my main narrator teach what I always needed to hear from My Savior Best Who Thinks Marshal Myers

Is in Him and Righteous. Jesus: You like old Denmark, jah, Marshal. Then Let It Go Bye bye guilty heart,. You have no power over Marshal. God's Most Authoritative "Rule" for Marshal Myers has always been Go ye forth, play hard and laugh in the Perfect Will of Christ. It's not naïve or bad to have fun . Heavy Heart. Jesus Christ taught me again the Theology of Playtime. I think for this reason mainly, God made me a storyteller, a dreamer, a romper in spirit, don't matter the physical limitations I have on this earth.

Reaffirming Christ's for me, Marshal "Bubby' Myers And I am ashamed of the Godspell of I shall be Holy Fun-Timers in Jerusalem, Judea and Samaria, Spreading Christ-Joy worldwide. I already know you're with me. Let's Play Divine Dressup to the very End of the Age.

Amen! Let's Cosplay, Lord Jesus!

Also by Marshal Myers

visit www.marshalmyers.com

Sword Dreamer

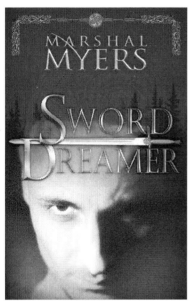

Young Léofric is troubled with strange visions of battle he does not understand. But when two warriors – an elf and a man – arrive to lead him away to war, Léofric learns that he is the Sword Dreamer, the legendary seer whose visions of pending battles are vital for brining an end to the civil war that rages Irminsul.

Now he must train for his role, use his visions to aid the Kind's Army, and defeat the vengeful and power-hungry Gollmorn and his evil army. But can Léofric's burgeioning skills help stop the war and defeat Gollmorn, or will the towering Silver City of Auraheim fall under the shadow of a madman's tyranny? More importantly, will Léofric finally learn who he is and find his place with the True King, the almighty King That Is?

Lady of Naofatir

Miriam O'Connor is a young Victorian Irish school teacher with an avaricious love for reading and mythology. She is overjoyed when she inherits a mansion in northern England filled with a treasure trove of mythological texts. What she truly desires, however, is to find a man like those in the old stories, who will love her truly and defend her honor.

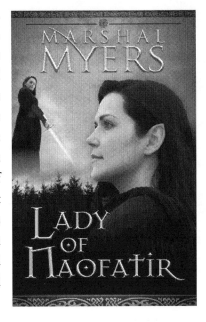

One day while reading in the attic of the library, she finds an old book filled with cryptic writing. When she opens it, it whisks her off to the beautiful golden green country of Naofatir, where the fairylike inhabitants are caught in a battle against their terrible Enemy, the Dorchadas. There, she meets the great prince of Naofatir, and comes to discover how she can play a part in helping him save the beautiful land from destruction.

Light Bringer

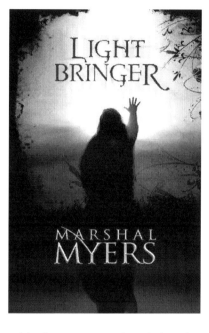

For centuries, the city of Silvardrassil has been cut off from the rest of the world and thrust into a state of eternal, starless night because of the folly of Fehar, who opened a connection between the city and the realm of the Shadow King.

The Legion of Silvardrassil has fought the forces of the Enemy with the magical aid of the Light Bringers, a holy order of mage-priests whom the Radiant King has endowed with the power to bend the elements. The people of the city are slowly dying, but prophecy foretells that the last and greatest Light Bringer is coming.

Made in United States
Orlando, FL
18 December 2024

56051498R00150